# Prais

"With great affection and an aplomb reminiscent of the glory days of detective fiction, Michael Allan Mallory has penned a mystery that's a joy to read. Police detective Henry Lau is a man with a heavy stone on his heart, but lightning in his body thanks to a deep knowledge of the martial arts. Carefully navigating between clues and red herrings, with beautiful pools of ancient wisdom to refresh him, Lau is as captivating a protagonist as you'll find anywhere in the genre. His police partner, niece Janet Lau, adds her own deft touches to the action. The result is a winning duo involved in a fast-paced double-murder investigation that's sure to please even the most demanding of mystery fans."

--William Kent Krueger, *New York Times* Best Selling Author, Edgar and Anthony Award Winner.


"Michael Allan Mallory deftly weaves murder, Asian history brought to life, and what honor truly means into an unputdownable mystery that kept me turning the pages deep into the night. Mallory tosses in some fascinating Wing Chun kung fu, awesome and sometimes hilarious turns of phrase, the strength of family, and some sticky affairs of the heart into a book I can't recommend more! This is an incredible follow-up to the award-winning first installment in the Henry Lau mystery series *Lost Dragon Murder*. I can't wait to devour the next one!"

--Jessie Chandler, author of the Shay O'Hanlon Caper series

# TIGER CLAW

## A Henry Lau / Janet Lau Mystery

**Michael Allan Mallory**

BookLocker

Trenton, Georgia

"The path that leads to truth is littered with the bodies of the ignorant."

--*Miyamoto Musashi, Japan's greatest swordsman and duelist.* (1584-1645)

# CHAPTER 1

The dumbest thing you could do in front of Henry Lau was to pick on someone unable to fight back. The next dumbest thing was to do it with a sense of entitlement.

The arrogant loudmouth four tables away was doing both.

Until that moment, Henry had been enjoying a late afternoon latte at his favorite neighborhood coffee shop. Minutes earlier, two men had noisily entered Windjammer Coffee House, ordered hot drinks, then took them to the little table. A guiding principle of Henry's was to be careful about judging people on first impressions, though some folks made it too easy. The older man, clearly the one in charge, was like a faulty cast iron radiator, giving off nothing but heat and noise. Fiftyish, condescending eyes, a sharp nose, and a brutish cleft of a mouth, he wore a tan sports jacket over a black polo shirt and faded jeans. Taking up most of the other side of the small table was a large, brawny, much younger man who listened to the other talk but contributed little to nothing to the conversation as if in deference to him. During their exchange, Henry heard the younger man call the other "Mr. D."

And then it happened.

Mr. D removed a cigar from his jacket, shoved it into his mouth, flipped open a lighter, and began puffing out streams of acrid blue-gray smoke. Not much later, one of the baristas, sweet-faced and barely on the cusp of adulthood, hovered apprehensively by his table.

"I'm sorry, sir, smoking isn't allowed," she said in a voice as fragile as butterfly wings.

She might as well have been talking to the table for the response she got. Ignoring her, Mr. D inhaled a lungful of stogie smoke and expelled a pungent cloud of blue-gray contempt.

"*Sir?*" she prompted, shifting uncomfortably.

The obstinate patron turned to her and spoke through the cigar. "Go away, little girl."

She swallowed, wavered for a second before slinking away, her lower lip quivering.

The rude son of a bitch threw a self-satisfied smirk to his associate and took another puff on his tobacco roll.

Henry stared at him. He hated bullies. They spat on the rules of common decency. Henry made a barely audible low growl, being of an age when his tolerance for rude behavior was worn paper thin. He was inclined to give this jerk a piece of his mind. But his inner voice cautioned him to let the situation play out. He waited. Ground his teeth but waited.

Moments later, the coffee house manager, Glenda, arrived on the scene. As a regular customer, Henry knew her, and he could tell she was not happy. Big-boned and stocky, her gray-streaked wavy hair was pulled back into a dense bunch that tried to be a ponytail but was too frizzy to behave. Glenda wiped stubby fingers against a green apron. In a throaty voice that struggled to be polite, she confronted the smoker. "Sir, I'm the manager. Smoking isn't allowed here. Signs are posted on the walls. My employee asked you to comply. Other customers are complaining. You can smoke outside, just not inside."

The offender sneered in a voice loud enough to carry to the four walls and beyond, "I don't give a flying fuck about the other customers. I'm enjoying a smoke. Leave me alone. It's a free country."

"Not when it comes to smoking. It's state law. The Minnesota Clean Indoor Act says you can't smoke indoors in public buildings except in designated areas. That includes us. We don't have a smoking area, so I need you to put out your cigar or go outside."

No reaction.

After a count of six, Glenda heaved an impatient sigh. "Sir…"

Mr. D blew a column of smoke into the air.

Glenda had reached her limit. "You were also rude to my employee. I gave you a chance. I want you to leave. *Now.*"

With a look of total disdain, Mr. D rested his forearms on the small table and looked back spitefully. "I'll go when I'm good and ready, dearie. Not before."

*Now he'd done it!*

That was the last straw for Henry. The arrogant shithead had gone too far. Nearby customers, who'd watched the exchange with varying degrees of discomfort, looked appalled but did nothing, afraid to get involved. Henry pushed back his chair and surged to his feet. Seconds later, he stood beside the man with the smoldering tobacco torpedo.

"You heard the manager," he said in a voice like flint. "It's time for you and your friend to leave."

"Who the hell asked you?"

"You're not moving."

"Get lost, pal. I'm not done with my cigar."

With startling quickness, Henry's fingers plucked the cigar out of the other's hand and crushed it against the wooden tabletop. "There, you're finished. Now get out."

Indignant, beady eyes bore into him. "*Do you know who I am?*"

"Yeah, a self-important asshole who thinks he doesn't have to obey the law."

"Nobody talks to me like that!"

"Shut up and show some respect. The manager told you to leave. Now get up. Or do you need help?"

Mr. D swung toward his barrel-chested associate. "Lou."

Lou lurched to his feet like a trained grizzly bear. He lumbered over to Henry, towering above him by at least seven inches and easily carrying an extra fifty pounds of bone and muscle. He brought up a paw of a hand to grab Henry by the shirt, warning ominously, "You should stay out of things that don't concern you."

Glenda's eyebrows shot up in alarm. "Stop! I don't want trouble. Don't hurt him."

"Too late, lady," Lou jeered with relish. "This schmuck needs to learn to mind his own business." He clenched the fabric tighter.

Rather than looking afraid, Henry turned to Glenda. "You're a witness to what he's doing?"

The coffee house manager nodded back slowly with worry-filled eyes.

Having anticipated a move like this, Henry could have intercepted the grab but didn't, not wanting to appear as the aggressor in so public a venue. He was also glad Big Lou hadn't sucker punched him, which would've been tough to deal with. The shirt grab was easy.

Much to Lou's annoyance, Henry didn't flinch or tremble with fear. Instead, in a calm yet menacing voice, Henry instructed, "Let go of my shirt."

Lou mocked, "Or what?"

"Or I'll help you let go."

Iron fingers clenched the fabric tighter.

Henry clamped a hand over Lou's fist to anchor it, swinging his free arm over and against the big man's forearm while twisting his waist. This cranked Lou's arm and entire body, dropping him to his knees. Henry's hand slid to Lou's throat, whose face contorted in silent agony as claw-like fingers dug into his carotid artery.

Big Lou was subdued. Not wasting a second, Henry's eyes flicked to a startled Mr. D, whose hand slipped into his jacket. *For what? A gun?* His heart thumping, Henry—fingers still locked on Lou's throat—shifted his stance to kick the small table into Mr. D's chest, pinning his arms.

"That better be another cigar you're reaching for," Henry warned. *"Don't move."*

A startled Mr. D froze in place.

Henry looked back at the muscleman. "If you promise to behave, I'll let go. Do you?"

Watery, pain-filled eyes blinked as the color-drained face bobbed up and down.

Henry released his grip. On his knees, Lou gulped in lungfuls of air as the blood returned to his pallid complexion. Stepping around him, Henry moved the table back a little.

"Show me your hands," he said to Mr. D. "Slowly."

A pair of rough, empty, pudgy hands came into view.

A distrustful Henry patted his jacket and pulled out a switchblade. With a press of the button, a nasty-looking blade flipped out. He gave its owner a disapproving look. "This would've been a very bad idea." He closed and pocketed the knife. "Now gimme your wallet."

"What for?"

"Shut up and do what I tell you. Your wallet. Or do I have to take it from you?" Henry feigned a move toward him.

Mr. D shied back. "Okay! Okay!" He tossed a bifold leather wallet on the table.

Henry snatched it up, removed the New Jersey driver's license, memorizing the name, city, and state before tossing everything back. "I know who you are now, Frank Del Gatto of Jersey City." He paused to let the point sink in. "Don't ever come back here. Don't threaten anyone here—*ever.* If there's any trouble, I'll hold you responsible. You got that?"

Seething yet compliant, Mr. D nodded.

"Good," Henry grunted. "You're not so tough without someone to do your dirty work." Some might consider the last comment overkill; he didn't care. Reason and courtesy were wasted on men like them. Henry didn't like sinking to their level, but he knew the only way to reach some people was in a language they understood. With this jerk, it was threats.

From his peripheral vision, he noticed Lou was having trouble getting to his feet, so he went to help. "Give it twenty minutes," he said to the big man, "and you should feel okay." A bit green around the gills, Lou offered no resistance as Henry pointed him toward the exit. "You too," he motioned to Mr. D. "The manager told you to leave. Move it. Or am I gonna have to get you started?"

With malice oozing from every pour, the boss man hoisted himself out of his chair. "Can I get my knife back?"

Henry shoved the switchblade into Lou's back pocket where he thought it would be safer than in Mr. D's hands. The men walked toward the exit. The moment the door closed behind them, Henry was there, watching through the window as they went to an oversized SUV. He waited for the car to drive away, every muscle in his body still alert. The threat wasn't yet over. He wanted to be certain the men didn't grab guns from the vehicle and come back shooting. He'd seen it happen before. A warning his first kung fu teacher had branded into him was never *to assume your opponent can't hurt you even when he looks beaten.*

Only after the SUV was out of sight did he feel the threat was over, and his heart stopped thrashing against his chest. He took a moment to catch his breath and settle his nerves. Turning away from the door, he was met by a burst of applause from the coffee house staff and customers. At a table off to the side, an attractive Asian American woman with lustrous, straight black hair gawked at him with incredulity. Her companion, much older, had Cherry Kool-Aid hair, a square jaw, and an animated face that regarded him as if he were some magical apparition. Shrugging past them and others with self-deprecation, he returned to his table.

Just then, a short man with glasses emerged from the restroom, turning his head every which way at the fading ovation as he walked to Henry's table.

"What'd I miss?" asked a puzzled Alan Zhu.

Henry updated his friend on the encounter with Mr. D and his goon.

"For real?" Alan's eyes widened behind his black-framed glasses.

"Ask around."

"I step out for one minute and look what happens."

Henry laughed. Friendly digs from his lifelong pal were typical. Alan had known him since grade school. A tad shorter, skinnier, and rounder in the shoulders than Henry, Alan was the poster boy for kind-heartedness. He teased with affection. The man didn't have a mean bone in his body.

"You have all the fun," he mocked. "If not for the call of nature, I could've helped you with those guys."

True enough. Alan was also a highly skilled kung fu adept who'd been Henry's training partner since their teens. His go-to guy.

"*Henry!*" a voice called over the whirl of a juice blender. Windjammer's manager shuffled over, looking overwrought and still finding her equilibrium. "Thanks so much for helping! I was freakin' out."

"How's the young lady?"

"Julie? Pretty shaken. I thanked her for doing her job. I just hope the experience doesn't sour her on people. For crying out loud, this is her first real job. She's been here less than two months, and *this* had to happen!" Glenda sighed as if trying herself not to sour on the public.

"Tell her from me she handled the man well."

"She'll appreciate that. And as thanks, let me get you and Alan coffees on the house."

"That's so nice of you, but I have to decline."

"No?" Her voice was heavy with disappointment. "Please. You have to let me do something."

Reluctantly, he said, "Really, I can't. You know I'm a police detective. I can't accept gifts."

"If you insist. But if you change your mind, there're jumbo lattes waiting with your names on them." Glenda squeezed his shoulder and smiled at Alan before returning to her duties.

Alan cocked an eyebrow. "Way to go, buddy. I would've enjoyed another coffee."

"Life is tough."

"Change of subject," Alan said, turning serious. "Those guys you encouraged to leave. Wouldn't it have been easier if you'd flashed your badge?"

"Maybe. The thing is, I don't want to be that cop who abuses his position by threatening people that he's a cop. I don't like using my badge to intimidate people."

"No, you'd rather use your fists."

Henry laughed uncomfortably. Then said, "Joking aside, I like giving people a chance to realize they're doing something wrong. Or that there are bad consequences if they do."

Alan, who'd been fingering his coffee's cardboard sleeve, stopped to look up. "Does that work? Does some guy drop the brick he's about to chuck through a window because you tell him it's wrong?"

"Not often but sometimes."

"That's good of you."

Henry liked to think so but knew every situation was unique. He did what he thought was right. And fair.

A companionable silence fell between them. After a while, Alan stirred. "I should hit the road. Mei-Yin'll be starting dinner soon, and I'm in charge of the salad and getting the kids ready." He seized his jacket from the back of his chair and slipped it on. "Will I see you in class this week?"

"I plan on it."

Whatever the vagaries of life and work, one constant in Henry's life was his workouts at Alan's studio. Although it was Henry who'd introduced his friend to the kung fu style of Wing Chun back in high school and Henry who was the more experienced and skilled practitioner, it was Alan who'd opened his own *kwoon* (training hall).

A ping came from inside Henry's bomber jacket. Slipping out his smartphone, he read the text message. The timing for his departure couldn't have been better.

He had a murder to get to.

# CHAPTER 2

Detective Janet Lau strode across the lobby on a mission. Images of the past forty minutes flashed before her eyes as she ticked off the boxes on her to-do list. Then double-checked them, not wanting to mess up. This was only her second homicide as an investigator, her first since returning from a short medical leave, and she didn't want to disappoint her partner or her boss. Or herself. For the moment, her mind was clear and sharp; she hoped it would remain that way. Casting a long shadow over her was the reality that she still suffered brief bouts of mental fog and occasional headaches from her recent injury, which could rear up at any time.

That bothered her.

Normal stuff, her neurologist had explained. Recovery from even mild concussions took time. A kick to the head had jostled her brain. Not seriously, though enough to trigger her symptoms and warrant the appropriate care. Except at twenty-seven and having the impatience of youth, Janet was more than ready for this remnant of her first homicide case to be over and done with. Now. She'd been raised to always do her best and make a good impression. And these annoying mental fog spells made her feel she was letting people down.

*Did you forget something?*

She stopped dead in her tracks.

*Crap. Wait. No...that was another thing. You're good.*

*Focus!*

She expelled a frustrated sigh.

Janet approached the glass lobby doors. Catching her reflection, she was troubled by the woman looking back at her. Beneath the sleek, dark bob brushing against her collar, a delicate face of Scottish and Chinese ancestry appeared stressed and tired. Not good. If she were to inspire confidence in others, she'd have to staple on her game face and be ready to take on the tasks ahead.

Gazing through the door into the darkness, she frowned at the empty parking lot. *What was keeping him?*

Movement on the wide concrete steps caught her eye. Officer Felicia Chavez was walking to the doors, visibly cold in her winter jacket. Hours earlier, a light dusting of snow had fallen, which Chavez now stomped off her duty boots at the threshold before entering the lobby along with a cold blast of air.

"You look chilly," Janet said.

"I don't like winter," Chavez announced, snuggling inside her coat collar.

Janet made a sympathetic noise. She thought it prudent not to inform Chavez it was technically autumn, Thanksgiving being less than two weeks away. Felicia Chavez, a recent transplant from Florida, was experiencing her first northern cold snap. Twenty-six degrees. Downright frigid to a West Palm Beach girl, although a mere chill to a native Midwesterner. Janet didn't have the heart to tell her that harsher—far, far harsher—temperatures were on the way, frostbite-inducing temps that would make a beach-loving Floridian freakout. No point in alarming her; Officer Chavez would learn the hard way come January. Besides, a change of subject had just rolled into the parking lot.

Earlier, the sun had closed shop for the day, turned out the lights and gone home. The ensuing darkness was depressing to those who thought sunset before 5 p.m. unconscionable. Welcome to mid-November in the northern hemisphere. Twin headlights swung into view out of the gloom, making the fresh snow glisten like a field of jewels. A black Chevy Malibu came to a stop by the front entrance next to several police cruisers. Janet broke into a smile as the driver emerged. Youngish-looking mid-forties, slightly under average height, a black shag of hair fluttering in the wind as the lean, athletic body took the steps in a smooth wolf-like lope.

Detective Henry Lau pulled open the door and entered the lobby.

But it was much more than that.

A knowing smile tugged the corner of Janet's mouth. Despite the grim task ahead, she allowed herself a private moment of indulgence. It wasn't that her uncle had opened the door; *it was how he had done it.* The casual observer would have missed it. Not her. She'd first noticed it as a little girl when he'd visited her home.

"Why did you open the door like that?" her eleven-year-old self had wondered.

Her uncle, on the back side of his twenties, was impressed. "Good eye. You're the first person ever to notice."

"Yeah, but why do you do it?"

He explained how most people use their hand and arm muscles when pulling open a door. He didn't. He tried to incorporate his kung fu skills into everyday moments. A key element in Wing Chun was instantly connecting and disconnecting different parts of the body. When he opened a door, he engaged his ankles, knees, hips, and shoulders. The only job of his arm and hand was serving as a connecting rod. It was his body opening the door, not his hand. Quick and fleeting as the beat of a wasp's wing, muscles were engaged and released, an action beyond the notice of the average person.

None of that mattered to her. "Yeah, but why do you do it?"

"I just told you."

"No. You talked about arms and stuff."

"Okay. Have you ever seen a bamboo forest?"

"Not for real. Just pictures."

"Close enough. Bamboo is flexible and tough. In heavy winds, big, stiff trees break or fall over. But bamboo doesn't fight the wind; it bends to it and stays standing. I try to be like bamboo. What I do teaches me to use different parts of my body without thinking."

"But *why?*"

There was a long pause before he said, "So I can stop bad guys from hurting people."

"Oh. Okay."

*Stopping bad guys.*

Janet never forgot those words or that moment. It was only later, as a teenager, that she understood the lengths to which Henry went to hard-wire his body to react to danger, how intense and persistent his training had to be to achieve his level of skill. A level of commitment that inspired her. She liked to think she could be as committed and passionate about something someday, yet not from a passion driven by tragedy as was his.

The lobby door closed behind Henry. He unzipped his jacket and nodded a greeting to Janet and Chavez. He ran a hand through his wind-blown hair to smooth it out. "What's up? Your text mentioned a 10-89 but no details. What kind of homicide are we looking at?"

"A different one."

"Different, how?"

"You'll find out," Janet promised. "We're in the lobby of a knife factory, Hancock Blades. Our victim was stabbed by one of their new products."

"Seems eerily fitting." He slipped on the nitrile gloves and disposable shoe covers she'd handed him.

Janet led him through a propped open door to the executive suite wing, where they walked along a corridor lined with colorful abstract art paintings illuminated by nickel-plated wall sconces. This was no fly-by-night operation. "You familiar with the Hancock product line?"

"They make high-end sports and hunting knives."

"Why am I not surprised you know that? I'm told they have factories in two other states. We're in their headquarters and main facility."

"The parking lot's empty. No weekend shift, I take it."

"Nope."

They paused in front of an office whose frosted glass door was kept open by a rubber wedge. Entering, the detectives stopped after a few steps to survey the room. Opposite them was an adjustable height desk upon which stood two widescreen LCD monitors, a tablet, and a cordless mouse. A Hancock marketing poster hung on the wall behind. A Korean moon jar painted with a school of fish sat on a nearby sideboard.

The body lay on the carpet away from the desk amid a litter of paper and pens.

Looking in his late forties, the man had rugged though handsome Korean features: thick black hair, wide-spaced eyes, a high nose, a narrow chin. He wore a long-sleeved flannel shirt, gray chinos, red socks, and penny loafers. The body lay on its stomach, the right arm extended beyond the head and resting on the page of a large open book. What grabbed your attention was the deep red stain on the lower back and the curve-bladed knife on the floor next to him.

"Name's Samuel Park, Chief Operations Officer." Janet's gaze lingered on the red-stained shirt. She could imagine the confusion, the shock, and the pain he felt as life ebbed from him. Death was her business, but that didn't stop her from feeling like a voyeuristic intruder at times like this. It was unsettling. Made her feel a little tainted, even though she was there on Park's behalf. She was getting better at handling her emotions and hoped never to become jaded at the sight of death. She knew her Uncle Henry never did. How could he, with the murder of his college girlfriend scorched to his bones? That one terrible event had changed the trajectory of his life to create the man standing beside her. Solving the homicides he worked on, Janet believed, was his way of paying tribute to Kay McAdams, whose killer was never known, let alone caught and brought to justice.

Janet watched him survey the room with an analytical eye, taking mental snapshots, trying to get the "vibe" of the crime scene as he called it. Moving near the body, he leaned in closer. "Looks like Park was stabbed near the kidney, maybe even in it." His eyes narrowed on the weapon, lying a foot away on the carpet: a five-inch curved blade attached to a curved black polymer handle that ended in a finger ring. A thin stripe of dried blood smeared the shining blade. He grunted in recognition. "A tiger claw."

Janet swung toward him. "You know this knife?"

"It's Indonesian, a *karambit*, a favorite among martial artists and tactical fighters."

"It's part of Hancock's new product line."

He nodded. "Nasty things. I saw them years ago…in Hong Kong."

A rare reference to long ago days. For reasons Janet never understood, her uncle didn't like talking about his time in that distant city. Too many unpleasant memories?

She indicated a two-drawer filing cabinet behind him, atop which sat a large acrylic stand supporting a colorful rigid foam board display. Emblazoned across the top in big, bold, colorful letters was "Hancock Blades." Printed in bright graphics were actual-sized photos of three knives. Mounted above those photos were the knives themselves: a deer antler blade, a fish filleting knife, and the noticeably absent top spot. "The tiger claw knife was attached there. Way too convenient!"

"Too easy not to grab for someone already riled up. Suggests the murder wasn't planned but a heat of the moment thing."

"Yep." Janet detailed what she thought happened. "Park and his killer have a confrontation. It gets out of hand. Enraged, the killer sees the display, snatches the tiger claw, and goes after Park, who was moving away from his desk."

"And gets stabbed in the back." Henry lowered to a squat to examine the carpet. Scattered pens, Post-it note pads, paper clips, pushpins, and a Sharpie marker were strewn near the body. "The struggle started at the raised desk, which is how all this stuff got here."

"Looks that way to me."

"Any defensive wounds on Park?"

"None that are visible."

Henry nodded, rising to his full height. "The atlas is interesting, don't you think?" His gaze fixed on the open volume under the dead man's hand.

"Very," she said, excited he'd noticed.

"What d'you make of it?"

She'd been waiting for that! Janet continued with restraint as if giving testimony in court. "Mr. Park is stabbed and drops to the carpet. To all appearances, he's dead. The killer is unnerved, frightened at what they've done. Drops the knife and runs off. *Except Sam Park isn't dead.*" Her eyes blazed, underscoring the importance. "There's a tiny spark of life left in him. Alone now, with only seconds left to live, Park rallies enough strength to crawl a few feet to the book stand. You can just see some marks on the carpet. There, he pulls down the atlas."

She gestured at the nearby wall where stood a slender walnut book lectern, glaringly missing its book. The missing volume, a folio-sized hardcover world atlas, lay open on the floor beneath Park's outstretched hand. With care, Henry stepped around the litter of pens and paper for a better view of the large atlas. "Must be a special book."

"I'm told it's a special edition reproduction. Looks hefty. The maps are gorgeous."

"So I see. It's open to…South America." He crouched closer. "What's his hand on? Looks like Argentina?"

"Uh-huh."

"Does that mean anything?"

"No idea. It might."

Something in the way Janet said that made Henry look at her oddly, his eyebrows lifting.

"Bear with me," she said, barely reigning in her excitement. "Sam Park went to all that trouble getting the atlas. Placed his hand on that page? Why? He's telling us something!"

"Leaving a message?"

"Yes."

"A dying clue?"

"Possibly."

"Very Agatha Christie."

"I know," she agreed with restraint and a solemn expression. Inside she was squeeing, "Holy crap!" A tantalizingly bizarre clue left by the murder victim. How interesting! Stuff like this never happens in real life—

*Whoa…Slow down. Keep your head.*

A man had died. She needed to treat his death with the proper gravitas, regardless of other considerations. Janet cleared her throat, looking to her partner for his insight. "Your thoughts?"

Henry was noncommittal. "You could be right." He studied the large atlas with a thoughtful scowl. "Although something's not right about this."

"Like what?"

"That's just it. I don't know. The atlas means something. Maybe Park *is* trying to leave a message. But something's off." Henry shook his head, annoyed. He stood up and looked at her. "What else you got?"

Maneuvering to the spill of paper and pens by the desk, she pointed to a yellow Post-it note pad with writing on the top square.

Henry stepped over. Printed in block letters were the words: *An Actionable Crime.* Below it was a name: *K.J. Hazzard.*

Janet said, "This *is* in Mr. Park's handwriting, I'm told."

"Which may or may not have anything to do with his death," her partner cautioned.

"Yeah. Curious all the same. Makes you wonder what the 'actionable crime' is. And is Hazzard the one who committed it?"

"Or has info on it." Henry gave an understated sigh. "A lotta stuff to process." He glanced round the room again without enthusiasm.

"Speaking of process," Janet chimed in pleasantly, trying to lift the mood, "DeMarco's outside." The CSI team was waiting for the go ahead to process the crime scene.

"Tell her to come in."

"Will do."

"Who found the body?"

"Park's boss, the factory owner, Aimee Hancock. She's waiting for us in a conference room."

"Then let's not keep her waiting."

# CHAPTER 3

Aimee Hancock looked like a natural disaster survivor. Her face bore the same dazed and disoriented appearance of having just crawled out from under the splintered debris and broken glass of a tornado-ripped house. Exhausted. No makeup. A platinum layer cut and fringe bangs disheveled from repeatedly running fingers through them. Embattled blue eyes stared blankly into space, looking as if all the fight had been pounded out of her and she was just getting by. Drooping shoulders were covered in a ratty, loose-fitting Ohio State sweatshirt. Below this were black yoga pants and canvas shoes.

Watching her through the glass wall of the conference room, Henry couldn't blame her for looking so defeated. A Mack truck of bad news had hit the CEO of Hancock Blades.

The factory owner sat alone in the big conference room, a showy affair meant to impress clients with its elegant furnishings and appointments but now seemed starkly gauche. She'd been kept from her office as a matter of protocol, it being across the hall from Sam Park's. She was—it had to be understood—herself a person of interest in the murder of her employee. It was vital for the investigators to maintain control of who had access to the crime scene and related areas.

As the detectives entered the room, Hancock's sky-blue eyes glommed onto them in anticipation before morphing into puzzlement after Janet introduced her partner.

"Another Detective Lau?"

"My uncle," Janet explained in her soft, cultured voice. "Also, my senior partner."

"Ah," an enlightened Aimee Hancock returned, taking stock of Henry. Life was beginning to percolate back into the empty husk.

Henry saw a middle-aged woman shaking off her earlier miasma and trying to be alert and engaged. A sleeping lioness had been awakened at the movement of prey. She sat upright, eyes now brimming with curiosity, if not a little defiance, ready to bare her claws.

The detectives settled into faux leather chairs across a large cherry wood table from the factory owner. Before getting on with the bitter details, Henry acknowledged her emotional state. "This must be difficult for you. We appreciate your patience."

Hancock gave a leaden nod. "It's shitty," was all she could say, her jaw muscles tightening, her impatience with them starting to show.

"Death of a friend is never easy. Can you tell us about Mr. Park?"

The eyes behind the fringe bangs flashed with annoyance at Janet. "I already gave her my statement."

Henry replied, "I'd like to hear it directly from you if you don't mind." He was polite yet stern to remind her which one of them was in charge.

For an instant the CEO looked to challenge him but reconsidered. "Fine," she capitulated with an eye roll. "Sam was our operations manager. A great guy. Really good at his job. There're a hundred different balls you have to keep in the air when running a manufacturing plant. Sam Park kept things running smoothly. I can't believe this happened to him!"

Henry could hear the admiration and sadness in her voice. Anger too.

"Sam had a great relationship with the department supervisors," she went on. "The way he worked with them—with everyone, really— to solve problems. It's what he did best. The man was like a dog with a bone. If an issue came up, he wouldn't give up until he or someone had found a fix. We even joked about it. This thing"—she waved her hand toward his office—"makes no sense. People liked Sam."

"Can you think of anyone who'd want to hurt Mr. Park?"

Glacial blue eyes held his gaze. "Bosses don't win many popularity contests. They make tough decisions, often delivering bad news. Sam did that without making it personal. I can't imagine anyone wanting to…hurt him." In the last second, her voice faded to almost a whisper, as if saying the word 'kill' was unthinkable.

"What about his personal life?"

Her shoulders rose and fell under the ratty sweatshirt. "Can't really help you. Sam kept his private life private. I know he liked camping and reading—histories, biographies, and mysteries, especially detective stories. He played pickleball and drank craft beer. Beyond that…" Another shrug.

"Did he often work weekends?"

"Not so much. I mean, we all do from time to time. At this level, it comes with the job. Long hours and occasional weekend work are standard. However, we're more likely to work remotely from home these days."

"Yet today, Mr. Park was in the office."

Hancock was unfazed. "From my own experience, there are times when it's easier to pop into the office when no one's here. The place is shut down. It's quiet. No interruptions or distractions. All the stuff you need is here. You can focus on the work. Bang it out and be done with it."

"Is that why you came in?"

"Me? No. I forgot something. I'd jotted down a phone number on Friday and forgot to take it home. I popped in to grab it."

"On a Sunday?"

Aimee Hancock placed her hands on the tabletop and looked back with an inscrutable smirk. "I'm funny that way, Detective. Once I get an idea in my head, I want to get it done there and then." She seemed to take extra pleasure in saying that.

From what he'd seen so far, Henry could easily believe she wouldn't wait to act if she could do something immediately. The CEO was a mover and shaker who wasn't afraid to shake things up. "So you drove to the office to get the number."

"No big deal. I live close by."

"And how did you discover Mr. Park?"

"His car was outside, so I knew he was here. His office lights were on. I ducked in to say hi and…well, you know…"

"Quite a shock."

"It was."

"Was he still alive when you found him?"

"No"

"How do you know?"

"No pulse. I checked." She shot Henry a look as if expecting a rebuke. "I know you're not supposed to touch the body, but if Sam was alive, I was calling for help."

"Of course."

"I didn't touch anything else," Hancock affirmed, glancing between the detectives. Maybe a little defensively.

Calmly, Henry continued the thread. "Just to be clear, Ms. Hancock, when you say you touched nothing else, does that include changing the position of the body?"

"That's right."

"Including Mr. Park's hand on the atlas? That's exactly how you found it?"

"*Yes.*" Her eyes flared. "I just told you I didn't touch anything else. That's annoying."

"My job is asking annoying questions. Answers matter, Ms. Hancock. We need to know what we're dealing with."

For that, he earned a glare of disapproval. It faded quickly as the factory owner remembered the gravity of the situation. "Sorry. You're right." Hancock heaved a full-throated sigh that shook platinum blonde bangs as she collected herself. "Sam's hand is where I found it on the atlas. I checked his neck for a pulse."

"Thank you. That was important. We suspect Mr. Park might've been trying to leave a message. If so, perhaps regarding South America or Argentina?"

She gave a head shake.

"Did either of those places mean anything to him?"

"I've no idea."

"Did he ever talk about those places?"

"Not to me."

Henry swung toward Janet to see if she had any questions. She did. Leaning forward slightly, she asked, "Ms. Hancock, what about webcams or CCTV? Are they any on-site?"

"Only in the back by the loading dock."

"Nothing at the other entrances or inside the building?"

"No."

Janet scratched a note in a little spiral notepad. "And you saw no one else in the building or outside while you were here, apart from Mr. Marsh?"

"That's right. Only Tom."

Janet explained to Henry, "Tom Marsh was in the loading dock area; he's the shipping and receiving manager."

Henry seized on this. "Hold on, this Mr. Marsh was in the building when you found Sam Park?"

Aimee Hancock edged forward to prop her elbows on the table. With some irritation, she emphasized her following words. "Don't jump to conclusions. Tom Marsh isn't a killer. After I saw Sam had no pulse, I went to my office to make a phone PA broadcast to see if anyone else was in the building. Tom answered the PA and came running."

"The loading dock is at the other end of the complex?"

"It is."

Henry frowned at a thought. "Why did you go to your office to use the phone? Why not the one in Park's office?"

"*Because I'm not supposed to touch things at a crime scene.*"

It was a direct dig at him, which she enjoyed doing. Henry came back with a muted chuckle. "*Touché*, Ms. Hancock. Good thinking. What happened after Mr. Marsh joined you?"

"Not much. Tom was as shocked as I was to see Sam. He'd heard nothing. Saw no one. Not in shipping or other parts of the facility. As far as we know, we were alone."

"Where is Mr. Marsh?"

"Not here," Janet jumped in, knowing Henry might be irritated and wanted to explain. "He had to rush to the hospital. His wife called. Their daughter tripped and broke her arm. The girl was in a lot of pain. Marsh went to be with them."

"I said it was okay," Hancock interjected, making it clear she didn't care if he approved. "I'd just called the police. Tom hadn't seen anything, so I let him leave. That probably was wrong. Too bad. The guy was worried sick about his kid. Tom Marsh is no flight risk. He's a hard worker, and Becca's his only child. I wasn't going to make him agonize about her while waiting for you guys. You can talk to him later." The CEO shot a look at Henry as if daring him to criticize her for making that call.

"Understandable," he agreed amicably, which seemed to appease her. "Then perhaps you can answer one question for me. What was Mr. Marsh doing when he heard your PA announcement?"

"He was prepping a shipping pallet for pickup today."

"You mentioned a camera?"

"Outside the loading docks. Helps us know when trucks get here."

"That gets us back to access security. The doors I've seen have electronic locks. Do all of them?"

"Yes, all of them. A key card is needed to gain entry."

"Every employee is assigned a key card."

"Correct."

A thoughtful pause.

He looked at her pointedly. "You realize this suggests the killer is one of your employees?"

The statement caught the CEO off guard. A hand came up to rub her forehead. "Shit. I hadn't thought of that." She groaned, shaking her head.

The detectives gave her time to consider the significance of this.

After a minute, Janet spoke up, eager to confirm an idea. "Ms. Hancock, am I correct in saying that each key card is coded for a particular employee?"

"Uh, yes," she answered after a pause, her mind elsewhere.

Janet tossed an eager glance at Henry before continuing. "So your security database should record who came in and at what time."

"Oh, right."

"Can we get printouts of the key card swipes? Is that a problem?"

The factory owner looked back sheepishly. "Our human resources director handles that. Lalani's on vacation. She's back tomorrow. And I don't know how to work the system."

"The sooner we get the data, the better. There's no one else who can get us the report tonight? Your HR director doesn't have a backup?"

"She does. Sam Park."

An awkward silence followed.

"Ah…well," Janet conceded, "tomorrow'll have to do."

Henry cleared his throat. A question was still niggling at him, and he wanted to address it before it was forgotten. "I'd like to return to the world atlas for a minute."

"What about it?"

"I'm told the atlas had special significance to Mr. Park."

Hancock smiled, recalling. "Sam loved books. Old books were a passion. The atlas was special, a gift from his daughter. It wasn't only a reference book but an art object." Her hand flipped back dismissively. "Personally, I don't see the appeal when it's so much easier to look things up online."

Easier but not always better. Henry wasn't going to disagree with her, though he felt her world was much smaller because of her utilitarian view of books; she was missing their ineffable appeal beyond the practical. Staying on topic, he asked, "Did the atlas mainly sit on the stand, or did Mr. Park use the atlas often?"

"Often," she said without hesitation. "I've seen Sam with the atlas a few times. It's more than pretty maps; it's got charts, diagrams, and tables. And before you ask, I still don't know why he had the book open to South America."

Fair enough, though he was pleased to learn Park was familiar with the reference book. That might be helpful later. For now, there were more pressing matters.

"You mentioned a daughter," he said. "Is she local?"

"No, she lives in Arizona...Prescott. She's a nurse."

"Any family in town?"

"No. The only other family was his wife, who died some years back of ovarian cancer—" Hancock stopped abruptly, her body jerking upright. "Hold on...Jim...no, not Jim. Joe! Joe Prescott!" She whacked the tabletop in triumph.

Janet's eyes narrowed. "Who's Joe Prescott?"

"Oh, sorry. A former employee. Earlier, you asked if anyone wanted to hurt Sam. Joe Prescott would be at the top of the list. I'd totally forgotten about him until a second ago."

"What about him?" asked Janet.

"He had anger issues." Hancock shuddered at the memory. "Some mental health thing. He got so bad we had to terminate him for cause. It was not pleasant. The man was angry and threatening. Even after he was fired, he kept showing up in the parking lot and badgered staff. We had to get a restraining order, even hired a security guard for two months to deal with him in case he came back."

"Did he?"

"No, thankfully."

"And you think Prescott blamed Mr. Park for his dismissal?"

"It's a long story, but, yeah, I think so. The guy blamed everybody for his problems except himself."

"How long ago was he terminated?"

"Six months. Maybe seven."

Henry looked at Janet. He could tell they were both thinking the same thing. "We're going to have to talk to Mr. Prescott. We'll need the details of his dismissal and any contact information."

"No problem. Lalani can give you all you need, as well as her thoughts. She was there for part of the termination. Sam was with her to make sure Prescott didn't do anything."

"That sounds ominous. Prescott was that bad?"

"Believe me, he was."

Henry thanked the CEO. Things were starting to look up. The bellicose Mr. Prescott was now at the top of their person of interest list.

# CHAPTER 4

Early morning was Henry's favorite time of day. Before the world awoke, the day was fresh, and the sins of the previous night were not yet revealed. Morning was a time of peaceful reflection with a mind not yet soured by bad news or ruined expectations. In the morning, all things were still possible.

As usual, his day started well before sunup in his basement. He'd just concluded the Wing Chun third form set, *biu jee* or shooting fingers, the problem-solving set with numerous elbow strikes, diagonal rotations and leg sweeps, useful when the practitioner got into trouble. Some called them the emergency techniques. He'd conclude his two-hour workout with a twenty-five-minute run outside. One way or another, this had been his daily routine for nearly three decades. Now, in the fourth year of his fourth decade, he needed to put in extra effort to maintain his skills, let alone improve them. Fortunately, his branch of Wing Chun, the Leung Sheung branch, cultivated the use of "soft" energy rather than "hard," which meant he was less likely to wear out his body. Muscle strength and stamina were still vital in a street fight. Skill deteriorated in an exhausted fighter. He'd learned long ago that a fit body was the first and most important weapon in a martial artist's arsenal. Henry's body was aging and he knew it. Near-fatal injuries seven months earlier had done him no favors. Compound fractures and ruptured organs were a significant setback to one who'd been in prime physical shape. He'd healed quickly but knew his body didn't feel the same. Even now, he had to make accommodations for his current physical reality.

His eyes flicked to the analog clock hanging on the cinder block wall. Almost finished. Legs were stretched in preparation for his predawn run. Before that, though, there was kung fu shadowboxing.

While doing squats, he noticed his lower back felt tighter than usual, a misaligned vertebra, another token of his injuries. Good thing he was seeing his chiropractor later. Cassie would pop the troublemaker back in place.

Henry was a pattern guy who liked doing things in a predictable manner for a predictable result. These early morning workouts were his rock. His way of getting ready for a new day.

Janet Lau was not a morning person. Willpower alone got her out of bed every day. That and a dread of being late to work or appointments. She hated letting people down, and being tardy was a sure way of doing that. For this reason, she didn't waste a lot of time getting ready. A quick brush through her jaw-length bob, a dab of makeup—enough to make her presentable and feminine. Not that much was required. Genetics had gifted her with a pleasing face with graceful contours. Good thing she didn't like fussing with face paint; it didn't take much to achieve a decent result. She was too practical for anything else and turned off by excessive showiness. A rib-knit turtleneck and navy slacks prepared her for a quick breakfast of yogurt, blueberry toast, and cranberry juice.

Then came her cognitive exercises.

For the past three weeks, Janet had forced herself out of bed thirty minutes early to make time for them. Brain games with playing cards and logic puzzles ended her morning prep. She couldn't wait to wave buh-bye to the effects of a mild concussion, an injury from her first homicide case, which had concluded successfully with an arrest, though she could've done without this souvenir. Starting the day with mental clarity mattered; it galled her to think her coworkers might doubt her ability to perform her job.

Janet was her own worst critic.

Then again, she had high standards.

Walking into the police station later, she hoped for an uneventful morning that might let her slide into the demands of the day. Crime in Gillette, Minnesota, usually dropped this close to Thanksgiving. Even criminals took the holidays off. Some of them. She hoped to get a running start on the Samuel Park homicide.

Nope. Not gonna happen.

Seconds after hanging up her jacket and greeting Henry, he informed her they'd been summoned to Chief Bowman's office. Before morning roll call, which was unusual.

"Close the door," Bowman's silky voice directed. His stocky frame sat stiffly behind his desk.

Janet's chest tightened. *Something's up. Bowman's not smiling.*

She cautiously lowered herself in a chair beside Henry, surreptitiously searching the chief's face for a hint of what to expect. The Black man's rugged face revealed nothing of his mood save for a twitch of the full dark mustache that suggested he was displeased. On the window ledge behind him rested a framed photo of his family. Next to this was a bobblehead of actor Samuel L. Jackson glaring back disapprovingly.

Chief Frederick Douglas Bowman waited a minute before clearing his throat. Twice. Janet's gaze wandered to the bobblehead, where the Jackson figure seemed to be glowering at the chief's back for him to get on with it.

"It's been a while since I checked in with you two," he began. "You've both recovered from or are recovering from injuries. How're you feeling?" Inquisitive eyes shifted between them.

"Doing fine," Henry said, offering nothing else.

Janet was only a month into her convalescence and was stingy about specifics. Nobody wants to tell their boss what they're really feeling.

Bowman appeared satisfied. "Good. No lingering effects, Henry?"

"I'm good, Chief. Pretty much my old self."

"And you, Janet?"

"Improving every day. Maybe ninety-five percent."

Well, that might've been a tiny exaggeration. Her mental clarity varied from day to day. In truth, she was more like eighty-five to ninety percent if you included the temporary bursts of fuzzy thinking and headaches. Still, she didn't want to give the chief any reason to treat her with kid gloves. She trusted he understood it took time to recover from a blow to the head. *Had it been only four weeks?* It seemed longer. She bit her lower lip, worried the point of this meeting was to review their mental health status.

Bowman's granite face gave away nothing. He sat back a little. Hands large enough to palm a grapefruit settled on his leather desk pad. "Glad to hear things are going well. What about caseloads?"

"Manageable," Henry supplied. "Slowing down with the holidays."

"Good." Bowman looked pleased. Cleared his throat again. Chit-chat time was over; he wheezed in a preparatory breath in a more serious vain. "You recall that partnering you two was always a temporary assignment."

Icy fingers clutched Janet's heart. *Crap! Was that what this was about? Was Bowman splitting them up?*

"Ninety days," Bowman went on. "That's what I said. Special circumstances, what with Henry's return from long-term disability and you, Janet, newly promoted. Well, given current conditions, I've decided to extend your partnership until sometime early next year."

"Oh!" said a delighted Janet. A reprieve. She loved being mentored by her uncle. They got along great, and these months working together had given her a chance to learn more about him. The bond she had with him had only deepened.

Henry's reaction was more circumspect. While he nodded at the news, he also eyed the chief with an air of suspicion as if he expected something had been left unsaid. Janet reminded herself that her uncle had far more experience dealing with their boss than her.

Bowman was saying, "You two work well together. No point in stopping a good thing. As Henry said, we're heading into a quiet time of the year. No need to make any unnecessary changes."

There came an awkward pause.

Chief Bowman, a big, solid, middle-aged man, shifted uncomfortably in his chair as if a pinecone was stuck in his butt crack. "The mayor called this morning," he divulged in a strange voice.

The statement hung in the air like the smell of a wet dog.

What, Janet wondered, did the mayor have to do with anything? She started getting a bad feeling when she noticed Henry give a low grumble. His suspicions confirmed? She decided to pretend the call was a good thing.

"What did the mayor have to say?" she said with bright eyes.

"He wanted to know how the Hancock case was going."

Henry frowned. "Seriously? We got the case yesterday afternoon."

"I know," Bowman said.

Henry wasn't leaving this alone. "Why is the mayor of Gillette interested in an active homicide investigation?"

"Aimee Hancock is his sister-in-law."

Janet's eyebrows sat up. "His sister-in-law? That could get awkward."

"Tell me about it," Bowman complained. "Stenson is married to Aimee Hancock's younger sister. He heard about the killing from her. I shouldn't have to tell you he's interested in a good outcome."

Henry's eyes narrowed. "What does *that* mean?"

"Your guess is as good as mine. I think his definition of a good outcome is one that doesn't get his sister-in-law or her company in trouble."

Henry made a face.

"I know!" Bowman came back.

Puzzled, Janet voiced her concern. "So how does that affect us? The mayor's 'interested.' Is he trying to influence our investigation?"

Bowman's brow furrowed. "He better not. He says he wants to be kept informed of our progress."

"Only informed?"

"That's what he said."

Janet wasn't convinced. "You believe him?"

The chief spread out his hands. "Stenson said all he wants is to know what's happening before it gets to the media."

She snorted derisively. "Oops, sorry. I didn't mean for that to sound so skeptical."

"No worries. You're in good company. If I have anything to say about it, Stenson'll keep his distance. I won't stomach any outside interference. I'm simply giving you two a heads-up that we're being watched closely on this one. Be careful."

Great, Janet thought, more pressure. Just what she didn't need right now.

Bowman noticed her reaction. "The situation sucks but can't be helped. I'll do my best to keep Stenson off your backs. Bear in mind Hancock Blades is a major employer in this town, and the owner has a direct pipeline to City Hall. Try not to step on too many toes."

From outside came the rumble of a passing heavy truck that made the miniature Samuel L. Jackson nod in agreement.

On the way back to their alcove, Janet felt Henry tug her elbow. He pulled her into an empty interview room and closed the door. It was a stark, tiny space with room for a small table and several chairs.

"What d'you make of that?" he said in almost a whisper.

Janet was relieved he'd asked. Felt like a co-conspirator. "The mayor doing what he did, calling Bowman like that. Is that normal?"

"No. For him, this case is personal."

"For sure. So what's our plan?"

"Don't do anything different. We do our jobs."

She liked the sound of that. A little rebellious, but it was her senior partner's recommendation. By nature, Janet wasn't a rebel, being more of a go-with-the-flow gal—whenever possible. That said, a good chunk of her DNA came from her obstreperous Scottish grandmother, Aileen Kerr Campbell, a fiery Aberdeen girl, born and raised, and proud to let you know it. There was enough Nanna Aileen in Janet to not take kindly to an interfering politico keeping her from doing the right thing. She doubted she'd be bold enough to take a page out of Aileen's book and tell an interfering mayor to *"G'wa ya gype!"* ("Go away, you silly person!") But she enjoyed thinking she could.

The detectives emerged from the interview room, barely stepping into the hall as a voice called out:

"Oh, you *are* here!"

Half-turned toward them stood a uniformed officer whose boyish Celtic features appeared relieved and cocky at the same time. Officer Ken Ferguson approached, a mischievous twinkle in his eye.

"Detective Lau, Henry, been looking for you; you got some groupies in the lobby," he wisecracked. "Don't keep 'em waiting. They're hot to see you." The impertinent mouth mocked.

Henry glared at him. "What the hell are you talking about, Ferguson?" Ken Ferguson was a recent hire to the Gillette Police, a fairly likable recruit who fancied himself a funnyman. Loved to tell jokes and pull occasional pranks. Henry didn't know him well and found the man annoyingly unfunny. He couldn't tell if the newbie was serious or pulling one of his lame pranks.

"No joke, I'm serious," the other insisted. "Two women asked to see you. They're waiting in the lobby."

"Okay...thanks."

Having delivered his message, the snickering officer continued on his way. "*Two* women! Must be nice!" he insinuated in a voice like a braying donkey.

Henry was not amused.

Exiting through the bullet-resistant security door, the first thing Henry noticed was a mass of Cherry Kool-Aid hair, one he'd seen recently. It didn't take much effort to recall when and where. The woman, pushing fifty, full of life and an expressive face, perked up when she saw him. Bundled in a puffy coat in deference to the weather, she nudged her companion, younger by more than a decade, tall and slender with an elegant jawline. She wore her lustrous black hair long and straight, offering a muted smile in greeting.

"I'm Detective Lau," he said. "What can I do for you?"

"My name is Dorothy Travers," announced the older visitor. "This is Wendy Chu. We were at Windjammer Coffee House yesterday afternoon."

"Yes, I remember. Are you here to file a complaint?"

"Oh, no. Nothing like that. I have a request."

"Request? Of the police?"

"No, of you."

He regarded her curiously, wondering what could've brought them in so early on a Monday morning. He motioned to a table and chairs a short distance from the public reception desk.

The women didn't remove their coats, which hung unzipped from their shoulders. The laugh lines in Travers' maternal face deepened as she smiled. "First, thanks for dealing with that jerk at the coffee shop. He deserved tossing out, and you did it so nimbly, almost dancelike."

Henry cocked an amused eyebrow at her choice of words. At the time, being dancelike hadn't been part of his action plan.

"After you and your friend left," Travers added, "we spoke to the manager. Glenda said you're a regular customer. Told us about you. I wanted to talk with you, and she suggested we get here before you started your shift."

"Good idea. Although a phone message would've worked."

She shrugged. "Yeah, but I'm old school. I like dealing with people face-to-face."

"Well, you've gone to a lot of trouble. What is it you want?"

"Glenda said you're some kind of kung fu master."

"Not a master," he corrected, too humble to assume that honorific. He'd run into too many self-proclaimed martial arts *masters* who didn't measure up and diluted the respect due to legitimate masters. "I'm pretty good," was all Henry would say.

"Okay. Um, Glenda said you've practiced Wing Chun for almost thirty years. Is that right?"

"It is."

A pleased Travers exchanged looks with her companion. "Wonderful! Have you ever choreographed a fight? A pretend fight, I mean."

"No."

"Not important," she dismissed as if anticipating his reply. Setting her elbows on the small table, she propped her chin on her hands and fastened eager eyes on him. "I'm the director of the Dorothy Travers Dance Company. Wendy is one of my lead dancers. We're putting on a big show at Northrop Auditorium next month. The University of Minnesota's hosting a huge holiday cultural event with bands, singers, and dancers. Our segment is a celebration of Chinese culture through dance, a martial arts dance."

"It's like nothing seen here before," Wendy broke in, unable to hold back her enthusiasm. "A dramatic story told through stylized martial arts, backed by traditional Chinese musical instruments."

Now he was curious. "Which martial arts?"

Wendy ticked them off on her fingers. "Southern Preying Mantis, Tai Chi Chuan, Tibetan White Crane, Baquazhang, and Wing Chun."

Wing Chun.

That last piqued Henry's attention. He sat back, understanding their interest in him.

Merely talking about the dance lit up Wendy's pretty face, which became more beguiling as she spoke. "The dance tells the story of a martial artist's journey. Dottie's done an incredible job."

Travers made a deprecating gesture. "The lead character is a young Wing Chun master. Detective Lau, what I came to ask is if you'd be our Wing Chun consultant."

Henry's eyes grew wide. "For a show going live in a few weeks? Uh, you want me to teach your dancers Wing Chun? There's not enough time!"

"No, no, you're right. The dance moves are an interpretation, an artistic impression of the specific fighting style. Justin Huang, our lead male dancer, already got instruction from a different local Wing Chun consultant who had to bow out."

"Who was this?"

"Fernando López. You know him?"

"I know him. Good guy. Why'd he drop out?"

"Family crisis," Travers said. "His brother in Georgia fell off his roof. Broke his hip and can't work or do much else. Fernando went out to help the family."

"That's tough."

Travers reached out to touch his hand. "Please think it over," she implored, "I'm not asking you to start from scratch with Justin. You'd correct his movements or answer questions. The hard work's already done. The upcoming rehearsals are for technical execution. May I show you something?"

"Sure."

From her shoulder bag, she pulled out a 10-inch tablet. "Our show's inspired by one performed in Beijing last year. I contacted the dance company to get permission to use some of their ideas." Travers slid the tablet closer to him. "This is a short segment from their show. Three minutes of the Baguazhang performers. It'll give you a good idea what we're aiming for."

She started the YouTube video.

A dozen female dancers stood in front of a background as black as endless night. They stood illuminated, each clad identically in formfitting black satin *hanfu* dresses with white collars and cuffs, black leggings, and kung fu slippers. They wore simple makeup, looking elegant and statuesque—

With arms and hands raised in a ready fighting stance.

In their center stood their master, a woman who stepped toward the camera and began a slow, circular, spiraling dance to the pulsing, haunting rhythm of *tanggu* drums, the violin-like *erhu,* and the bamboo flute. The others followed her movements in perfect unison, stepping, circling, and kicking. The flick of their hands looked like birds in frenzied flight. Stepping from the darkness, a man approached the Baqua master. They fought in a dramatic, thrilling dance of attack, parry, and counterstrike until their mock battle ended in a peaceful acknowledgment of the other's ability.

By the end of the video, Henry was grinning, moved by the beauty of what he'd just seen. The challenger to the Bagua master was doing

Wing Chun or a version of it. For a moment he was transported back to Hong Kong and his youth. "That was wonderful!" he said.

The dance director looked at him with hopeful eyes. "Does that mean you'll do it?"

"What kind of commitment are you looking for?"

"A few evenings over a couple of weeks."

Henry considered this. "I'm willing to give it a try. The catch is I do have active investigations. They sometimes require unexpected evening work." He looked to see how she'd react to that.

"Whatever works," she came back. "We can be flexible. This is short notice. So…is that a yes?" A wishful lilt shaded her voice.

"Yes, I'll do it. When do I need to show up?"

"Tonight?"

His eyebrows stood up.

"*If you're available*," Dorothy Travers hastened to add.

"I'll see what I can do."

"Great! We're still rehearsing at my studio. I'll give you the address and other details."

Well, he thought, this'll be a new experience.

# CHAPTER 5

From a distance, the Hancock Blades factory complex resembled an upscale fashion mall; its several gabled blue-metallic roof elements, large windows, and arched roof portico looked nothing like the typical manufacturing plant. The uniform dusting of snow on the parking lot from the day before was broken by lines of parked cars and footprints.

The Malibu doors closed. As they marched up the broad granite steps to the front entrance, Henry noticed how Janet kept looking at him.

"*What?*"

"You and a dance company. I'm still enjoying that."

"I'll be a consultant."

"A *dance* consultant," she teased, launching into a playful twirl.

"Uh, again, not the dance part, for the kung fu movements."

Janet snorted, "For kung fu *dancing!*" Another twirl before she squeezed her uncle's arm. "I'm just pulling your chain. You'll have fun."

He let the remark go without comment; they were about to enter the lobby and had to transform into dignified representatives of the law for the interviews ahead. The greeting from the receptionist was subdued. News of the death must have spread, he suspected. Henry announced who they were, and they signed in. He and Janet were attaching their visitor badges when the security door to the executive suite creaked open.

Out stepped Aimee Hancock. No sweats or yoga pants today. The CEO was dressed for battle, decked out in a crisp white shirt blouse, dark gray trousers, and black pumps. Her snow-white hair was styled, her makeup tasteful and attractive. Alert and put together, she effused professionalism, a far cry from the disarrayed, embattled-looking woman from the day before. "Detectives, I was told you'd arrived." Even her greeting was a turnabout from yesterday, welcoming, as if pleased to see them.

It was a difference Henry appreciated. Often in his work, he saw people at their worst moments while he peppered them with deeply personal questions they were in no mood to answer. He suspected the factory owner's pleasant manner was more for show than it was sincere, a bit of public theater done for everyone's benefit on such a grim occasion. To rally the staff. Keep up spirits.

She said, "Just so you're both aware, this morning, we had an all-company meeting. I broke the news about Sam. I told the staff to expect a visit from you today and to cooperate fully with your investigation."

Henry and Janet nodded in appreciation.

The knife factory executive swung out a well-manicured hand to follow her. "Our HR director is ready to see you. I texted her last night. Lalani came in early to work on your request. This way." Aimee Hancock led them to the first office past the security door, where she made introductions. "I'll leave you in Lalani's capable hands. With Sam gone, I need to review what he was working on. If you need me, I'll be in my office." The CEO flashed a tight smile and tramped away as one with too much to do and no time to do it.

Lalani Dunne's office was compact but alive with greenery she nurtured in rows of narrow trough containers, small terra cotta pots, hanging planters, and a Mason jar. The woman standing behind the desk was in her mid-thirties, with an oval face, a pert nose, and enormous dark eyes that pulled you into them. Her wide mouth smiled sunshine. Long black hair draped across her shoulders. With a figure that filled out a dress like nobody's business, she pulsed with vitality. For a brief instant, Henry forgot why they were there. All he wanted to do was just look at her; she was a living, breathing work of art. But gawking at her would've been wrong for so many reasons, as well as just plain rude. What could he say? He appreciated beauty and was not immune to the antediluvian impulses of biology.

Pulling himself together, he focused his attention on the business at hand.

"Please sit," Lalani waved them to a pair of clothbound chairs. "Pardon me if I'm a little out of it." She managed a wan smile. "A mix of the news about Sam and jet lag. I was up for thirty hours straight."

Janet tilted her head. "Thirty hours? What were you doing?"

"I was in Maui."

"Nice! Vacation?"

"This trip was only partially a getaway. I grew up there. I was also visiting family."

Henry smiled. "Grew up on Maui? What motivated you to move to Minnesota, the frozen north?"

"I met a man."

"Ah."

"And married him. We're still married. That was twelve years ago. Terry said he'd move to the islands, but he had a great job here and, except for a trip to Seattle, I'd never been to the mainland."

"Well, you can't get much farther into the mainland than the Midwest."

A playful glint warmed Lalani's eye. "My parents are still confused why a girl from Kahului would choose to live in a place where the air hurts your face for a quarter of the year."

"And yet here you are," Janet said, impressed.

"It took getting used to, and I don't mean just the cold." Lalani's tone darkened. "Things are getting tougher on the islands. Real estate prices are insane. Regular working people can't afford to buy a house. Native Hawaiians are forced to leave our homeland. I was open to change. I'm a Minnesotan now," she added with pride. "I take walks when it's ten below zero, learned how to ice skate, and do cross-country skiing—" She stopped abruptly at a realization, her smile fading. A heartfelt sigh followed. "I'm rambling. Sorry, it's the jet lag. You're here about Sam."

Indeed they were. Which was too bad. Henry could've listened to her ramble longer. Lalani Dunne had a lively and soothing voice. But the spell was broken. Time to get serious again. "Take your time," he said.

She reached for a mug of coffee and took a long, indulgent sip. "That's more like it." She smacked her lips. "I'm ready. What can I do for you?"

"Tell us about working with Mr. Park."

"Operations and human resources go hand in glove. And Sam's fingers were in a lot of company pies. Sam was good at his job."

"Did people like him?"

"I'd say so."

"Any ideas on who'd want to hurt him?"

She speared him with a look. "You want to know about Joe Prescott. Aimee asked me to dig up his file. And before you ask if anyone else had it in for Sam, there isn't. He's the only one that comes to mind, a real piece of work."

"We heard Prescott left under a cloud."

"A very dark one. The man was disruptive. Made violent threats."

"How violent?"

The HR director squinted at the ceiling, recalling. "I can't remember him physically hurting anyone. He threw tantrums, made wild accusations, gave you the stink eye if you looked at him the wrong way. Threatened to 'get even' with people."

"'Get even,'" Janet interjected, leaning forward. "He actually said that?"

"Oh yeah."

"But you don't think he ever attacked anyone?" Janet pressed.

Lalani shook her head. "As far as we know. No complaints were made. Seems he was all talk, but we couldn't take any chances. We had to terminate him before he got violent. The man was screaming at people." She shuddered. "He has mental issues."

Henry said, "He sounds dangerous."

The oval face gave a conciliatory nod. "Prescott was spouting all kinds of anti-government conspiracy theories and radical views. You couldn't shut him up. A nutjob, as my husband says. It got to a point where Prescott's supervisor had to pull him aside and warn him about his behavior. He was put on probation and told to keep his opinions to himself. Focus on his job. He didn't. Got worse, so he was terminated and escorted off the premises." She breathed in a shallow breath and let it out. "Except he didn't stay away; he kept showing up in the parking lot yelling at people as they came to work. We had to get a restraining order and hire a security guard."

Janet blurted, "I see why!"

"The man was scary."

An uneasy lull followed in which no one spoke. It was evident the memory of dealing with Prescott was still too fresh for the HR director.

Henry waited a few seconds to let Lalani settle her thoughts. Then he asked, "Who gave Prescott his marching orders?"

"His supervisor, Matt Johnson."

"The same guy who put him on probation?"

"Right."

Henry frowned. "That doesn't quite fit." His eyes flicked to Janet. "Why would Joe Prescott kill Sam Park if it was his supervisor who canned him?"

Janet shook her head.

The HR director stirred. "This might not be important…"

Henry straightened. He couldn't recall how many times he'd heard those words casually tossed out, words that would later have an impact on a case. "Please, go on," he prompted.

Lalani said, "There was concern Prescott might get violent at his termination, so Sam was in the room with Matt. Sam was also with me when I gave Prescott his termination package. Believe me, I'm glad he was."

You could practically feel the distress in her voice.

Henry said, "Perhaps Prescott targeted the one person he kept seeing: Sam Park. Mislaid blame? Does that fly?" This last to Janet.

She mulled it over. "Some bizarre blame transference. I suppose."

Lalani's nostrils flared. "Let me tell you, nothing about Joe Prescott would surprise me! He was living in his own warped conspiracy world. And something else I just remembered. This was before the probation thing. Line workers on the factory floor have a dress code. OSHA safety rules. One morning, Sam was walking by the hafting area, which is where the handles are attached to the blades and custom fitting and shaping are done. That's where Prescott worked. He was a hafter." Revved up by the memory, she rushed on breathlessly. "Okay, so Sam saw Prescott at his station wearing flip-flops on the factory floor. A big no-no. Sam chewed him out."

Henry's fingers curled into a fist. *Now we're talking!* "So there was already bad blood between those two before the termination."

"Yes," Lalani confirmed.

Janet made a sound of approval. Not just liking this train of thought, she jumped on board. "Let's see. Prescott, a die-hard conspiracy nut, blames Park for all his troubles. Yeah, that works."

The HR director reached behind her for a computer printout. "Here's Mr. Prescott's last known address. Aimee said you'd want it. Do you really think he killed Sam? Am I in any danger?"

Henry wanted to give her peace of mind without false assurances. "We don't know enough right now, but I think you're safe. There's no cause for alarm."

The tightness in her face eased. She visibly relaxed.

"One other thing, Ms. Dunne—"

"Please call me Lalani," she insisted with a smile as inviting as Maui sunshine.

"Lalani, do you know if there's any connection between Joe Prescott and South America?"

Her lips pressed together thoughtfully. "That doesn't ring a bell. Oh, is this about the atlas? Aimee told me."

"It is."

"You think Sam left a message?"

"Maybe." A big maybe, Henry had to admit, one he couldn't ignore. He was reminded of an aphorism by the great fictional Honolulu detective Charlie Chan: *Every maybe has a wife called Maybe-Not.* Worth remembering.

"Well, I'll ask around."

"Thanks."

Then Lalani retrieved a purple folder from which she handed a single page to the detectives. "This is the key card data you asked for."

"*Mahalo*," Henry thanked her.

Lalani Dunne's face burst with delight. "*'A' ole pilikia.*" ("You're welcome.")

Janet studied the sheet, which didn't take long. "Pretty short. Only a few entries."

Lalani explained, "It was a Sunday. No shifts. And the system only records the key card when a person enters, not when they exit."

Janet said, "Your system still records when people leave, just not who."

"Correct. Just that the door opened, and the date and time."

Janet passed the report to Henry, who gave it a glance before handing it back to her, a tiny show of confidence. He trusted her insights.

She gave the report a quick study. "The first person in yesterday was a Susan Zelinsky at 11:37 a.m. That's a new name. Who's she?"

"Susan works in accounting."

Janet returned to the report. "The next person came in at 12:05, Sam Park. Then someone exited at 12:34. I'm guessing Zelinsky because the next time anything happens is at 1:58 when Tom Marsh enters by door three."

"That's shipping and receiving," Lalani supplied. "At the back of the complex."

"Okay, and finally, at 2:21, Aimee Hancock enters." Janet raised her eyes. "That's it. Only those four until 2:56 when the police arrive. No other records. We need to talk to Marsh and Zelinsky."

"Tom's in the factory. I don't think Susan's here yet."

Janet straightened. "It's after 9:30 on a Monday. Is that usual?"

"It isn't. Susan's very dependable. Perhaps she told her supervisor she'd be in late. That'd be Jim Karjala, our chief financial officer. If you're finished with me, I can take you to him. He's just down the hall." Lalani smiled as if nothing would give her greater pleasure than assisting them further.

This woman's damn good at her job, Henry mused. Attentive, efficient, personal to the max, the consummate human resources manager. Lalani Dunne made you comfortable in her presence, so comfortable he didn't want to leave but needs must when duty calls. "I've got nothing else. You?"

Janet shook her head.

The journey to Karjala's office took less than a dozen seconds. The office was empty. Empty of Jim Karjala, that is. Instead of the chief financial officer, they happened on a woman leaving a note on his desk. Turning to go, she halted when she saw the others. Short in stature and fine-boned as a house finch, her long hair was pulled up in the back and held with a large leopard claw clip. Delicate eyes regarded the newcomers with polite interest.

"Evelyn," Lalani said, "these folks are from the police. About Sam. They'd like to talk with Jim."

She replied in a reedy voice that was a touch defensive. "He's at the Monday morning sales meeting. Should be back in fifteen minutes. I can tell him you were here." Watchful, avian-like eyes darted between the detectives. Henry could almost feel the distrust in them.

"If you'd be so kind," he said. "We have another stop. We'll come back. Could you let Mr. Karjala know we'd also like to talk to him about one of his employees, Susan Zelinsky?"

*Did her face curdle when he mentioned Zelinsky?* Or was it for another reason? he wondered. He decided to explore that further. "A quick question, Ms...."

"Brown, Evelyn Brown."

"Am I right that you also worked with Mr. Park?"

"I'm the executive assistant to all upper management. I often worked with Sam."

"Was he a good boss?"

Barely above the five foot mark, she squared her small shoulders, bristling. "Sam Park wasn't a *boss;* he was a manager. A very good one. A wonderful man."

*Okay, a little too much emotion for a simple question.* More was going on here than was evident on the surface. "I meant no disrespect; I can see his death hit you hard."

One talent Henry had was the ability to put people at ease in tense situations. Something in his sincerity and affable face made people believe this man would do them no harm. It didn't always work, but often did. He could tell Evelyn Brown was teetering on the brink. The petite woman regarded him hesitantly before she relented. A pained expression replaced her earlier brave front. "I'm devastated," she said, her voice surprisingly raw. "Sam Park didn't deserve this. Whoever killed him is a *monster*."

"No doubt. Mr. Park sounds like a good man. Maybe even a friend. Someone you respected. I didn't mean to upset you." It was an apology that seemed to placate her.

"I don't feel up to talking." Just like that, the stony façade was back up.

"You've had a terrible shock. We won't trouble you further." Turning to Lalani, he suggested, "Perhaps you can take us to Tom Marsh."

"This way," the HR director said with a parting glance at the tiny woman now standing as impassive as a Roman statue, any trace of her previous emotion ancient history.

Lalani Dunne led the detectives back toward the lobby in a rhythmic stride that caught Henry's eye. The sway of her backside was nearly hypnotic. Then he remembered: this woman is a native Hawaiian; these people know a thing or two about pelvic locomotion. Lalani's undulations continued as they returned to the lobby. After a few steps, she slowed and said over her shoulder, "That was Evelyn, as you heard. She's an ace at caring for top management. They don't come much better."

Janet quickened her pace to keep up with the HR director's brisk stride. "Mr. Park's death really shook up Ms. Brown. She was like a little pressure cooker, ready to burst. Was she and Mr. Park particularly close?"

"Can't say. Although Evelyn can be a little protective about Sam."

"Why is that?"

"She cares more than she shows; that's all I meant."

"We noticed."

Lalani offered nothing further, smiling enigmatically. Seconds later, with a swipe of her key card, she led them through another security door into the factory area, an auditorium-sized space packed with machines and line workers. A relentless low drone filled the air. Staccato thuds and pings of heavy equipment came as they walked along a black and yellow striped-bordered safe zone. Henry craned his neck to see, having never lost a boy's fascination with big machinery.

Lalani took note of his interest. "We're in the assembly area. Way in back is the fabrication wing. Most of the noise comes from the punch presses and grinders. These workers are the finishers. They put together the knife blanks and handles, sharpening, buffing, making adjustments. All done by hand here, though we do have CNC machines."

"What are those?"

"Computer-guided milling machines. Watch your step."

They'd entered an archway labeled Shipping and Receiving, where a man contemplated a bale of flattened cardboard boxes. Broad in the chest, square-jawed with a rugged outdoorsy lumberjack face, he analyzed the cardboard cube. A glance toward the visitors and the rough features softened. "Hey, Lalani, welcome back. Have a nice vacay?" he said in a voice like a rusty rasp.

"Hi, Tom, it wasn't long enough."

"It never is. Who're your friends?"

Introductions followed.

Marsh expelled a breath. The smile faded. "You're here about Sam. Let's move away from the pallets to somewhere more private. And quieter." He ushered them to an area behind huge rolls of thin steel 440C high-carbon high chromium. "How can I help you?" A pair of bushy eyebrows lifted attentively.

Henry opened with something personal. "How's your daughter?"

Marsh hadn't expected this. The rough persona melted like a gob of butter in a hot saucepan. "Yeah. Man, that was scary; broke her arm. Was in a lot of pain. She's doing fine now." A calloused hand came up to rub the back of his neck.

"Her first bone break?"

"Yeah, she's only ten."

"The first break's always unsettling."

Henry's was the voice of experience, having had a few broken bones over the years. With the niceties covered, he moved on to business. "Mr. Marsh, you were here yesterday when Ms. Hancock found Sam Park's body. Can you add any details?"

"Not much to tell," the raspy voice replied. "Got here after lunch to get some pallets ready to ship when Aimee's voice came over the PA. She sounded upset. Asked if anyone else was in the building. I answered. She told me to get to Sam's office immediately. When I got there, she showed me his body." Marsh paused, shaking his head. "It was surreal. About then, my cell rang. It was my wife calling about Becca. Aimee told me to get my butt to the hospital. She'd deal with the police."

A straightforward story, Henry thought. "How about what you saw in Mr. Park's office? Did anything strike you as odd? The position of the body? The wound?"

"Not really. It was just a shock to see Sam like that."

"What about the blood?"

"What about it?"

"Was it fresh?"

"No, the blood looked separated and dry."

Which indicated the stabbing had been done at least thirty minutes earlier. "Good observation," Henry said.

Big shoulders shrugged. "I'm a deer hunter. I've gutted plenty of animals. I've seen it all."

"One other thing," Janet broke in. "You were alone in the shipping area yesterday. Could someone have entered without you knowing?"

"Not likely. Besides the security lock, the door in the back has a bell and a light to alert workers that someone's come in. Also, it's a heavy metal door. The hinges groan like your granddad climbing out of his rocker."

She slipped him a side-eye. "Would you have heard that?"

"On a weekend with the assembly lines shut down? You bet. The place is a graveyard. You can hear that door open and close three hundred feet away."

Janet had no further questions and turned to Henry, who thanked the shipping and receiving manager for his time, adding, "Let us know if you think of anything else."

"There is one thing," Marsh's raspy voice growled. "Get the son of a bitch who did this."

# CHAPTER 6

Lalani led them back to the lobby, where Tammy, the fresh-faced receptionist, waved to get their attention. "Oh, Detectives, Jim's waiting for you."

Without missing a beat, the HR director moved to the security door, key card at the ready. "I'll take you to him."

The CFO also had a height-adjustable desk identical to Sam Park's from which he stepped away to greet his visitors. Plain looking, average height, his thinning brown hair was graying at the temples. Karjala wore a pressed blue shirt and dark dress slacks. Neat and tidy, looking the picture of an older, successful man of finance. Hospitable gray eyes welcomed them from behind metal-framed aviator glasses.

"Thanks, Lalani," he said.

With a bob of her head, the HR director turned and departed.

"Sorry I missed you earlier. Jim Karjala," he introduced himself with an extended hand. Squeezed Janet's then turned to Henry, wincing afterward. "That's some grip." He shook out his fingers lightheartedly.

A puzzled Henry looked back. Janet understood his confusion. From experience, she knew her uncle had a firm yet benign handshake. No kung fu death grip his—although she had no doubt he was capable of it—so she was as bewildered as he by the finance man's reaction.

The answer was revealed a second later.

Karjala raised his right hand. The little finger was held snugly against the third finger by two strips of first aid tape. "Not you, me. I fell last month and dislocated my pinkie. It's still tender."

Henry said, "Only dislocated? You're lucky it didn't break."

"I'll say!" Karjala laughed. "It was freaky enough popping this guy back in place. Please, sit." He returned to his desk and pressed the button to lower it to the same level as his guests, after which he eased himself into a leather chair. Once in his comfy zone, the CFO adopted a more appropriate demeanor. "How can I help you, Detectives?"

Janet took the interview lead, starting with the obvious. "Mr. Karjala, you're the money man for Hancock Blades. Chief Financial Officer."

"That's what it says on my business card."

"How *are* the company's finances?"

The money man's forehead creased, caught off guard that this was her first question. "The financials are fine," he answered tersely, a little too knee-jerk in Janet's opinion. Distrustful eyes narrowed on her. "I'm not sure I understand how that's relevant to Sam's killing?"

It wasn't. Not directly. The question had been an opening pitch, a curve ball to see how he reacted in case he'd had a pat answer prepared. Janet preferred the direct approach of asking a question and getting a straight answer, but, as she was learning, some people became more evasive when expected questions were put to them. Starting with an anticipated question only reinforced their resistance.

In reply to the CFO's question, Janet offered a disarming smile. "Your knowledge of the company's financial health may be relevant. If Hancock Blades is struggling, that could mean employees are working under some stress. Stress can cause conflict. And conflict can lead to violence."

A confident Jim Karjala held her gaze. "I can assure you the company is doing fine; we've had twenty-one consecutive profitable quarters. We're quite healthy."

A bit defensive, she thought, feeling the heat of his gaze. Did the CFO resent an outsider questioning how he did his job?

"The company's doing well then," she acknowledged.

"Very."

She tried a different tack. "Your office is next door to Mr. Park's. You didn't overhear anything he might've said recently that could have any bearing on his death?"

"Like eavesdropping? I don't do that."

"Not intentionally. People's voices carry. Mr. Park might've been on the phone or talking to someone." She looked at him in hopes he might resurrect a half-forgotten memory.

Karjala shook his head. "Sorry, nothing comes to mind. Jim's voice did carry, but I usually tuned him out."

She followed with standard questions of how Park was to work with and if the finance executive could think of anyone who'd want to hurt him, neither of which produced anything helpful. Curiously, the more Karjala talked, the more he reminded Janet of her junior high art teacher, Mr. Darby. Mr. Darby had a tone that sounded like he was correcting you for some misapprehension. You must be mistaken. And then he'd enlighten you. Which almost always came up when he embarked on the merits of fan brushes. The man loved painting pine trees with a fan brush. His lamest joke was he was a fan of fan brushes.

Shoving Mr. Darby back into the memory closet, Janet moved on. Cleared her throat. "We wanted to ask you about Susan Zelinsky."

"So I heard. My senior cost accountant."

"Has she made it in today?"

"Not yet."

"Does that surprise you?"

"It does. She's almost always in the office by now."

"She's not working remotely from home?"

"That needs to be preapproved by me, and it wasn't discussed."

"Susan didn't let you know she's running late?"

Karjala shook his head. "Evelyn mentioned you wanted to talk about Susan, so I texted her earlier. Called a few minutes ago, when she didn't get back to me. I left a message."

"And she hasn't responded?"

"No."

"Is that unusual?"

"It is. Susan's very conscientious."

"A good worker?"

"My best employee. Nose to the grindstone. Very thorough. She'll keep digging until she finds the answer." The CFO made a deep-throated rumble. "This is so unlike her."

There was another possibility. "Perhaps she had an emergency."

Karjala considered this. "I suppose…although she still would have notified someone."

*Unless she couldn't.*

*Or didn't want to.*

Although Janet wasn't going to go there. Not yet. She had a more pressing question in mind. "Susan was briefly in the office yesterday, thirty minutes before Mr. Park arrived. We think she left a short time later. Do you know why she came in?"

Karjala's shoulders rose and fell. "No. There was nothing on her plate requiring her to work extra hours."

"She was in the building at the same time as Mr. Park. Any significance to that?" Janet dangled her baited hook in the water. This fact and Zelinsky's no-show the following morning made Zelinsky a person of interest in Samuel Park's murder, perhaps *the* person of interest.

The CFO was taking too long to respond. Janet found that interesting. Zelinsky's supervisor had removed his eyeglasses and thoughtfully chewed on the metal bow. Seconds later, he straightened as though having made a decision. "I might have an explanation," he said reluctantly. "I don't like gossip, but one hears things." He slid the aviator frames on again. "There's been some talk those two were having a personal relationship."

"Park and Zelinsky?" Janet repeated.

"Yes."

Janet stole a glance at Henry, who looked back with interest. Then back to Karjala. "Any truth in that, the relationship talk?"

"I can't say. What I can say is the two of them were spending a lot of time together recently. In the lunchroom, Sam's office after hours. None of it seemed work-related."

Janet's lips parted with a quick intake of air. *This must mean something!* In a rush of excitement, she could see the dots starting to connect: Park and Zelinsky had a budding romance; she was meeting him off-hours at the knife factory when something turned sour between them; it escalated; they argued, and in anger or self-defense, Zelinsky grabbed the knife, killed Park, and now was on the run.

It fit. Was a definite possibility; however, she shouldn't get ahead of the facts. Taking a mental step back, Janet tried a different angle. "You're Ms. Zelinsky's supervisor. Was she working on anything requiring her to consult with Mr. Park?"

"No, not at all."

"Perhaps Mr. Park requested her help?"

Karjala shook his head. "He wouldn't, not without asking me. Susan's my employee."

Janet nodded. If true, this made a personal connection between them a more likely scenario, although verifying it could be difficult. But it was early days yet; one thing at a time. More to add to her to-do list. Janet turned toward Henry to see if he had anything to add. He didn't. Although the corner of his mouth tugged back a fraction. A tiny gesture of encouragement. She could read the sign. When Bowman first assigned Henry and Janet together as temporary partners, Henry had taken her aside. "Ask questions. I'll help you when you want help or I think it's useful. But I won't tell you what to do or boss you around. If you wander too close to the cliff's edge, I'll pull you back. You're smart. You're ready for this." Janet loved him for that and thrived under his mentorship, even though it had been only a few months. His covert smile was the boost she didn't know she needed until she saw it. She'd been fighting an uphill battle with *something* all morning: a vague tightness in the chest, a little trouble breathing. It'd happened just now with Karjala; she'd pushed the thought aside, thinking it a bit of indigestion. Now, she didn't know.

Having finished with Zelinsky's boss, the detectives returned to the lobby, stopping at the workstation of Evelyn Brown, gatekeeper to the executive suite. That was not her official title, but, in Henry's opinion, she seemed to serve in that capacity. Her space was across the hall and down from Human Resources, steps away from the lobby security door. Behind her was a roomy alcove with a multifunction copier, a large format high-quality inkjet printer, and well-stocked doorless cabinets of paper and office supplies. Ms. Brown barely glanced at her visitors, either too busy or too disinterested in them to bother. Over the years, Henry had cultivated some skill in reading faces and body language. He sensed an internal struggle was being waged behind the woman's pinched features and decided to address her antipathy toward them.

"Ms. Brown," he said, "it must be difficult for you to concentrate on work today after what happened to Mr. Park. I think you want to help us find out who did this terrible thing. Do you have a minute?" His voice ended on a soft note, appealing to her better nature.

She didn't look up. Kept her eyes on the printout. "No."

It wasn't a convincing 'no.' She wavered. Perhaps with gentle persuasion, she might agree.

"I'm sorry, then," Henry said, disappointed. "I get the feeling you want to tell us something about Mr. Park. Too bad. Every bit of information gets us closer to finding his killer." He inched closer. "Perhaps somewhere more private?"

He was hopeful when she didn't immediately shut him down. Brown was thinking it over. After a moment, she gestured toward a small glass-walled conference room down the hall.

Janet closed the door behind them. She and Henry remained standing. The executive assistant perched her small backside against the table, delicate fingers gripping the edge to brace herself. Safe now from unwanted ears, the small-framed woman scowled thoughtfully before muttering, "I don't know if I should say this…"

Magic words.

*I don't know if I should say this.*

Words, Henry knew, that almost always preceded something interesting.

Swallowing her initial trepidation, Brown went on. "You wanted to ask Jim about Susan Zelinsky. I caught part of what Jim told you. I walked by his door," she explained, although Henry suspected the small woman might also have big ears when it came to eavesdropping. "Jim told you he thought Sam Park and Susan Zelinsky might be in a relationship. Well, the answer is they were."

"You sound pretty positive about this."

"I am."

"How, if I may ask?"

"I've heard them talking. Saw them in Sam's office, the lunchroom, and the parking lot."

"I'm not quite following. Ms. Zelinsky is the senior cost accountant, and Mr. Park was the chief operations officer. Finance and Operations. Wouldn't those two talk often?"

Ms. Brown shook her head so emphatically it threatened to loosen the leopard shell hair clip. Loose clumps of hair dangled by her ear. "Not the way you think. Jim's head of finance. Everything goes through him. He makes sense of all the reports for senior management. If Sam wanted specifics about company finances, he'd go directly to Jim. And if he wanted something from Susan, he'd also go through Jim."

Henry nodded. Which was what Karjala had told them. Regardless, it still left the question of Park and Zelinsky's meetings unanswered. He looked carefully at the woman making the relationship claim about them. "You say you saw something?"

The cords in Ms. Brown's neck tightened. "They—Sam and Susan—weren't talking about work; that's all I know. The way they were looking at each other. Their voices. It wasn't about work!"

"What in particular?" he coaxed. Details were helpful, not innuendo.

A cloud of suspicion fell across her face. "It was after Labor Day when I saw them together. Before then, they'd hardly ever spoken except in passing like people do in the office. For a while, they sat at the same table in the lunchroom. Sometimes in Sam's office after 5 p.m., just as I was leaving. They'd be laughing, getting excited about whatever it was they were talking about. It was clear to me they were having an affair!"

"You're sure of that? Did you see them holding hands or looking at each other a certain way?"

"Not exactly."

"What does that mean?"

Pencil-thin eyebrows formed a V of consternation. "I want you to know I'm not a person who sticks my nose in other people's business. Understand? All I'll say is the way Sam and Susan behaved together was different in the past month. Noticeably different. After a while, they stopped meeting at work as often and got together after hours or on weekends."

"How d'you know this?"

Rather tartly, she said, "I heard Sam talking to Susan about it. As a matter-of-fact, Jim also mentioned it to Sam. He knew something was going on between those two. After the first couple weeks, Jim was in Sam's office, and I heard him joke to Sam about his meetings with Susan. He wondered if there was anything he should know about. Sam laughed and told Jim there wasn't, that he and Susan were working on a 'private project.'" Brown's eyebrows arched meaningfully.

A private project.

Now there was a phrase brimming with innuendo if ever there was one. Which all but guaranteed Henry's next question. "Any idea what this private project is?"

"No. Strange, though, considering Susan's direct supervisor knows nothing about it. If you ask me, their 'project' was just them humping each other."

Well then!

Henry and Janet turned to each other with the same muffled look of amusement.

"Um, thank you for sharing this," Henry said.

"*I'm not finished.* There's more." For a woman who was hesitant to talk earlier, Evelyn Brown wouldn't shut up. "The project thing," her voice sharpened, chin thrust forward, "I just remembered something I heard last week in the lunchroom. Sam and Susan were talking. I happened to walk near their table to get to the microwave. Sam said they—he and Susan—needed to get this thing done for someone by the end of the month."

Henry cocked his head to the side. "Did they say what it was?"

"I missed that. But I did hear a name. A Filipino woman, Ann Oreino."

"Ann Oreino?"

"Ann or Nan. It was a little noisy. I think it was Ann."

"And you know she's a Filipina, how?"

"My neighbor's daughter-in-law is from the Philippines. Her maiden name was Oreino."

"Does anyone by that name work for Hancock Blades?"

Evelyn Brown shrugged.

Henry turned to Janet. "We'll need to check with Lalani." Janet already had her little spiral notebook out and was taking notes.

Then back to Brown. "Just to be clear, you're positive you heard Sam Park say to Susan Zelinsky that they—together—needed to do something for this person?"

"His exact words were: 'Get this done for Ann Oreino.'"

"By the end of the month?"

"Yeah. And I wasn't the only one there," Brown added with a note of vindication. "Lalani was there. Jim, too, though he might've left just before; he loves the new coffee maker and his late-morning lattes."

"This is Jim Karjala?"

"Right." Like a winded little bird, she gulped in hurried breaths as if the last minute had sapped what energy remained in her diminutive figure.

Henry's smile encouraged her. Now that the information spigot was gushing, he didn't want to shut it off prematurely. "Was there anything else?"

She shook her head.

Kindly eyes assessed her. "I know this was difficult for you. What you told us may help break the case. Thank you."

"What d'you make of that?" were the first words out of Janet's mouth in the car. The doors to the Malibu were closed. "Juicy stuff! An affair between Park and Zelinsky."

Henry agreed. "Though we don't have confirmation. Did you notice how Brown's statements nullified each other? First, she was certain the 'project' reference meant her two coworkers were hooking up. Seconds later, the same word came up again to prove Park and Zelinsky were working on a project."

"For a mysterious Filipina who Karjala knows nothing about."

"Who isn't a Hancock employee." A fact established after a detour to the HR director's office. "Makes you wonder what's going on."

Janet laughed. "Oh, it's obvious, isn't it? Evelyn Brown's got a crush on her boss. She's jealous of Zelinsky."

"Yeah, she was protective of Sam Park."

"And dismissive of Zelinsky. You could hear it in her voice. She dislikes that Zelinsky was spending so much personal time with Park."

"Even more of a reason to get a statement from her. Get Zelinsky's side of the story. Where does she live again?"

Janet faltered. *What? A memory test!* It took her six seconds to recall it from Lalani's printout. "Bloomington."

"If Zelinsky doesn't show up for work by lunchtime or doesn't call in, get on the horn with Bloomington PD and request they do a welfare check."

"Roger that."

"In the meantime, we have a new name to research: Ann or Nan Oreino."

"Yep, I'll jump on that back at the station."

Janet was happy to tackle the assignment; she loved doing research. Unlike Henry, she got a kick working out brain teasers and puzzles. These odd scraps of information were like manna from heaven. Her muddle-headed self could use a stimulating challenge.

And who knows? Maybe she'd even solve the case.

# CHAPTER 7

Henry Lau lay face down on the drop table. Standing beside him, the woman placed her palms strategically on his L2 vertebrae.

"Breathe in." Cassie's voice soothed like hot honey tea. Then, "Breathe out." Both palms pulsed down. Exploratory fingers ran along his spine. Satisfied, she said, "On your left side, please." She placed a knee on his thigh, a hand on his shoulder, the other on his crossed arms. Her knee pressed down twice before getting the muffled pop she wanted. The other side followed. Several adjustments later, Cassie checked his skeletal alignment. Pleased, she stepped away, signaling the end of the session.

"Your lower back's a little tight today, Henry. You don't look like you've been in any fights."

A joke.

Cassie would know, having worked on his body over the years; she knew at a touch when something was off. He stood to put on his shoes. Balancing on one leg, he lifted the other foot, keeping it in the air while bending forward to tie the laces. Then switched legs to tie the other, again standing on one leg. He made it look easy. Afterward, he smiled at the chiropractor. "No fights. Just road wear."

"Uh, *yeah.* April wasn't that long ago, my friend. You may feel back to normal, but your body's still recovering. You need to take care of it." Cassie's round face scolded affectionately as dark, Mediterranean eyes drove home the point. Her straw-brown hair was styled in a pixie cut that boosted her already sprightly personality.

Henry wouldn't contradict the person whose hands had helped guide his body through the final stages of his recovery from ICU earlier that year. "You're right. I'm not a hundred percent."

"Damn straight! Your body was a mess. Broken bones, ruptured organs. Recovering from all that damage is the greatest challenge of your life."

On that she was wrong.

Another event deserved that honor, one from long ago and too personal to mention. He wasn't going to correct her, letting the comment pass.

Cassie's face and tone softened. "I don't want to come down hard on you. I know you take good care of yourself. Hell, you're the most physically fit client I have!"

"Really? Aren't some of them professional athletes?"

"A few. But even they don't keep in top shape year-round like you."

"Off-season."

"Right. You don't get an off-season." She formed a cheeky grin. "They also don't get as banged up as you."

"Not even the football players?"

"Pads and helmets. They work. If I get footballers, it's usually for knees and ankles or the odd hinky shoulder."

"Don't you have other martial artists?"

Cassie paused, catching herself before she spoke. Diplomacy was also part of her makeup. She never spoke ill of anyone, which was part of her positive energy healing philosophy. Negative thoughts breed negative energy that turns on the body unless released. However, speaking the truth also mattered; the trick was in how you expressed it. "Three others," she acknowledged. Her eyes targeted his. "The thing is, you're the only one who gets in real fights regularly. You have the scars to prove it."

"It's why I keep coming back to you."

The chiropractor smiled. "You do put yourself out there, so I'll cut you some slack." She laughed. "You also have the best sense of balance of anyone I know. I saw the way you put on your shoes."

That she'd noticed did not surprise him. Cassie's particular skillset involved body alignment and wellness. She'd worked on his body every six weeks for over a dozen years. Her comment made him feel he'd done his first teacher proud. He fondly recalled Sifu Chiang-Li emphasizing the lesson to his sixteen-year-old self: *Before you can control your opponent's body, you must first control yours. Find your center and master it. Do that and it will be hard for your opponent to move you. But you will move him.*

His first sifu would've been pleased at how far he'd progressed since that first month.

Henry's eyes flicked up. Cassie was talking, asking about his plans for Thanksgiving. "Staying in town," he said. "I usually go to my brother's for dinner."

"We don't travel either. Try to keep it simple." Proof of that was her one concession to seasonal decorations: a long, solitary string of lights hanging in her front window. Nothing else. Keep it simple.

There, in a nutshell, was Henry Lau's philosophy of life. He didn't make a big fuss about many things. Took things in stride. As he got older, he found minor irritations and setbacks weren't worth wasting energy on.

A glance at his watch told him he had enough time to grab a quick lunch before returning to the station. Starting his car, he paused, leaving the gear shift in Park as Cassie's words came back to him that he was the most physically fit of her clients. How long that would last, he couldn't say. At best, he figured he had five to seven years left at his current fitness level before age began to assert itself. Over time all things wear out, including him.

One thing Cassie had been wrong about was the most challenging moment in his life. It wasn't recovering from the broken bones and damaged organs. No, his greatest challenge had been living life after the heartbreak of Kay's death, the love of his life. The pain of losing a loved one—especially so suddenly and violently—is one that never goes away; it simply becomes part of you. Twenty-two years after she'd been taken from him, Henry still felt the crater-sized hole in his heart. Yet along with the bitter memory of losing her, there were also precious moments he did not want to forget. One could not be there without the other. He could bear the loss, knowing that he'd once been blessed by the love of this remarkable young woman.

Deep wounds always leave their imprint. One either learns to live with them or to perish by them.

Henry Lau endured.


Janet eased her car into the parking bay and killed the engine. Her eyes dropped to the bag on the passenger seat containing her uneaten lunch, and she sighed. Her tuna fish on wheat would have to wait. During the drive back from the sandwich shop, her phone had pinged, a text message notification. She pulled out her cell and read the message.

*U gonna make it 2 nite?*

A reminder from Dani Montanaldo about their dinner date. Janet's thumbs tapped out a reply: *Intend 2. So far, so good!* That was her plan if nothing important from her current cases reared its ugly head. It'd been way too long since she'd seen her best friend. Texts, emails—yes, they still did emails for longer convos (as Dani called conversations) where juicy details mattered. The occasional phone call but no actual face time in months. Now that Janet was starting to get the hang of being a homicide detective, she felt more in control of her work schedule and less guilt for not pushing herself. Chief Bowman was a big believer in work-life balance, as far as the job allowed. Even so, homicides still need to be investigated and solved in a timely manner. Distraught families expected no less. Her head injury had disrupted that. Concussion protocol required mandatory time off, which Janet had taken. Back on the job, she didn't want to fall behind. Didn't want to disappoint anyone. Didn't want to look bad.

Putting away her phone, she remained in her car for a quick meditation. Over the past few minutes, she'd felt a light pressure in her head. Closing her eyes, she continued her breathing routine, glad to be away from everyone in the quiet shell of her Mazda compact SUV. Five minutes later, feeling better, she emerged into the cool kiss of a frosty November day. With her lunch in hand, she hustled across the parking lot toward the station door.

"Detective Lau!"

She stopped and turned. Saw the owner of the voice and felt pressure on her chest. The public entrance to the Gillette Police Department shared a large parking lot with the back entrance to City Hall. Waving at her was an overweight man in a long wool coat. Although she'd never met him, Janet instantly knew who he was from his photos.

Larry Stenson, the mayor of Gillette.

*Now what? She didn't have a good feeling about this.*

*Better see what he wants.*

Janet breathed in and strode across the blacktop.

Stenson's chubby face brightened at her approach with a politician's easy, vacuous smile. Bushy white eyebrows arched like albino caterpillars. Chunky and oozing with discount store likability, he greeted her like a long-lost friend.

"Happy to make your acquaintance!" Stenson said, pumping her hand and introducing himself.

"Same here," she answered guardedly.

"I recognized you from your photo."

*And why were you looking at my photo?* Her chest was as tight as a bowstring. "Is there something I can do for you, Mr. Mayor?"

"Please, call me Larry. One of my projects has been trying to get to know city employees. Not so easy. We have so many! I saw you and couldn't pass up the chance to say hello." Earnestness practically oozed from him. His expression suddenly changed at a thought. "I'm not keeping you from anything, am I?"

Only from soothing the angry beast in my hungry belly, she wanted to say but held her tongue. Abby Lau hadn't raised her daughter to be impolite. Instead, Janet replied, "Just my lunch," holding up her bag.

"Oh, okay, I won't keep you long."

*Good. It's cold outside and I'm hungry.*

Stenson enthused, "I read a report on the dragon head homicide you and your partner resolved last month. Good work. Chief Bowman has nothing but good things to say about you. I hope you're doing well after your concussion."

"Thank you," she said, distrustful of this man she'd just met who had information about her personal health.

"Good news, then. Before I let you go, I was wondering if you're making any progress on that Hancock knife factory killing. Chief Bowman and I were discussing it the other day."

*Okay! Now she understood the real reason Stenson had waylaid her.*

She did not want to show her cards, not here, not now. "We've only just started, sir; the homicide happened yesterday. We're still getting statements from people and processing evidence."

A flash of annoyance appeared behind Stenson's mask of friendly curiosity. "Of course. You're right, it's too soon. I'll let you get on with your day. A pleasure to have met you, Detective." The mayor tramped off toward City Hall.

Janet remained standing in the cold parking lot and purged a deep breath, replaying what had just happened with Stenson. She'd been ambushed and was not happy about it.

# CHAPTER 8

"You'll never guess what just happened!"

Henry looked up from his desk computer. "Then you might as well tell me."

Janet set down her lunch and shucked her jacket. Too amped to sit, she stood behind her chair, fingers clutching the chair back as she relayed her encounter with the mayor. By the time she finished, her sense of moral indignation had spiked. Stenson's poorly veiled ruse to 'chat' with her still left a rancid taste in her mouth.

Henry was also none too pleased. "Stenson's supposed to deal with Bowman, not us. We need to tell the chief."

"I suppose…"

"You don't want to?"

She made a face. "Getting Bowman involved could stir things up. Maybe this was a one-off with Stenson; he might never talk to me again."

"C'mon, d'you believe that?"

Nope. Just wishful thinking, which seldom worked anyway. A hand came up to smooth back dark brown curtain bangs. "I guess not. We'd better talk to the chief." She blew out a breath.

He threw a chin jut toward her chair. "That can wait. For now, sit down and eat your lunch. We've got a list to work through. We'll deal with Bowman later."

At that moment, a resonant voice boomed out of the ether. "*And what exactly are you going to deal with Bowman about?*" The man himself then materialized from behind a cubicle. Chief Bowman parked his portly rear end on the edge of a nearby desk, arms folded across his broad chest, eyes shifting between them.

A mortified Janet slid down in her chair.

Henry took the interruption in stride. "Chief, I didn't hear you coming."

"Obviously not." Bowman looked pleased. "Good to know I'm still light on my feet. Not as much as in my patrolman days." He patted his round belly. "Yet light enough to surprise a highly trained martial artist with rabbit-like hearing." He glanced inquisitively between them. "I believe I'm interrupting," he said as one trying to diplomatically enter a conversation in which his name was dropped loud enough for him to have heard.

Janet hesitated, needing time to wade into those waters lest there be alligators, unsettled her boss would criticize her for speaking with THE mayor.

Not sharing her concern, Henry jumped in with both feet. "Larry Stenson approached Janet in the parking lot just now." He summarized the encounter.

Bowman frowned, stroking his broad black mustache. "I wish he hadn't done that. He's supposed to keep his distance." Annoyed, the chief wheeled toward Janet. "I'm sorry if Stenson made you uncomfortable, though it sounds like you handled the situation."

She bobbed her head in appreciation and relief that Bowman wasn't chewing her out.

The chief made his stance clear. "Next time I talk to the mayor, I'll strongly insist he refrains from directly talking to either of you unless you initiate the discussion. If Stenson bothers you again, Janet, remind him you're not at liberty to discuss the case with any outsiders, including him. And if he has a problem with that, he knows where to find me."

"Thanks," she smiled.

"Was there anything else?" Bowman half-turned, gearing up to leave. "No? Then I'll be on my way." As he receded into the background, his voice floated back toward them. "Consider me *dealt with.*"

Janet released a torpid breath and leaned forward, lowering her forehead onto her desk. Dark brown tresses formed a curtain around her field of vision. Fine with her. She'd just wanted to crawl into a hole and hide. Why had she been worried about what Bowman thought? It had worked out; he'd even complimented her. So why was she feeling anxious?

She groaned into the desktop, a groan of frustration and plain weariness of dealing with the world.

"You okay over there?" Henry asked.

"Yeah." Her voice filtered through the curtain of hair, face still planted against the desk blotter.

"You don't sound okay."

Slowly, she raised her head, sat up, tucking back errant locks behind her ears. Her sweet face looked back more agreeably. A faint, closed-mouth smile assured him. "I'm good now." Scrunched her nose.

"Want to talk about it?"

"It's nothing," she dismissed. "Just tired." Tired and feeling inadequate, she figured. Too many balls to juggle and not all of them getting their due attention. Her post-concussion symptoms were responsible for that, thank you very much, but she wasn't going to use that as an excuse.

Henry didn't press her further. That he didn't was one of the things that made working with him enjoyable. He gave her her space. Yet he cared enough about her well-being to have *asked.*

That he'd asked was enough for now.

A rumble in her stomach reminded Janet her lunch was still waiting. The sandwich wasn't going to eat itself. For the time being, hunger elbowed other matters out of the way. The beast in her belly needed attention. She couldn't think straight on an empty stomach. A hand stretched out for the paper bag from which she pulled a tuna submarine sandwich and a bag of sour cream and onion potato chips. Only then did she notice the bare status of her partner's desk. "You already eat?"

"I did. On the way back from the chiropractor. Want to go over stuff now or wait?"

She waved him on. "You talk. I'll eat." Slender fingers peeled back the wax paper wrapper. Sandwich in hand, she took a hefty bite, chewed, and swallowed before settling back to give him her full attention.

Distant voices filtered out from the dispatch room as someone opened the door. Next came the metallic clank of handcuffs from a passing uniformed officer adjusting them in his belt holder. A desk phone from one of the night shift detectives chirped before going to voice mail.

Janet took another bite of her sandwich.

Henry pushed back his chair and got to his feet. "Before I start, how'd your call go with Prescott PD?"

Janet uttered a sigh of relief. "Yeah, they agreed to make the death notification. I gave 'em the details and Jennifer Park's contact info." *At least there was that.* Janet didn't have the lousy job of delivering the worst possible news on Sam Park's daughter. The Prescott, Arizona, police were handling it, for which she was grateful. Death notifications were the absolute worst part of her job. Nobody in law enforcement liked doing them.

Henry nodded. "I'll start then."

"Good idea," she said. Although with a mouth full of tuna fish and bread, what came out sounded more like "Gud ID." Not very ladylike, her Grandma Lau would say. Too bad. Janet had more important things to deal with than proper dining etiquette. And for the record, she could be as ladylike as anybody. Poise, charm, manners, Janet had those in abundance, as well as a pleasant, cultured voice (she'd been told). Her delicately shaped mouth tore off another hunk of sandwich as she fixed her attention on Henry, whose backside leaned against the wall, hands jammed in his trouser pockets.

"The ME's report came in while you were out," he said. "Park died of a penetrating trauma to his kidney, rapid organ failure, and blood loss."

"Which matches what we saw."

"Yep. He also had superficial scratches on an arm and a small contusion on the back of the head. Cause of Death, though, was from the knife wound. It went deep."

"Forensics have anything yet?"

"Still processing. DeMarco reminded me we might not get much from Park's office. A bounty of fingerprints and DNA from employees and visitors. Too many to process quickly. The karambit knife handle was wiped. Crudely, though well enough. No prints or DNA."

"What about Park's home?"

Sam Park lived in Blaine, a suburb in the north metro area. "Blaine PD did the walkthrough. Haven't turned up anything useful yet."

Janet exhaled. "Not very promising. D'we know if Susan Zelinsky made it into work?"

"She didn't. Just before you got back, I got a call from Lalani Dunne. Zelinsky's a no-show. Hasn't answered texts or her phone."

The tuna sub lowered. Troubled eyes looked back. "Has she done a runner?"

"It's looking that way."

"I'll contact Bloomington PD and request a welfare check." Susan Zelinsky lived in Bloomington, an inner ring suburb of Minneapolis to the south of Gillette, yet another city out of their jurisdiction.

Henry shook his head. "I don't like that she's dropped out of sight. What do you think?"

*What do you think?*

The words, while simple, touched her heart. It showed respect. Her senior partner, a man with over twenty years of experience, had asked for her opinion on a question he likely already had the answer to but, nonetheless, had *asked for her opinion.*

"It looks bad," Janet agreed. The tuna fish sandwich hovered by her mouth, the next bite on hold. "Since we're talking about Zelinsky, one thing's bothered me about the key card list."

"What's that?"

"We touched on it with Lalani. Nobody uses their key card to leave a building, only to get in. What if someone was already inside?"

"Like from the day before?"

"Like walked in with Sam Park." Janet reached for the potato chip bag. "More than one person can enter on the same key card. You see it all the time. The first person opens the door and others follow them inside." Having made her point, she rewarded herself with a handful of sour cream and onion goodness.

He squinted thoughtfully. "Meaning the killer isn't necessarily someone who works at Hancock Blades."

"Yeah." Janet dabbed her mouth with a paper napkin. "If the killer walked in with Park."

They looked at each other.

Here was a potential game changer, one whose ramifications needed time to consider.

Janet's gaze drifted to her lucky bamboo plant, the only decoration she kept on her desk. Ten four-inch green stalks stood inside a pebble-filled ceramic container. From the tops of the stalks grew a bushy cluster of tall green leaves. The little plant gave her joy. She didn't know if she believed in *feng shui,* the idea that the placement of objects in a room influenced positive and negative energy. However, her spirit nearly always felt lighter when she looked at the little green shoots. The plant made her feel better. "What else we got?" she asked.

Henry said, "Speaking of forensics, they're analyzing Park's work laptop and cell phone records."

"Good."

"How about the name on the Post-it we found in Park's office? Making any headway?"

She shook her head. "No K.J. Hazzard works or has ever worked for Hancock Blades. A national search found five K.J. Hazzards. Two are dead. One is ninety years old in Waterville, Maine, one is in grade school in Mobile, Alabama, and one is in the U.S. Navy in Guam. I'd be surprised if any of them had anything to do with Park's death."

"Any thoughts on the words on the note: An Actionable Crime?"

"Makes you wonder, doesn't it? Was Park accusing Hazzard of a crime? If so, did Hazzard kill him?"

"Or," Henry countered, "was Hazzard the one making the accusation?"

Janet sat up. "You think?"

"What if he or she was, and Sam Park was looking into the allegation?"

"Yeah, but what does it mean? What crime? And who committed it, if not Park or Hazzard?"

"Exactly."

Anticipating his next question, Janet waved a potato chip at him. "And before you ask, it's the same for Evelyn Brown's mysterious Filipina, Ann Oreino. Can't find anything on her." Janet tossed the chip in her mouth. Nosily chewed and swallowed, realizing he hadn't yet mentioned the elephant in the room—literally in the room: Park's office.

"Aren't you going to talk about the atlas?" she asked.

"Nothing new," he sniffed. "So far, I can't think of an explanation for it."

"You don't think Park was trying to tell us something?"

"If he was, I don't know what. A dying message? Something to do with South America?"

"His hand was on that open page," Janet pointed out. "It must mean something."

"Perhaps. *But what?*"

Janet's hands spread in an I-have-no-idea gesture.

He acknowledged her with a sympathetic nod, reaching for his jacket. "Well, while you work with Bloomington PD, I'm off for a chat with Joe Prescott. Unless you'd like to come along."

*Let's see. Tag along to confront a disgruntled knife factory employee terminated for making violent threats? No, thank you.* "I'll pass," Janet replied sweetly.

"I figured." Henry smiled and shrugged on his jacket.

In Mandarin, Janet said, *"Wán de kāixīn!"* ("Have fun!")

"Yeah," he snorted, "We'll see about that." Half-turning, Henry stopped and swung back. "Oh, I forgot to mention. Lalani Dunne dropped another tidbit about Prescott. Another reason he was let go was he'd been harassing Susan Zelinsky. He'd asked her out, and she said no, and Prescott wouldn't take the hint. Kept bothering her and she complained to HR."

"Well, well, well." Janet livened up. "Lemme think this through. So Prescott has the hots for Zelinsky. Gets fired. Later, he finds out— or thinks— she's having an affair with the guy who helped get him fired: Sam Park." A host of possibilities danced before her eyes. "Oh yeah, that's a peachy motive for him to kill Sam Park!"

# CHAPTER 9

The Malibu was parked. Henry gazed through the windshield at Green Heron Lake. Near him, fields of brown cattails wavered in a light breeze by the lakefront. By a stand of river birches, three dark-eyed juncos foraged on snow-dusted grass, the first of the little migrants from the north. The dark gray and white songbirds were his favorite winter visitors; they signaled the impending change to cold weather. He found peace in watching them forage for food.

Peace.

Nature did that for him better than anything. On his worst days, walking among tall trees or along a city park lake was enough to lighten the weight of living in a world heavy with complications and unpleasantness. Being in the natural world helped clear his mind and lighten his heart so he could focus on things that mattered.

Such as his partner and her health.

The good news was Janet's concussion was mild. Her symptoms were on the wane and no longer as severe. Over the past week, he'd been observing her on the sly and was heartened by what he'd seen. There were fewer lapses in answering an easy question and fewer anxious moments. The latter she'd tried to conceal, but he knew. She never complained. Hid her frustration. He offered support but saw his role as guiding her with a soft touch, leaving her room to figure things out on her own. Gave her room to fail. He wasn't going to micromanage her but would do everything he could to help her.

For now, he could let that go. Thought Janet was doing well enough.

Was he?

Henry sat back and closed his eyes, flushed his mind of thoughts of work, in need of a mental reset. Lately, he'd felt bombarded by divergent images and emotions. Too many to deal with. He inhaled slow, deep, meditative breaths and absorbed the peaceful surroundings outside. Tried to be in the moment. Unfortunately, that peace was cut short a minute later by the loud squeal of heavy brakes. His eyes flew open. A garbage truck had grumbled into the lot and wheezed to a stop near a trash container. The driver climbed out of the cab. Mid-thirties, overweight. A dour face focused on his task. He wore a neon green safety vest over a flannel shirt, trudging to the trash bin as if he were mad at the world and everyone in it.

*This had to be his man.*

Henry stepped out onto the asphalt and quietly shut his car door, then strode toward the trash hauler, who was lifting a black plastic bag from the bin. He tossed it into the back of the truck and was in the middle of placing a new bag in the container when he realized he had company.

"Hello, are you Joe Prescott?"

"Who wants to know?" challenged the other.

"Detective Henry Lau, Gillette Police." He presented his badge wallet.

Most people gave the creds a passing glance; the trash hauler leaned in to inspect them. Satisfied, he straightened, eyes hard. "Okay, you're a cop. What d'you want?"

"First, *are* you Joe Prescott?"

"Yeah."

"Thank you. And you used to work at the Hancock Blade factory?"

Prescott's reply dribbled with suspicion. "Yeah…What's this about? I've been gone half a year."

No point bringing up his ugly dismissal. Antagonizing him so soon wouldn't accomplish much. Henry decided to get straight to the point. "You remember Samuel Park, chief of operations?"

A grunt of disdain followed. "Oh, I remember him."

"There was an incident at the factory yesterday. Park was killed."

For several heartbeats, no reaction came from Prescott, although Henry could tell something was boiling behind that bellicose stare. Then the garbage collector uttered a grunt of enjoyment. "Park's dead, huh? I'd say I was sorry, but I ain't."

"You didn't like him?"

"Uh, no. That fucker got me fired. But I'm guessing you already know that, so how about cutting the bullshit? You wanna know if I killed Park."

Well, since he'd asked, Henry obliged. "Did you?"

"No!"

"You do have a history with Park. Not a good one."

"Old news."

"Is it? You left the company on bad terms. Made threats. You threatened Sam Park, who's now dead."

"Whoa!" Prescott edged back, waving his hands in protest. "You ain't pinning his murder on me. I had nothin' to do with it!"

"Who said he was murdered? I said Park was killed."

The trash hauler worked his jaw. Looked angry enough to chew nails. "Why else would you be here? You wouldn't be talking to me if Park died by accident or suicide."

Fair point. Henry was impressed. Unexpected logic or an insider's knowledge of what happened.

Prescott huffed out a breath. In the cold air, it streamed as white vapor. He'd come to a conclusion. "You're settin' me up."

"No, I came to take a statement from you. That's all."

"Bullshit! I know how cops work."

"No, really. Just a statement."

Distrust crouched behind the combative eyes, ready to pounce before a new thought occurred to him. "Say, how'd you find me here?"

"Your boss emailed me your pickup route. I could see you hadn't been here yet. I've been waiting."

"How'd you know where I work?"

"I'm a detective. I have resources."

"The government! Shoulda known," the other jeered.

Henry softened his manner to come across as less threatening. "A man is dead. You knew him. I'm not accusing you of anything. Standard procedure is to interview people who've had recent or fairly recent dealings with him—*if only to eliminate them as suspects.*" This last was always a popular method to nudge people into cooperating, though usually done in hopes of getting DNA swabs from suspects. "As I said, I came here to ask you a question," he continued. "Answer it and I'm outta here."

Prescott shifted his weight, scowling. After an indecisive second, he grumbled, "Ask your question."

"Where were you on Sunday between 10 a.m. and 2 p.m.?"

"Home watching the Vikings game. That includes the pregame show."

"Can anyone vouch for you?"

"No. I was home alone."

Of course he was home alone. They always are.

A defiant Joe Prescott grunted. "I answered your question. Why're you still here?"

For half a tick, Henry debated whether to mention Susan Zelinsky before dismissing the idea, doubtful if anything this guy said could be trusted. He'd made first contact, gotten a statement, and seen what the man was like. Enough for now. "Thanks for your time," was all he said before walking back to his car.

It was nose heaven the instant Janet entered Marcello's Bistro and Bakery. The enticing aroma of freshly baked baguettes pulled her in further. Night had fallen an hour earlier. Inside Marcello's, the lights blazed invitingly as the dinner crowd gathered at this popular eatery in Richfield near the Southdale Shopping Center. Janet unzipped her jacket. Standing by a display case of pastry confections, she scanned the seating area for Dani. It didn't take long; Dani Montanaldo's laugh was one you never forgot once you heard it. Loud and boisterous with an occasional snort, her laugh bounced off the Parisienne-postered walls. She was six tables over, a lively woman on the back side of her twenties. Long, thick red cinnamon hair, an impertinent nose, a full-figured body draped in a pullover cardigan sweater and stretch canvas pants. Lively arms gestured at the man sitting across the table.

*Man? There wasn't supposed to be a man.*

Janet's jaw muscles tensed.

Dani's husband Dustan was out of town on a work assignment. The dinner was supposed to be a chance for the old friends to catch up on their busy lives. A twosome, not a threesome.

*Who was this guy?*

It wasn't that Janet suspected her friend of having an extramarital affair. No way. The Dani and Dustan she knew were happily married. On top of that, Dani Montanaldo would never cheat on her husband, having a strict code of conduct. No, Janet's misgivings came from another possibility. Dani fancied herself a matchmaker. Was this a hookup ambush? Janet's heart sank; she wasn't in the mood for a dip in the dating pool. Not now. No way would she make a good first impression still dealing with bouts of brain fog. And if she vomited in front of her date, well, he might take that the wrong way.

*Not so fast. Don't jump to conclusions. Maybe it's nothing.*

Janet sucked in a breath that went down to her belly, put on her game face, then threaded her way between the white-clothed tables.

"Hey, Dani."

"Janet!" Dani jumped to give her a bear hug. Afterward, she swung toward the smiling man she'd been entertaining. "This is Jay Kapur. We used to work together ages ago. It's been like three years since we've seen each other. And the dude just walks in here two minutes ago!"

Kapur stood and shook Janet's hand. Tall and fit looking, a chiseled face, curly black hair, and dreamy dark eyes, as Dani would later describe them. "Nice to meet you," he said with a charming British accent.

Everyone sat. From the nearby kitchen came the clank of a metal pot and the scrape of ceramic plates being stacked into a column. The lively chatter among a group of friends two tables away drifted over.

"Jay's a graphic designer," Dani informed. "He was sharing the latest low down on our old company."

Janet listened with a polite smile, on guard for the inevitable shoe to drop, namely for Dani to mention—surprise!—that Jay was currently unattached.

Surprise followed, though not what Janet had expected. Jay leaned toward her, saying, "Don't worry, I'm not intruding on your dinner. I just popped in to pick up some apple cream cheese Danishes for tomorrow." He nodded at the white bag on the table. "I'm leaving in a minute."

Janet did her best to hide her relief. Likewise, when Dani didn't insist on him sticking around. Janet wasn't in the mood to meet anyone new. Did that make her a bad person? she wondered with a tiny pang of guilt.

A very tiny pang.

But then Dani threw out a restraining arm at Jay, even though she was on the other side of the table, a symbolic gesture. "You can't go yet! Jay's working on something. It's so exciting. Tell Janet."

Jay hesitated, but Dani Montanaldo, like the moon's tidal pull, was an irresistible force. He gave a nod, lowering his voice as if confessing a murder. "I'm writing a book, a science fiction novel."

"Oh." Janet was impressed. "That's a lot of work. Have you written other books?"

"No, this is my first one. I've started others but never finished them. This time's different. I'm doing NaNoWriMo."

Janet blinked. "Sorry. What?"

"NaNoWriMo is short for National Novel Writing Month."

"That's a real thing?"

"Totally. It's been around for over twenty years. It's held in November. The idea is to write a 50,000-word novel in one month."

"A month?" Janet's eyes flashed wide. "A whole novel?"

Jay Kapur's mouth pulled into a sardonic grin. "It's not like you've got a polished, ready-to-publish book at the end. What gets written is mainly a load of rubbish. And that's okay. The idea is not to correct yourself as you go but to keep writing whatever comes out. Don't stop. At the end of the month, you have a very rough first draft." His eyes twinkled. "Now you have something to work with. You polish, make corrections, add things, remove things, play with the manuscript until you get a proper book."

Janet was charmed by his accent. "I get it. How do you eat an elephant? One bite at a time."

"Brilliant! Yes, that's it. I've busted my arse to get this done in time. Previously, I'd get distracted when I wrote alone on my own schedule. Things always managed to go a bit pear-shaped. With NaNoWriMo, you make a commitment, posting your progress online. It keeps you motivated. Thousands of people do this."

"What happens if you don't finish by the end of November?"

He gave a little laugh. "Nothing. No one is punished. It's all quite civil. If I need more time to finish the novel, I continue." Kapur shrugged. "The idea is to incentivize writers to keep working toward a goal. Which is why, ladies, I must be on my way. I still have two hours of work to put in this evening, or I'll fall behind. Nice to have met you, Janet. Dani, we need to have a proper dinner with Dustan now that I have your number. Perhaps after New Year's."

On her feet, Dani pulled Jay to her like she was a drowning woman and he a life vest.

"He seems nice," Janet said after he'd gone.

"He is. Great guy."

"And handsome."

"That too, but don't get your hopes up. Jay plays for the other team."

"Pardon?"

"You're not his type. He's gay."

"Oh."

"Wait," Dani tossed her a glance, "did you think I asked you here so I could friengineer you with Jay?"

"What the hell are you talking about?"

"Friengineer is urban slang for a planned hookup. Engineering a friend. Get with the times, girl."

Janet rolled her eyes. "The idea you even know the word is telling."

Dani pooh-poohed the thought. "It's like I said. Jay showed up on his own. Not because of me. No lie!"

"Okay, okay, I believe you."

And she did. Their friendship had been forged as teenagers. At face value, they didn't appear to have much in common. Brassy Dani and soft-spoken Janet. One an impetuous risk-taker, the other thoughtful and measured. But they liked the same music, books, movies, and engaging in the art of conversation. Moreover, they shared a similar worldview of how people should be treated. They also laughed at the same things.

"Let's order dinner," Dani was saying. "We've got too much catching up to do. Tell me what you've been up to." She waved over a waiter.

If Janet had hoped this get-together would be a distraction from the day, she was in for disappointment. She brushed lightly on her current cases without giving any details. When it was Dani's turn to lunge into her adventures in offroad fat tire bicycling and her new pottery class obsession, Janet's mind drifted back to work. Bloomington PD had done their welfare check on Susan Zelinsky. They'd found nothing. She wasn't home. No signs of trouble. The house was neat and tidy, the garage empty. Her car wasn't parked outside. Zelinsky's neighbors hadn't seen her in several days, which wasn't out of the ordinary. Where was she? Was she on the run? Or something else? The news had triggered Janet to issue a BOLO. A notification went out to all law enforcement agencies to Be On the Look Out for the missing cost accountant.

So much for a relaxing, carefree evening. One thought kept echoing in Janet's mind:

*Where the hell was Susan Zelinsky?*

# CHAPTER 10

It was a dark drive across the metro. Sporadic flurries drifted down, though not heavy enough to engage wipers. Henry could see well enough through rush hour traffic. As he neared downtown Minneapolis, he searched for the top of Target Corporation's world headquarters. The top section of the thirty-three-story building was a giant public art display. Engineered by 3M with over 680,000 LEDs, seasonal images and animated holiday scenes moved across all four sides of the enormous display. In the bleakness of late fall and winter, the skyscraper was a lighthouse of bright scenes cast into the dreary darkness. This week's motif was colorful autumn leaves drifting in the wind. He enjoyed a quick glimpse or two as his car skimmed by the outer fringe of downtown. It was a pleasant distraction from the update about Susan Zelinsky. The woman needed to be found and questioned as either a key witness to the murder of Sam Park or as the prime suspect. One way or another, she was involved. With luck, the warrant to access her cell phone records would get approved tomorrow. Which could help them track her location.

But that was tomorrow.

For now, there was nothing more he could do. Or wanted to. He was tired and looking forward to getting his mind off work. Compartmentalizing his life into separate boxes was a skill Henry had been forced to learn long ago to preserve his mental and emotional health.

*Don't worry about the things you can't control.*

The words had become his mantra. Not that it always worked, but more times than not that mantra kept his emotional footing on even ground. All stress did was bring frustration and heartache. His younger self had taken far too long to figure that out.

Even a raging hurricane has an eye of calm.

Henry worked to cultivate serenity. The best decisions are made with a calm mind and a tranquil heart. Sometimes, he cared too much, which often got him in trouble. Sailing through life's swells and tempests without crashing on the rocks was an ongoing trial. At the ripe old age of forty-four, he remained a work in progress.

Tonight, though, his plan was to unwind and relax. Let his mind go on a journey. His hands lightly touched the steering wheel to make the final turn toward his destination. Funny, he thought; despite his initial reservations, he found himself looking forward to the evening now that he was almost there.

The Dorothy Travers Dance Company was housed in an abandoned supermarket in the Northeast Minneapolis Arts District not far from the banks of the Mississippi. Neighbors in the "Nordeast" locale included a popular microbrewery, a national award-winning Thai restaurant, a Polish cultural center, and several recently built upscale apartment buildings. The tired old supermarket was given a facelift outside to help it blend in with its trendy and more youthful neighbors. The space inside had been completely gutted and redone. Flat black interior walls and ceiling. Dozens of hanging lamps from the ceiling rigging. The centerpiece being a spacious ground-level stage flanked on three sides by large blackout curtains. Facing the stage were two large stands of theater seat risers.

The custodian who let Henry in escorted him to the stage area. People were everywhere. Most looked in their twenties, men and women in T-shirts, cropped knit sweaters, sweatpants or leg warmers. From their physical appearance and stretching, there was no doubt they were dancers. All of them looked Asian. Some gathered in groups of four or five. Others stood in pairs to go over movements. In the near distance, an older woman with Cherry Kool-Aid hair waved her arms to gather an enclave of performers. Her voluminous Moroccan caftan sleeves fluttered like flags. Assertive and joyful, she instructed her youthful charges with boundless energy. Turning, she noticed Henry and burst into a delighted smile. She strode over in quick little steps.

"Detective Lau! I'm so glad you could make it."

More likely relieved he showed up, he suspected. "Call me Henry."

"Henry, please, make yourself comfortable." Travers led him to the nearest riser and a clothbound seat on the first level. Front and center. Slipping off his jacket, he draped it across the back and plonked down onto the cushion.

"Since this is your first time, we're doing a rough run-through of the entire performance. There are five sections." When she got excited, Travers tended to speak a little too fast. She paused to catch her breath. "The idea's for you to get a general picture of what we're attempting. No pressure. Just sit back and relax."

That he could do; he excelled at doing nothing.

Travers continued. "We have a few weeks before rehearsals move to Northrup Auditorium."

The venue impressed him. Northrup was an old and venerated concert hall on the main campus of the University of Minnesota. In addition to UofM events, rock concerts, films, dance, and other performances were held there. Such an illustrious location meant this show was a big deal. The Travers segment was one part of an international cultural celebration.

"We'll start shortly," the doyenne of dance informed. "As I mentioned the other day, our performance is a tribute to Chinese martial arts and culture for Westerners who've had little to no exposure to them. Please bear in mind this is an interpretive dance, not a documentary. Many of the martial movements are stylized or exaggerated for the sake of art. To juice it up. We're not aiming for one hundred percent accuracy. Though we do want the fighting moves to look authentic." Hope shined in her eyes. "If you have any suggestions for Justin—Justin Huang dances as the Wing Chun master—please let me know. I'll bring him over after the run-through." Travers explained the plan for the evening before tramping off to the stage to round up the performers for last-minute instructions.

As he waited for things to begin, Henry let his gaze roam the expansive hall, the black-painted ceiling and network of pipes that supported the lights, a side wall where the dancers' coats hung, below which were stashed rows of street shoes and bags. And then there was the colorful letterman varsity jacket. Gold arms, black body. A large blood-red disk dominated the back. Inside the disk was a silhouette of a man executing a flying kick. Above and below this, Henry saw two other design elements he couldn't make out. Too far away. Stitched in large curving burnt orange letters above the red disk were the words: Taketa-Ryu Karate. The name meant nothing to him, which he found curious as he was familiar with most of the martial arts studios in the region, at least by name. The jacket looked expensive. High quality. Showy. It screamed, "Look at me! I'm a karate guy!" None of the high-level martial artists he knew would be caught dead wearing so garish a jacket. It put a target on their backs. Brash advertising that invited trouble from bad players who saw the jacket as a boast that you thought you were a hotshot fighter. Bad players who would like nothing better than proving you weren't. The other thing this jacket did was give away your advantage. The bold design declared you had fighting skills. Or thought you had.

It was a young man's jacket. Cocky. Immature.

Henry believed his assessment was on the nose, not just conjecture. The reason?

The jacket was occupied.

The wearer couldn't have been older than twenty-six. Solid looking, hefty shoulders, a long face with a ruddy complexion, and lank, pale blond hair that needed a wash. All told a hard-hearted face.

The guy couldn't stand still. Was constantly fidgeting, shifting his weight back and forth, moving his hands. Too much nervous energy. Jacket Dude just gave off bad vibes. Why was he here? He couldn't be another consultant. The performance showcased Chinese martial arts. The lettering on the jacket implied that his was a Japanese-based art. Because of where he was standing, Henry figured Blondie was the boyfriend of one of the dancers.

Further musings had to wait. The house lights were dimming, and stage spots came on to create a mysterious background of light and deep shadows. Off to the corner, five musicians played an enchanting melody on bowed strings, flute, and drums, accompanied by the occasional percussive clank of steel rods. The cutouts suggested Chinese urban rooftops, a house, a back street, a temple. In the next minutes, Henry was swept up into the journey of a talented fighter in search of his place in the hierarchical martial arts world of the early twentieth century. The Wing Chun master engaged in thrilling and beautiful battles with four kung fu masters and their followers: Southern Preying Mantis, Tai Chi Chuan, Tibetan White Crane, and Baguazhang. The final segment, the Bagua sequence, was the most beautiful mini-story. All the fighters were female, led by their master, danced by Wendy Chu, the woman he'd seen with Travers at the coffee shop. The eleven women walked the Bagua circle, spinning, turning, and twisting with stunning synchronicity and elegance. Rapid palm strikes and whirling kicks followed as the challenger emerged from the shadows toward them. Wendy's Bagua master held her own but eventually succumbed to the Wing Chun fighter who, having proved his ability, was offered a seat with the other masters in the temple.

Dynamic. Thrilling. Beautiful.

The performance had taken Henry back twenty-two years to Hong Kong and the most intense and challenging days of his life. Memories, good and bad, flooded back. However, there was no time to dwell on those as the lights came up. Dorothy Travers made a beeline toward him. True to her word, at her side was the male lead dancer, Justin Huang, who'd portrayed the Wing Chun fighter; he had a dancer's perfectly sculpted body: muscular yet agile, neither bulky nor thin. Introductions followed. "I'll let you guys talk," Travers told Henry. "I'll come back in a bit." Her eyes crinkled at the fresh-faced performer. "Think of Jason as a lump of clay for you to mold. Ta-ta." Then off she went.

The lump of clay looked inquiringly at Henry. "What'd you think?" he asked with an artist's yearning for positive feedback.

"Great show. You're very good."

"Thanks! We're all super excited. Asian-based shows here are rare. The show's a huge opportunity for all of us. Dorothy's worked hard to make it happen."

"I can see that."

Jason changed the subject. "You're the replacement Wing Chun master."

In a quiet voice, Henry corrected, "I don't call myself a master."

"Oh, sorry. Didn't mean to—"

"No offense taken. Just a quirk of mine."

"Sure. That's kinda cool. I like that you're humble. Um, any suggestions for me?"

"One or two, if you're interested."

"Totally! I know we're taking some liberties, but I'd like to be as real as possible."

"What you're doing is excellent. Just a couple of small things."

Initially, Henry wasn't going to speak up. Nothing Justin had done was wrong. His Wing Chun stylings were close enough, just slightly different from Henry's. Different wasn't wrong. Every martial art has its families and off-shoots. Different styles stress different aspects. There are dozens of different styles of karate taught in the world, just as there are different factions of Wing Chun, each stressing its own particular insights. Divergent philosophies. A concept not limited to the fighting arts. Christianity, for instance, which has numerous denominations. Same religion yet different teachings. Likewise with Fernando Lopez, the original *Wing Chun Kuen* (Wing Chun Fist) consultant for the show. Fernando's branch of the art differed from Henry's. Not radically. Henry wouldn't undo Fernando's teaching; instead, he'd refine a few things, the reason he was there.

Henry led Justin away from the seat risers onto the main floor stage where Henry had the dancer lift his arm into a *bong sau*, the wing arm position with bent elbow and palm facing outward. Satisfied, he explained the concept behind the structure. "Imagine your energy flowing through your arm to and beyond your fingertips like water rushing through a hose. But not stiff. Relaxed yet firm." Then, with startling quickness, Henry fired a punch at Justin that effortlessly glanced off his forearm.

The dancer's eyes grew as large as bar coasters.

Continuing, Henry said, "Position is everything. So is intent. Used this way *bong sau* is a defensive deflection. Don't clench the muscles. That'll only weaken the structure. Instead, use the rest of your body with your arm. That's key. People don't see that. They only see the arm. But you, you must *feel* the connection inside, though not stiffly. My first sifu hammered that lesson into us. He'd say, 'Bend like a reed in the wind but stay rooted to the ground like a pine tree.'"

The dancer grinned; he was eating this up.

Henry spent another five minutes with Justin to work on his kicks before the latter went to a private corner to practice the changes. Feeling he'd made himself useful, Henry returned to his chair with the uncanny feeling he was being watched. A glance at the wall of coats confirmed his suspicion. Letterman Jacket Dude was eyeballing him hard. Brow furrowed in heavy concentration as though summoning up a dusty old memory. Henry settled into his seat, ignoring him. Unfortunately, that didn't last. In less time than it takes to fry an egg, the tramp of purposeful steps approached to stop a sofa length from Henry.

*Now what?*

Henry lifted his eyes to see Jacket Dude in a militant stance. A human roadblock. A contentious glare and hard mouth. Not even the pretense of a polite preamble, the man spit out a question that sounded like a demand.

"Are you Henry Lau?"

"Yes."

"The Henry Lau who was profiled in Kung Fu World magazine?"

"Eight years ago. But yeah." The article had been the result of an incident when he was in San Jose visiting Sifu Eric Kwan, a person who should rightly be called a master but who never referred to himself by that honorific.

Jacket Dude looked him up and down. The hard face hardened further, followed by a snort of confirmation. "You're supposed to be a pretty hot shit fighter."

A noncommittal shrug from Henry.

"Is it true?" the other persisted.

Henry returned a look as hard as granite. "Why does it matter to you?"

That wasn't the answer Jacket Dude wanted. "How about answering the question?"

"What if I don't want to?"

"Then I'd say you suck as a fighter."

Henry chuckled. He was already getting under this guy's skin. Too easy.

Jacket Dude bristled. "What's so funny?"

"You are. How about going back to your wall? Leave me in peace. No harm done."

"I ain't leaving. I asked you a question."

"And I gave my answer."

"Fucking asshole."

"Probably. And you are?"

"Name's Jake Bosko. I'm a fifth-degree black belt in Taketa-Ryu Karate. What rank are you? The article didn't say."

"No rank. Belts don't mean much outside your dojo. Traditional kung fu doesn't use them."

Bosko's jaw hardened. "Answer my question. You any good?"

"Why do you care?"

"Can't a guy be interested?"

"Sure. Doesn't mean you'll get an answer. And you're standing in my way, Bosko. I'm here on business."

Puffing out his chest, Jacket Dude sneered. "In your way, huh? Why don't you make me move?"

*Good grief! Not one of these bozos.*

Henry answered politely, "Do we really have to do this? Can't we sit and have a nice talk?" He padded the empty seat beside him.

It was not to be. Jake Bosko had a tree stump of a chip on his shoulder. "I'm not here to be your buddy. I'm here to challenge you."

"Challenge me?"

"To a fight. Right here. Right now."

"No."

Confusion, disappointment, then anger filled the long face. "What d'you mean 'no'?"

"I'm not fighting you."

"But I challenged you!"

*Oh, dude, grow up.*

Henry breathed heavily. This guy was getting tiresome. Like something out of an Old West dime novel where a baby-faced punk, desperately wanting to make a name for himself, goads a well-known gunfighter into a duel. Trash talk did not impress him. Trash talkers had a pathological need to stroke their egos. They were pathetic. Henry fixed a pair of stern eyes on the ill-mannered man-child. "I'm still not fighting you. I don't need to prove anything to anyone, especially you. Go away."

"You're not getting rid of me that easy."

"Don't waste my time, kid."

Bosko glared back. "You're afraid of me. That's what it is. I'll tell everyone you chickened out. You're a coward."

"Say what you want. The people who matter won't believe you."

Jacket Dude burned hot. His body stiffened with a new resolve. Rushed forward like a rolling thunderstorm—

Stopping in his tracks as Henry jumped to his feet.

With ice in his voice, he warned, *"No closer.* Do you really want to be humiliated in front of all these people? I don't fight for sport. It's not a game. Not a friendly contest of skills. It's about survival, kid. And I've been around a lot longer than you." Harsh eyes narrowed on him. *"I'll break you."*

The younger man remained where he was, a sliver of doubt appearing in his eyes for the first time. Henry could almost see the gears grinding in Bosko's head, weighing the odds of taking him on. Yes or no? In the end, sanity prevailed. Jacket Dude stormed off, though not before jabbing a warning finger at Henry. "We're not done here. This isn't over."

Which was what Henry was afraid of. When confronted, some hotheads back down and stay down. Others can't take the hint. They stew and won't be denied.

The danger had passed. But the threat was not yet over.

# CHAPTER 11

Driving home later, Henry's mind was peppered with images and half-forgotten memories from the past.

His Hong Kong past.

The original plans after college never included relocating overseas. The problem with Life is that it doesn't care about our plans; it does what it does, and we simply cope with the outcome. After earning his BS in Criminal Justice at Stanford, Henry was supposed to return to Minnesota with Alan Zhu, who'd also moved to San Jose to earn his advanced degree. Kay's murder changed everything. Brought the world crashing down. As Henry crawled out from the rubble of heartache, his friends assured him that he was not to blame for Kay's death, though in his heart, he knew better. While his hadn't been the finger that pulled the trigger, his actions—or inaction—had set events in motion that resulted in her death.

For that, he could never forgive himself.

*He wasn't there when she'd needed him the most.*

Worse was knowing the last words to pass between them had been strained.

Both thoughts gnawed at him for months, leaving no room for tranquility. His heart had been torn from him, and the will to go on was no longer there. But, with the help of friends, Henry managed to get by, if barely. In time, the ache blunted into something bearable, though he felt like a man wading through a swamp of self-reproach, never to see the other side and solid ground.

Then came a moment of clarity.

Three months into mourning Kay, an idea started taking root, giving Henry a new purpose. Which is why, shortly before receiving his college degree, he humbly approached his Wing Chun teacher after class one Saturday morning.

Sifu Kwan listened to the impassioned plea from one of his top students.

"You want more intense training?" Kwan said.

"Yes, Sifu."

"Why?"

"I want to use my skills to help people."

"Good answer. But you have enough skills now to do that."

"It's not enough. Guys in the street can be nasty. I need to understand that kind of fighting better."

"Because of Kay?"

"Yes."

Fatherly eyes rested on him. "You've seen a terrible side of life, Henry. You've changed. You're not the same person you were a year ago. You've grown up and, I'm sorry to say, for a tragic reason. Just now, I saw the old spark in you. It's different. I'm not sure how."

"Is that a bad thing?"

"No, not at all. Just an observation." Kwan studied him. "This matters a lot to you, doesn't it?"

"More than anything!" Henry returned with a twenty-two-year-old's resoluteness.

"You're a good student. Dedicated. Dependable. Most of all, you have a good heart. And you have a burning desire. That's important." Kwan made a dismissive sweep of his hand. "People don't understand martial arts. A good teacher means everything. But what the student does with that teaching makes all the difference. It's up to you to make the kung fu work. And I see something in you again I thought might be lost."

There came a pause. Henry didn't know what to say. Was afraid he was going to be turned down but showed respect to his teacher by waiting.

As if making a decision, Kwan nodded to Henry. "What you want is doable. The only way to improve your skill level for the kind of real-world challenges you're talking about is to train hard with people with similar goals who know the ins and outs of getting you there. Where your skills would be constantly put to the test."

Henry nodded excitedly.

A reluctant Kwan shook his head. "Unfortunately, that person can't be me."

"It can't?"

"No. Ten years ago, maybe. But I'm a middle-aged man with a wife and small children. My family needs me. I don't have extra time for the private lessons you'd need. And we're not talking about a few lessons. This would take many months, if not longer." A thought came to him. "What you're asking for is like going after a PhD in fighting. It's that kind of commitment."

A crestfallen Henry sighed. "I understand."

His disappointment was almost palpable.

Kwan's brow creased as he contemplated his impassioned student. "How serious are you? I mean, *how* hard are you willing to work for this?"

"As hard as it takes."

"Even if it means punishing your body and pushing it near exhaustion? Not just every so often, but every week for a year or two?"

"Yes!"

Kwan still had his doubts. "Henry…what are you trying to prove?"

He was ready for this. Had thought about it long and hard. "I'm not trying to prove anything. I want to help people who need help…against people who want to hurt them."

A nod of approval followed. "Another good answer."

Regardless, Henry was afraid he was making a bad impression, hastily adding, "I'm committed to doing this right. Whatever it takes."

"*Whatever it takes?*" Kwan tossed back at him.

"Yes."

"Even move to Hong Kong?"

"In a heartbeat!"

"You'd have to live there a year, probably two. A huge sacrifice and commitment."

One Henry was willing to make and said as much. The mention of Hong Kong had revived his hope, knowing his teacher's story. It was the 1960s. A teenaged Baak "Eric" Kwan had trained under Leung Sheung, legendary grandmaster Yip Man's first and most trusted Hong Kong student. Leung had trained intensively under grandmaster Yip, the latter eventually encouraging the former to teach publicly. Kwan had trained under the highly regarded and highly skilled Leung a few years after a teenaged Bruce Lee had departed the school for America. After Leung Sheung stopped teaching due to ill health, Kwan completed his training under one of Leung's top students, Lo Bai Hu.

Henry hoped his sifu saw in him a throwback to his own younger, hungry-to-learn self.

It seemed he did.

Kwan told Henry he'd contact his second *sigund* (master) to see if he'd take on Henry as a student. Under Lo's tutelage, Henry's Wing Chun skills would be further refined. He'd be continually under duress in realistic situations of hard-sparring and actual fights. As Kwan had alluded, this would indeed be Henry's post-graduate training in kung fu. But if he made it through to the end, Henry would be battle-tested. Very old-school stuff. Rarely done in the modern world of weekend warriors and McDojos, where sport was the primary objective. This real-world combat training had made Eric Kwan a superior martial artist with finesse, a surprising lightness of touch that could shut down an opponent, yet with a punch that could drop a mule. If Henry could come out of Hong Kong half the Wing Chun man Kwan was, he'd be satisfied.

The move across the ocean didn't come until the end of summer and was the single scariest thing Henry had ever done. Alone in a strange city in a different country. Culture shock. He spoke some Mandarin but needed a crash course in Cantonese, the dominant language, enough to get by. Also helping was his arrival not long after the turn of the new millennium, just a few years after the British had turned over governance of the old city back to China. English still served as a helpful back pocket language. He'd spent the summer after graduation preparing for the trip, working, saving money, and finding cheap lodgings with a fellow student in Kowloon above a congee and noodle shop in the Tai Kok Tsui district. There he'd live a bare-bones existence, but he was young and determined. Rough times lay ahead, which included facing what seemed an endless stream of full-of-themselves assholes like Letterman Jacket Dude.

Henry Lau had to learn the hard way how to handle them.

The call came early the following day. Susan Zelinsky's body had been found. Janet was at her desk, speaking to Bloomington PD. The detective in charge was Sergeant Cheri Hanson, who'd paused early in the conversation after passing on the grim news.

"Janet Lau?" Hanson had said with more than idle curiosity. "Any relation to Henry Lau?"

"My uncle."

"Aha."

Janet got that a lot. Henry was fairly well known among law enforcement in the metro area. Although Hanson's "Aha" seemed a bit more personal. Side-tracked momentarily, Sergeant Hanson resumed her update in her smoky voice. "The body was found on Sunday morning in an abandoned parking lot. No ID. She was processed as a Jane Doe. Then your BOLO came out. The description matched. We looked up her driver's license. The photo's a perfect match."

"Wait," a troubled Janet interjected, "you said she was found Sunday morning? What time?"

"Around 10:40."

"Cause of death?"

"Severe blunt trauma. She was hit by a car. Run over. Postmortem shows multiple lacerations, contusions, rib fractures, a punctured lung, and traumatic brain injury."

"Sounds nasty."

"Believe me, it was. The ME says the car didn't just hit her; it came back to finish the job."

"He knows this how?"

"Multiple tire treads on her clothes. She was found in a light sweatshirt, leggings, and sneakers. A wireless earbud was found in her left ear."

"Just the one?"

"Yeah, the other's missing."

"Any leads who did it?"

"Not yet. That's where I hope you come in. Zelinsky's a person of interest in a homicide in Gillette. Am I right?"

"She is—was." A thought raced through Janet's mind. Something didn't add up, and it bothered her.

"There's a chance her death is connected to your homicide."

"Yeah. Too much of a coincidence for it not to be. Can I see where the body was found?"

"No problem. Nothing much to see. She was killed someplace else and dumped at the site."

"Understood. Still might be helpful to take a look at it."

A grunt of assent came from the other end of the phone. Hanson said, "I'll text you the address. I need to deal with something first. I can meet you there in an hour."

"Perfect!"

At the appointed time, Janet stood on the cracked and crumbling pavement of Fast Louie's Auto Repair on Old Shakopee Road. Long abandoned and forgotten. Even the birds had disavowed the crumbling nest on top of the rusted signpost. The flat-roofed building next to it wasn't in better condition, having clouded windows and the peeling remains of painted lettering.

"Like I said, not much to see." The woman in the puffy coat swept out a mittened hand. Strands of barley-colored hair fluttered from under a wool country hat. Stylish, not police issued, but it was a chilly twenty-five degrees, and Sergeant Cheri Hanson was taking no chances. No fashionista herself, Janet admired the headgear. Made a mental note to research one for herself as Hanson went on. "The body was dumped over there behind the weeds. It wasn't visible from the street. A passerby was cutting across the lot when he saw what he thought was a bag of clothes."

"You weren't kidding." Janet's eyes did a rapid sweep of the area. Cracked concrete, an old, crushed beer can wedged into a space in the curb, the bent oil change sign. A light but steady breeze had blown away almost all of Sunday's dusting of snow.

"Too clean," Hanson said. "No tire tracks or skid marks. No blood. No scrapes or scuff marks. No debris. The location doesn't fit Zelinsky's injuries."

Janet nodded. "She sure didn't die here." Her gaze wandered to the boarded-up repair shop for anything useful. At her core, Janet was an optimist who thought the best of people and situations. Her mother had gone to great pains to ensure her daughter was raised with an appreciation of the larger world and how people are often connected in ways that aren't visible at first glance. Well, if there was anything here that could give insight into either of the two homicides, it was evident to Janet that she'd need a big fat spotlight directed on it for her to notice. She did a chin jut toward the dilapidated structure. "What about inside?"

Hanson said, "The place is empty. No one's been inside for years. We looked. A thick layer of dust's all over, undisturbed dust. No footprints. Only ours. So what now?"

Janet was slightly taken aback. "You tell me. It's your turf."

"Yeah, about that. Like I said, it looks like our homicides are connected. You've already got a head start on yours, Detective Lau. I was hoping you'd take the lead on this."

"Oh."

"We can work together. Coordinate efforts."

"Sure."

Hanson looked relieved. "Great. I got two other cases I'm about to close. They'll need most of my attention for the next few days. I don't know how much help I'll be. Just keep me in the loop, and if you need something, ask."

"Will do."

Traffic was picking up on Old Shakopee Road. A tree-trimming truck and its attached woodchipper rumbled by, scattering a flock of crows perched on the nearby telephone line.

The sergeant leaned in. Raised her voice over the road noise. "Yesterday, you requested uniform do a welfare check on Zelinsky. As you know, they found nothing odd. Now that her death is officially a homicide, I went back after the body was ID'd. Our IT guys'll be looking through her desktop PC."

"There're some names we're interested in: Sam Park, K.J. Hazzard, Ann Oreino. That last could also be a Nancy or some variation. I'll send you the list. What about her car?"

Hanson shook her head. "Hasn't turned up. Zelinsky drives a metallic blue Subaru Forester. It's not in her garage or near her home. Uniform did a sweep of the neighborhood. I've a BOLO out on it."

"Good."

"Wanna check out her townhouse?"

"Yeah."

"You available now?"

"Let's do it."

"You done here?"

"I'm good to go."

Cheri Hanson paused, looking curiously at Janet. "How's Henry doing?"

That wasn't expected. "He's well. Doing well."

"The buzz last spring was he got pretty banged up. I didn't know how bad until a few months ago. All that time in ICU! I can't imagine."

The incredulity in Hanson's voice came through loud and clear. *She really cares.* Janet made a closer assessment of the sergeant. She guessed Cheri Hanson was in her late thirties. Had a disarmingly up-front, I-mean-what-I-say demeanor with its own charm. Janet thought, I should be like that! Made a mental note on her Things to Make Janet Better list, which she'd started compiling at the tender age of ten and a half. This differed from the Things to Make Janet Happy list, where the wool hat purchase was noted.

"You know Henry well?" Janet ventured, never having heard her uncle mention the woman.

Sergeant Hanson puffed out a breath. In the cold air, it streamed out as a white cloud. "Nah. We've talked at events and things. Your uncle's a good guy. Some male cops can be...*difficult.*"

Janet pinged on that, listening with care.

Hanson straightened a little. "You know what I'm talking about, right? As a female detective, you must've dealt with some of the shit male colleagues give you. But I never got that from your uncle. He's always treated me with respect."

Sadly, Janet knew exactly what Hanson was talking about. Police culture was changing for the better, although enough old-school cops were around who had a distinctly paternalistic view toward women. Her first job as a uniformed officer was in a different city. Not even a month into her career, an eighteen-year veteran went out of his way to invade Janet's personal space and tell her women weren't tough enough to do the job. As a sweet-faced rookie trying to learn the ropes, intimidated by everything and everyone around her, how was she supposed to respond to that? She didn't. She bit her tongue. Three months later, a senior detective, a white supremacist, made a slur about her ethnicity. Yes, Janet Lau was half Chinese; she was also half Scottish. What did that have to do with anything? Thankfully, there'd been none of that at Gillette PD. Janet counted her blessings to be in her current situation and agreed with Hanson's comment about her uncle.

Janet spoke proudly, "Henry's a great partner, a wonderful mentor."

"You're lucky."

"I am."

The sergeant angled toward Janet to ask, "Is he seeing anyone?"

"You mean like dating?" Janet shook her head. He wasn't as far as she knew and said as much.

Hanson's mood was suddenly more buoyant.

Janet said, "I'll tell him you said hi."

She had known Cheri Hanson for only a short time but already liked her. Janet wasn't sure if the sergeant was Henry's type, but she'd leave that up to Fate. Turning to go, Detective Hanson stopped, remembering. "Oh, two things. At Zelinsky's townhouse, there's a large—I mean humongous—corkboard mounted on her home office wall. Dozens of push pins are stuck all over the place, but no paper. It's bone bare. Either she cleared away all her notes—"

"Or someone else did," Janet put in, a shine in her eyes.

"Maybe her killer, who, by the way, has her keys. They weren't found on her. Her townhouse doesn't have a keypad. Her purse wasn't at home. It could be in her missing car, although I bet her killer's got it, keys and wallet. Why bother dumping the body elsewhere and not holding onto the things that could ID her?"

Janet nodded.

"We also searched Zelinsky's trash. No scraps of paper with pin holes. But we found this." The sergeant fished out her smartphone and showed Janet a photo. "It's the bottom of a sheet of paper. Written in her handwriting. Notice how it's all crossed out like she decided not to use it."

Janet turned the phone at an angle to keep the sun's glare off it. The words made the hairs on the back of her neck stand up:

> *I thought I loved you, but I don't anymore. Not after what you did. You're not the man I thought you were. What are you hiding? If you don't go to the police, I will!*

"Wow…" Janet locked eyes with Hanson.

"I know! Makes you wonder what she'd gotten herself into."

What an adrenaline rush! Janet realized the investigation had just taken a sharp turn. If Susan Zelinsky's body was found in this abandoned lot at 10:40 Sunday morning, she couldn't have used her key card at Hancock Blades an hour later.

So, who did?

# CHAPTER 12

The text from Janet was eye-opening. Susan Zelinsky hadn't done a runner; she was the second homicide victim. Now, both deaths had to be viewed in a different light. It seemed insanely coincidental that two people strongly linked together should both die on the same weekend. The killings must be connected. While Janet was checking out the dead woman's townhouse, Henry had the unenviable task of sharing the bad news with her coworkers.

He asked the receptionist to let Jim Karjala know that Detective Lau was there to give him an update on Susan Zelinsky. Tammy reacted to the solemnity of his demeanor by making the call minus her usual friendly banter. "Jim will see you right away," she said. "I'll buzz you in." Her hand disappeared under the reception counter.

Karjala was standing near his desk in front of his desktop laser printer. The paper tray was open. The CFO held a ream of paper, fumbling to peel off the wrapper when the ream slipped from his fingers and dropped on the table. With a frustrated groan, he collected the bundle, tore off the remaining wrapper, and removed a hefty wad of paper to insert in the tray. "Come in, Detective," he said, embarrassed. "You've found me a little fat-fingered today." He flexed his hands before gesturing to the guest chairs. "Please take a seat."

"I'm good. This shouldn't take long. Oh, please stay, Ms. Brown. This concerns you as well."

Henry motioned for the executive assistant to stop. She'd just stepped through the doorway and, seeing Karjala was not alone, had taken a step back. Slightly startled, Evelyn Brown glanced at Karjala, who nodded for her to remain. She stood off to the side.

Karjala adjusted his glasses, his uneasiness evident. "Tammy said you had an update on Susan. Why do I think it's not good news?"

"There's no easy way to say this. I'm sorry to tell you Ms. Zelinsky's body was found."

"What? Wait." The color drained from the CFO's face. "Susan's dead? What happened?"

Henry said, "I can't go into details. All I can tell you is her death's now an active homicide."

"She was *murdered*?"

"I'm afraid so."

"Jesus! First Sam, now Susan. What's going on?"

"We aren't sure. The second death changes everything."

A troubled Karjala blew out his cheeks and rubbed his graying temple.

Brown stirred. "I'm sorry, Jim." Her tone was flat, somewhat distant.

What struck Henry was her reaction. Or lack thereof. She didn't seem particularly upset by the news and seemed to offer condolences as a matter of form. There was more emotion in the face of the Statue of Liberty than he was seeing in the small-framed woman, which was in stark contrast to her heated response to the murder of Samuel Park.

*What to make of that?*

"As before," Henry continued, "if you think of anything that might help our investigation, please let me know. We'll update you when we have further information."

"Thank you." Karjala swallowed with difficulty, looking like a man whose comfortable world was in freefall.

Meanwhile, Brown's face remained a stony mask of indifference.

On the way back to the lobby, Henry paused at the doorway of Human Resources. Lalani Dunne looked up from her computer screen. Recognition glinted in her expressive face. "Detective Lau, I didn't know you were here."

"Lalani, do you have a minute?"

"Of course. Please come in." The warmth of her smile beckoned. The smile vanished after he informed her why he was there.

"Oh no," she lamented. A shadow fell across her. "And you're saying Susan was murdered?" The idea seemed unthinkable to her.

He'd read the post-mortem earlier. "I'll spare you the unpleasant details. The ME—sorry, medical examiner—has no doubt. This was no accident. Someone went out of their way to kill her."

Lalani uttered a moan of dismay before her anger flared. "Fuck this! Susan was a good person. This is so unfair!" The HR director caught herself. Gulped in a deep breath and struggled to regain her composure.

Henry took note. Lalani's passions ran deep. He patiently waited for her good-natured self to return. Only her professionalism let her win the day. Mere seconds ticked by before the ready smile returned.

"Sorry for the outburst," she said, her cheeks flushing. "I liked Susan."

He found her embarrassment endearing. So honest. "No problem. It's never easy losing someone you care about."

Lalani nodded, eyeing him curiously. "You must do this often, deliver bad news to people."

"More times than I care to remember."

"Does it ever get easy?"

"No."

"I get that. It's not much different than when we terminate an employee. It upends their life. The worst part of my job is sitting across the desk from someone who's just been dismissed and explaining their benefits package, trying to ignore the stunned look on their face."

"I bet."

"You've got it worse. You tell people a loved one is dead. I can't imagine what that's like." She gave a little shudder, regarding him with a how-do-you-do-it? awe. The woman was charm personified.

Henry was disappointed their conversation had to end; being in Lalani Dunne's presence was like standing before a warm hearth on a frosty morning; you didn't want to leave.

"Detective," she said, "can I ask a question?"

"Of course."

"It was looking bad for Susan after Sam's murder. He's dead, and she's a no-show for work. People were talking. And not in a good way. Does what you told me mean it wasn't Susan who killed Sam?"

"It would've been impossible for her to have murdered Mr. Park. She was killed before him."

A relieved Lalani let out a breath. "Thank God for that! It makes a difference. People's imaginations go wild if you let them. Is it okay if I tell others?"

Henry thought it over. At this point, he didn't see any threat to the investigations by letting her share this one bit of info. "Go ahead," he said, happy to throw her this bone.

In the lobby, Henry signed out and flashed a brief smile at the receptionist, who was in an animated discussion with a chubby brunette in teal-colored eyeglasses. He was out the door and halfway to his car when he heard the rush of footsteps on the cold asphalt behind him.

"Detective!" called a breathless voice. "Please wait."

He stopped. Spun round to see the chubby brunette from the lobby shuffling coatless toward him, puffs of white vapor from her breath swirling by her face.

"What can I do for you?" he said cordially as she drew near.

She looked flustered. Hesitant. "My name's Lori Deaver. I work in accounting with Susan Zelinsky. Susan's my best friend here. I've been worried sick about her." Deaver wheezed in a few breaths, hand on her chest. "Tammy said you had news about her." Hopeful eyebrows crept above the teal eyeglass frames.

She had grabbed his attention with the words *work with* and *best friend*. He definitely wanted to talk with this woman! He motioned to the black Malibu, which offered refuge from the chill. "You look cold. Sit with me."

The doors were closed and the engine started. For good measure, he turned on the seat warmers, a cold weather must for those who lived in northern states. Henry took stock of Deaver: in her early twenties, she was like a puppy, earnest, a bit clumsy, and immediately likable, with a figure that used to be called pleasingly plump. (He had no idea what the current term was.) Her clothing was unseasonably light material. She shivered. Luckily, the car warmed up quickly, and within a minute, she seemed comfortable.

Henry didn't mince his words. "You might as well hear it from me." He told her the bad news. Shock and dismay were her first reactions before the wash of tears. He handed her a tissue from the box on the floor behind the passenger seat. Waited as she snuffled into it.

"Please excuse the blubbering." She wiped her eyes and then her glasses, slipping them back on. "You must think I'm a dork. I don't normally go Niagara Falls at bad news." Deaver looked sheepishly at him.

"No worries. Susan was your friend."

She flashed a tiny smile of appreciation.

For the next few minutes, Henry answered all the questions he could. When she had finished and seemed to have regained her composure, he decided it was his turn. However, he had to tread lightly, not wanting to trample on emotions that were still tender. One of the more unpleasant parts of his job was intruding into people's personal lives at the worst moments. He was calm in hopes of projecting calm. "When you feel ready, I have questions."

"I'm good," she said, spreading her fingers in front of the dashboard heat vents.

He started with something easy. "You said Susan was your best friend at work. You knew her well?"

"Uh-huh. Our desks are next to each other. We'd talk about work and life, the world."

"That include her personal life?"

"Sometimes."

"Private things?"

Deaver scoured her memory. "I can't remember anything super personal. Susan didn't talk much about herself."

"Can you think of anything in her work or personal life that might explain why she was killed?"

"Nah. We'd talk about hobbies and shit like that. Nothing deep or controversial. I know she was a runner. Got up every morning to run. Even in winter! She read a lot. Mainly biographies, histories, and mysteries. She did show interest in my hobby. I'm into e-bikes—a bike with an electric motor? I loaned her mine a month ago to try out."

Lori Deaver smiled at the memory. He thought now was the time to switch gears.

"You and Susan both worked for Jim Karjala?"

"Yep. Accounting. Susan's a senior cost accountant. She had tons of experience in other industries."

"And you're…?"

"Me? I'm a CPA."

"What's the difference?"

Deaver made a face. "Totally different skill set. Susan had a funny way of explaining it." She cleared her throat. "CPAs make sure the numbers are in the right boxes and that the totals add up. They don't care much about profit and loss. What matters is the figures are right and look good for external lenders and investors. A cost accountant goes into the details behind those numbers. We're a knife factory. So how much do raw materials cost? Like down to the tiniest screw. A good cost accountant can tell you what your company's profit is and exactly what everything costs. A CPA doesn't do that. Cost accountants dive deep into the details, looking for where the money really goes. *That* was Susan." Lori Deaver looked pointedly at Henry. "She was a digger."

"Sounds like she'll be missed."

"For sure. I helped. Was learning so much."

"How about work assignments? Anything out of the ordinary recently? Work after hours…private projects?" He'd deliberately used the phrase *private projects* to see if it would trigger a dormant memory.

Deaver frowned. Shook her head. "Nope. Third-quarter journal entries were posted two weeks ago. We've got a couple weeks to relax before the craziness begins—Oh shit!" she yelped, eyes wide. "Susan won't be here for year end!" There was something close to panic in Lori Deaver's voice, as if the end of the world was near. She lowered her head and groaned.

"You okay?"

"Yeah. Just thinking ahead." She lifted her head to look at him. "It's gonna be hell doing year-end without Susan. We'll have to hire temps. Even then, it'll be a bitch. Pardon my French."

"Isn't this where your boss steps in? Karjala's the main finance guy."

"Sure, Jim'll help, but…" She made a face.

"But?"

"Don't get me wrong. Jim's an accounting wiz. The thing is, he doesn't have the eye for detail Susan did. That woman was a hawk at deciphering irregular journal entries. Plus, our computer systems are a hodgepodge of different software that don't play nice with each other. Jim's been trying to upgrade our software for years. Some of our systems are older than me! There were plenty of times Susan had problems making sense of them. I've been with Hancock for ten months, and I'm still learning new stuff about our accounting systems." Deaver adjusted her glasses. "Getting back to Jim; he's been a little distracted lately, so I don't know how much help he'll be."

She had Henry's attention. "What d'you mean?" he asked.

"Um, I'm not sure. For the last couple of weeks, his mind's been somewhere else. I'd ask a question, and a second later, I'd have to repeat it."

"I take it that's unusual."

"Yeah, not like him."

"Any thoughts why?"

"Could be medical. His finger may be bothering him more than he lets on."

"Possibly. It takes months for something like that to heal. Maybe he doesn't like admitting a weakness. Some men are like that. What about his relationship with Susan?"

"It was good. Better than good. Susan was Jim's right-hand woman. His number one problem solver."

"How about on a personal level? Was there anything going on between them?"

"*Susan and Jim?*" Lori Deaver was aghast. "No way! Why? Did you hear something?" Intrigue colored her voice.

"No, just trying to figure out a motive for the killings."

A dark thought crossed her mind. "You don't think Jim's involved? Do you?"

Henry shrugged. "He's her supervisor. Gives her work assignments. We have to consider every angle."

"Every angle? Am I a suspect?"

"No."

The answer came so quickly it surprised her. Relieved, she slumped back against the seat.

By now, the interior of the car was toasty. Henry turned down the blower. Changed the subject. "As Susan's friend, you might be able to answer this question better than anyone."

Deaver looked pleased at the compliment, well-rounded cheeks stretching back.

He said, "Did Susan ever mention changes in her personal life? New relationships? Bad news? Frustrations?"

"Not that I remember. Sorry."

"It's okay," he assured her. Another dead end. Well, he figured, no point in holding back. "What about Susan and Sam? Were they in a relationship?"

Unlike before, Lori Deaver didn't immediately answer. Her forehead wrinkled. "Like having an affair?"

"You tell me. You saw them every day. I've heard Susan and Sam Park were spending extra time together, and it might not've been work-related."

"Yeah, they were hooking up a lot. A relationship, though? Nah, I can't see it. It had to be something else. But people see what they want to."

"Any ideas on what they were doing?"

"Oh, that's easy. Susan *was* working with Sam on something."

The back of Henry's neck tingled. "How do you know?"

"She told me."

"When was this?"

"Last week."

"Ms. Deaver, when I asked you earlier if you knew if Susan and Sam were working on a private project, you said no."

The CPA looked back ruefully. "Susan didn't say it was private. As far as I know, it was just work stuff. Sorry!"

*Done in by semantics!* "Okay, let's try this again. Susan told you she was working on this thing with Sam, correct?"

"Yes. And that they had to finish it soon. There was a deadline."

"Was there a reason she'd told you about this?"

"Yep. We were talking about weekend plans—"

"Hold on. When was this?"

"Friday."

"This past Friday?"

"Uh-huh. I asked if she had plans. Susan said her weekend was spoken for with this extra work but didn't go into specifics."

"Not at all?"

"Susan was like that. She didn't like talking too much about plans like it would jinx her."

"For real?"

"Oh, yeah. I guess when Susan was a kid, she'd tell people about all the stuff she was gonna do. Trouble was half the time she never finished those things. Made her look stupid, she thought. That's when she started to clam up. Wouldn't give away much on what she was up to until after it was finished. I got used to it." Deaver spread her palms in a there-you-have-it gesture.

Understandable, though not helpful. Henry had hoped for more. Closed-mouth people were anathema to an investigator. Give him a chatty suspect or witness any day; they made his world go round. The CPA hadn't totally let him down; she'd confirmed that Samuel Park and Susan Zelinsky were working together on some project, a project no one seemed to know anything about. He was now confident that whatever this mysterious project was, the deaths of two people were anchored to it.

# CHAPTER 13

La Pâtisserie was a popular bakery in Gillette, noteworthy for its mouthwatering eclairs and French opera cakes, tasty macarons, tarts, and other delights. Feeling a need to reward herself for a good morning's work, Janet detoured on her way back to the station for a bag of sweet almond croissants. Luck was with her. She snagged the last open parking spot in front of the bakery. Turned off the engine. She sat as a passing pickup's big chrome side mirrors reflected the bright sun. The blinding dazzle drove spikes into her brain. Hands flew to her face in a rush of vertigo.

*Shit. Shit. Shit this concussion.*

Her eyelids jammed shut against a kaleidoscope of sparkles bursting against her retinas. Rapid breaths pulsed in and out until the headstorm abated. It took three minutes before she started feeling like herself again. To make sure, she thought it best to remain in her Mazda for a while before going vertical. Janet slapped the steering wheel in frustration. How much longer would she have to deal with this? she wondered. Four weeks so far. Her neurologist had said it would take this long, and probably longer, for a full recovery. Her hope had been that her symptoms would diminish to almost nothing as time went on.

*Well, this attack busted that idea.*

It was discouraging.

*Yeah, so what? You're dealing with it.*

The little voice in Janet's head berated her for getting maudlin. She paid attention to that voice; it had guided her through difficult times since her injury. That and meditation got her through the last minutes in the car. Deep, tranquil breathing and emptying her mind. Be an empty vessel. She knew when Henry meditated, he envisioned standing in front of a clear mountain lake. She pictured a relaxing hot tub with massage jets. More her style. Opening her eyes again, Janet felt better, relaxed, and clearheaded. She was also famished. Those almond croissants were calling her name.

Happily, the line inside La Pâtisserie was a short one. In no time, she paid the cashier and started for the door with her sack of goodies when she came to an abrupt halt. At a table against the far wall, she recognized two familiar faces: Aimee Hancock and Mayor Larry Stenson, sitting together, having what looked like an intimate conversation. The CEO of Hancock Blades rested a tender hand on her brother-in-law's mayoral forearm in a deeply personal tableau. They turned and saw Janet. Didn't acknowledge her presence. Turned back toward each other and resumed their tête-à-tête, although Hancock removed her hand from Stenson's arm.

*Awkward!*

Janet made for the exit, her brain buzzing with fascinating scenarios from the little scene she'd just witnessed.

At the station, she found Henry at his desk, typing a report on his computer. She set down her bag of baked goods, hung up her jacket, then threw herself into her chair. "Guess who I just ran into!" she announced, eyes brimming with mischief.

He did what one was expected to do when lobbed a statement like that. He stopped what he was doing and looked back. "I'm listening."

Janet relayed her encounter at the bakery.

Henry laughed. "You and the mayor. Is this a thing now?"

"I hope not."

"What's your take on those two?"

"I don't know." She cast her mind back. Aimee Hancock and Larry Stenson. This was more than a casual late-morning breakfast between two in-laws. The way they'd leaned into each other suggested a level of…well, intimacy. Precisely what that meant, she didn't know. Had to be careful not to read too much into what she'd seen. And yet, she believed she'd witnessed a significant moment pass between them. Janet shared her opinion.

Henry agreed. "It's worth exploring. Lift enough rocks, and you'll eventually find something crawling underneath."

"Charming," Janet remarked. She was about to add more when the tromp of heavy footsteps stopped her.

"Ah, both of you *are* here. Good!"

Chief Bowman burst into their alcove. He stopped and struck a stance to give them the once-over. The stance reminded Janet of an old Polaroid photo of a much younger and far slimmer Fred Bowman. He was at a costume party posing as the Black Elvis. The pelvis placement was why she'd thought of the photo. Bowman fixed his gaze on Janet. "I just got a weird-ass call from Larry Stenson, *Mayor Stenson*. He said he just saw you at La Pâtisserie. Didn't go into much detail. Sounded a bit flustered. Stenson wanted me to make it clear to you that nothing inappropriate was going on between him and his sister-in-law." The chief jacked an eyebrow. "Which begs me to ask: what the hell did you see, Detective?"

Janet smiled. Well, well, well, Stenson hadn't wasted any time grabbing his phone to complain. *Was it a complaint?* It was presented as an "explanation," but she had doubts. Rather than pacifying her, the mayor's call had only stiffened her belief that what she'd witnessed between Hancock and Stenson had made them uncomfortable. Maybe even rattled them. Why, if the situation was innocent?

Janet told the chief what she'd seen.

A disappointed Bowman looked back in disbelief. "That's it?"

"Yep."

He rubbed the side of his face. "From how Stenson talked, I thought you'd caught them locking lips. Sounds to me like a whole lotta nothin'. Or is it?" he reconsidered.

Henry shrugged. "We were just discussing that."

"Something's going on," Janet put in. "I just know it. The call from the mayor. He sure went out of his way to insist on his innocence. Sounds like a man hiding something."

Bowman looked like the cat who ate the canary. "I might be able to help you there."

Janet sat up with interest.

He elaborated. "You know we have security cameras all over the building outside. One camera is above our front entrance; it shows who comes and goes. It also shows a section of the parking lot and the rear entrance to City Hall. Output from them is displayed in the dispatch room. One of the dispatchers commented yesterday that she's noticed the mayor's car leaving the lot every morning after 9 a.m. and returning around 10:20. Every day for the past three weeks."

Janet didn't know what that meant. "Is that unusual? He's the mayor. Doesn't he go out and do things, meet with people?"

"On occasion, yes. Though not every day at the same time for weeks."

"Like a regular appointment with someone." She studied him carefully. "Is that what you're saying, Chief?"

"I'm saying nothing at all. Merely passing along information about our security cameras. Make of it what you will."

She considered this. More than ever, Janet believed Mayor Larry Stenson was up to something, and she needed to know what it was. Which could get tricky. Sticking her nose deeper into Stenson's personal business could backfire.

Chief Bowman wasn't finished. "Speaking of His Honor the Mayor, got any updates on the Hancock case I can share?"

Henry deferred to Janet, who updated their boss on the discovery of Susan Zelinsky's body and its significance."

"Good. That's progress!" Bowman looked pleased. "So Zelinsky's key card could've been used by anyone, including someone who's *not* a Hancock employee. Possibly an outsider. Even an outsider from South America." This last a jab at Henry. "Still think your dead man was trying to name his killer with the world atlas?"

Henry took the teasing in stride. "The atlas is there for a reason. It has to mean something."

"Good luck with that," Bowman chortled. "Be careful the two of you don't dive too far down that rabbit hole." He straightened, emboldened by Janet's update. "The mayor will be pleased the field of suspects has widened beyond the knife factory workers. Or is it too soon to tell him?"

"I'm okay with it," Henry said. "Janet?"

The answer wasn't as clear to her. If she had her druthers, she'd prefer not giving away information this early. On the other hand, it was a small crumb they could toss to the politician and, perhaps, keep him at bay. "Sure, tell him," she shrugged.

"Excellent." Bowman could placate his boss with the update. With a departing wave, he started to turn—

"Chief, interested in an almond croissant?" Janet held out the white paper bag.

"From La Pâtisserie? Don't mind if I do!" His well-manicured fingers fished for a sweet pastry. "Thanks, Janet."

Henry coughed. "Hey, Fred, you sure you want that? Thought you were trying to lose a few pounds."

Bowman's broad back faded into the distance as his voice came over his shoulder, "A time and place for everything, my friend. Mmm, tasty."

What made Frederick Douglas Bowman a great leader was his sense of humor, and that he didn't take himself too seriously, that and the way he treated his staff and coworkers. It created a healthy and happy work environment. Janet had nothing but respect for the man. Owed him her promotion. Early on, he'd recognized her potential and encouraged her to pursue the detective's rank, which is why she worked hard to prove his faith in her had not been misplaced.

On the subject of hard work, there'd be more of it tonight at home. Perhaps charting the two homicides would help. Janet was a visual thinker. Drawing little boxes with notes helped her see connecting threads between them she might've missed before. A technique Henry never used. Not on paper. Somehow, he managed to keep all this information in his head and could flip through it like pages in a book. She envied him that. As far back as grade school, Janet had forced herself to be methodical and organized, drawing her little boxes or circles on paper and making her lists. Was teased about it but didn't care. She was damn good at it. The process had helped her get this far in life, and she wasn't about to abandon it.

She stopped. Realized she was lost in her reverie. Looking across her desk, she saw Henry sitting back in his chair, observing her with a thin, contemplative smile.

"*What?*" Her self-consciousness stood proud.

"Nothing. Just watching you think. You're working through a decision. About work, I'm guessing."

"Is it that obvious?"

"You were staring after Bowman as he walked off, holding onto that croissant for the longest time without taking a bite."

"Not bad. Now, if you can tell me what I was thinking, I'll be really impressed."

"Sorry, I don't do parlor tricks."

"Too bad. We could use one right now. How good are your reflexes?" She pitched the pastry bag at him, made a face, and took a chomp from her almond croissant.

Nothing happened after lunch except one curious incident late in the afternoon. Henry was rinsing out his coffee mug in the break room when Officer Ken Ferguson strode in to drop a crumpled bag into the recycling bin. The two exchanged pleasantries. Henry, trying to be sociable, asked Ferguson if he enjoyed patrolling the streets of Gillette. He got a standard, positive reply. Then, the latter veered the conversation into a different traffic lane.

"So, Detective, word around the station is that you're some badass kung fu dude. That right?" Ferguson, head tilted back, sized up the other. The problem with Ken Ferguson was that he had a reputation for being a smartass who liked to wind up people. Henry wasn't yet able to tell whether he was sincere, pulling his leg, or just being a dick. It didn't help that the guy generally gave off a smarmy air, making him difficult to read.

Wiping his ceramic mug dry with a paper towel, Henry said, "You can't always believe what people tell you."

Which wasn't enough for Ferguson, who pressed further. "You don't think the watch commander's a reliable source? C'mon, don't be so modest."

Henry gave an indifferent shrug.

Satisfied by this or just moving on, Ferguson hitched his duty belt, squaring his shoulders with the air of one expert conversing with another. "Yeah, I did martial arts when I was in middle school. Got a brown belt in Taekwondo. Good stuff, as far as it goes, but for real protection, I'll take a gun any day." His fingertips patted his holster.

"Sure," Henry said without further comment.

Unfortunately, Ferguson didn't know when to stop. "In a pinch, nothing beats a reliable gat," he pontificated and kept yammering about the advantages of a gun over bare-handed techniques against multiple assailants. Henry didn't disagree with him, but he was getting annoyed at the other's myopic view of handling troublemakers.

Finally, Henry had to shut him up.

"Look, Ferguson, what you're saying is fine. We have sidearms because they do the job when we need them. For some reason, you seem to be putting down the value of empty-hand techniques. Don't. They have value."

That was enough pushback for the young officer to get defensive. "Oh, they do. I've tackled and restrained enough shitheads to know that."

Henry was confused. "Then why bring up the subject?"

"Just sharing ideas. You do martial arts. I used to." Again, that smarmy smirk undercut the sincerity—if any—behind the words. Henry couldn't help thinking the other was toying with him. Maybe the jokester was unable to resist.

"Fine." Henry inhaled a calming breath. "All I'll say is you don't always have your gun on you. There are times when pulling a firearm is not appropriate. Or you don't have time. Having other skills is useful."

Ferguson said nothing.

Henry could have left things there and probably should have, except the man was annoying enough that he decided to go a step further: "Besides, some guys could take your gun away and use it on you."

"I don't think so," Ferguson scoffed, arms folded across his chest.

"It happens."

"In the old days, maybe. Not likely now."

"I wouldn't be too sure about that."

"Could *you* do it?"

"From here? No problem."

The confidence in Henry's voice and manner made the other blink. What Ferguson didn't know was that Henry had already gauged the distance between them: eight feet. Close enough for him to spring like a tiger at the dumbfounded officer and manhandle him.

Still miffed at the other's cockiness, Henry felt compelled to pour scorn on him. "You say it's unlikely. Standing here, right now, I could take your gun away. Look where your hands are. By the time you uncrossed your arms and reached to unsecure your gun, I'd be all over you. For instance, I throw this mug in your face to distract you. Before your hand got halfway to your holster, your arm would be pinned against your body."

"It's a security holster," Ferguson complained. "You'd have a tough time drawing the weapon."

Like many law enforcement agencies, Gillette PD used a security holster that required a two-step process to extract the firearm, making it nearly impossible for someone to grab it from an officer. Henry leaned forward to remind the cop, "But I know how it works. And if you're a curled-up heap of hurt on the floor, I have the time and angles to extract your weapon. Think about that, Ferguson."

Henry started toward the exit, thinking it was a good idea to escape this uniformed irritant before he said something he'd regret.

# CHAPTER 14

The remainder of the workday was uneventful, meaning Henry was free to visit the Dorothy Travers Dance Company after his shift and, he hoped, no appearance by Letterman Jacket Dude. It was probably too much to ask for the hot-tempered karateka to have realized the error of his ways. Troublemakers typically don't have common sense to begin with, let alone much in the way of soul-searching.

Seconds after he walked into the rehearsal space, he heard his name.

"Henry!" A thrilled Dorothy Travers hustled toward him, the Cherry Kool-Aid hair bouncing at each step. The laugh lines around her eyes crinkled. "You came back! How wonderful!"

"You didn't think I would?"

She winked at him. "There was a chance your experience last night might've spooked you. I told Karen her boyfriend is no longer welcome here." With surprising familiarity, the artistic director guided Henry to his seat in the risers, then plopped into the seat next to his, placing her hand on his arm. "You won't be seeing him anymore."

"Let's hope not."

Travers angled her body toward him. "Tonight'll be different. We're going over a few segments, trying to get the timing right for the moving scenery. It rolls in and around from different directions. A few changes are tricky with the dancers moving. By the way, Jason liked your suggestions. If you have more, please let him know. I'll check back later." And with that, she was off, a harried mother duck, rushing off to gather her fledglings.

Henry settled back and made himself a blank receptacle for the entertainment ahead. Emptying the mind of the day's troubles was an indispensable step in attaining inner peace, a practice he'd first begun after the death of Kay to get him through those first terrible months. Half a lifetime later and with a ton of experience, Henry Lau was still a work in progress.

Sustained inner peace was a long-term goal.

A quartet of dancers moved onto the stage, doing initial setups with three oversized, flat black silhouettes on wheels. The cutouts suggested buildings in a Chinese back street where menacing shadows lurked around every corner. Standing in front of the flats, Travers, the prop master, and scenery movers discussed an issue with a sticky wheel.

That was when Henry became aware of a figure settling into the seat beside him, the subtle scent of jasmine wafting in the air. Long, lustrous black hair swooshed by his shoulders. Wendy Chu, the lead female dancer who portrayed the Bagua master, turned to him and flashed a beguiling smile. "Ready for another fun evening?" she said with amused irony. No doubt she'd witnessed the incident with Jacket Dude.

"I am," he answered.

Leaning forward, Wendy pulled up a fallen leg warmer above her shapely calf. She straightened, then reached behind her head to gather her hair into a high ponytail, which sent a cascade of silky black tresses tumbling to the base of her neck. "Your job must keep you busy. It's so cool your taking time to help us. We really appreciate it."

"My pleasure. It's a nice change. I don't often get to see talented performers like you. Your dance was awesome. No, more than that, it was magical."

"Thank you! That's so nice of you to say. Of course, the difference for us is it's all make-believe, going through the fighting motions. For you, it's real."

"It can be."

"I can't imagine the risks of getting hurt—seriously hurt—from some street thug or a killer trying to get away." Wendy's dark eyes gave him a quick, appraising look. "Can I ask a personal question?"

The phrasing of that gave him pause. How personal would it be? he wondered. He barely knew this woman.

She hesitated at his reaction. "Let me back up. I'm getting ahead of myself. Earlier, I was talking to Lily Chen. I think you know her."

Indeed, he did. Lily Chen was a master of Tibetan White Crane, one of the five arts showcased in the performance. Lily was five years older than Henry and had taught at her St. Paul academy for over twenty years. Henry knew her well. Although their paths crossed regularly in the early days, it'd been far too long since he'd last seen her.

He sat up and looked around. "Is Lily here?"

"No. She left before you got here."

"Too bad. It would've been nice to catch up."

"She says hi."

That warmed his heart; he'd have to call her later.

Wendy turned in her seat to face him. "Word got to Lily you were helping us. She said we got a good man. Talked you up big."

"Nice of her to do that."

"She's such an inspiration. I've no reason to doubt her. I saw you deal with that jerk at the coffee shop. I told her what'd happened. Lily said that was just like you, putting yourself in harm's way for others. Then she told a story that made my skin crawl, of how you fought a bunch of guys with knives and pipes to keep them from hurting two teenaged girls they'd cornered."

"Oh, yeah. My sidearm was locked in the car. Bad timing. Got whacked hard with a pipe. My shoulder was sore for two weeks after that. Needed a few stitches from a cut to my arm."

Wendy's eyes filled with mixed awe and admiration and horror. "But you got those girls away from those creeps. You put your life on the line for them."

"I guess I did."

"Why do you do it? Put yourself in danger like that?"

"It's my job."

A decisive head shake. She wasn't buying it. "Not according to Lily. The story she told me happened when you were on vacation. She says helping people like that's a kind of personal calling. Is it true?"

Not wanting to take a deep dive into the subject, he replied with a noncommittal shrug.

"Anyway, back to my question: when you're in those dangerous situations, don't you get scared?"

"Yes."

From her look of surprise, Wendy hadn't expected that direct an answer. It took her a moment to process, coming back with, "You must be brave."

"I'm not brave," he replied.

Wendy Chu regarded him with friendly skepticism. As her gaze lingered, he couldn't tell what thoughts churned behind that lovely face. Finally, she stirred as if remembering she was needed elsewhere. She rose out of her seat. "I should go. We're about to start my section. Thanks for the chat." Wendy made to leave, then, on second thought, turned back with a furtive smile and said softly, "*I* think you're brave."

Detective Henry Lau watched the dancer's lithe figure withdraw, her black ponytail swishing from side to side with each stride of her long, perfectly proportioned legs. And he smiled.

In time, his thoughts returned to Lily Chen, who'd made him out to be a good guy. He hoped that was true.

He hadn't always been so altruistic. When he'd started his martial arts journey at the impressionable age of sixteen, such a high and mighty concept was not uppermost in his mind. The teenager viewed kung fu as this mysterious, hard-to-attain skill that would allow him to stand up to the bullies who'd occasionally pick on him. And for the first time in his life, he'd found something he was good at. Better than good. Only time and experience and the advocacy of his teachers opened the eyes of the self-absorbed teen to use his developing skills to help others. But the event that hammered the message home was the murder of Kay. Not being there for her—when his so-called fighting skills might have helped the person he cared about the most—was a bitter irony. Henry had failed her, the sting of that never distant in his thoughts. From this came the commitment to use his failure as a springboard to help those who couldn't stand up to bullies.

The road to atonement led to Hong Kong.

The impressionistic, moveable stage scenery recalled his neighborhood in Kowloon. Oddly enough, one of the male dancers bore a passing resemblance to his roommate, Archie Lee. Images of these ghosts from his past—the struggles, frustrations, doubts, and hard-won victories—launched a wave of other memories.

The first months in his new city were tough, devoted to getting acquainted with *everything*. It didn't come easy. The one constant was training with Lo Bai Hu and his students, the reason Henry had uprooted his life. These sessions were augmented by training with roommate Archie in hopes he would eventually participate in *beimo*.

*Beimo.*

The rooftop challenge matches were the fading remnants of a bygone time. In their heyday in the 1950s and early 1960s, these full-on contests between individual martial artists from different schools, thugs, and gang members were legendary. No gloves. No helmets. No padding. No protection of any kind. However, decades of urban renewal projects and sweeps by Hong Kong police to make the city safer had put an end to these contests.

In theory.

In reality, the fights moved underground, behind closed doors, became fewer and less conspicuous. While not as prominent as in the glory days, these martial arts challenges still drew in those who desired a place to test their skills away from the safe environs of the training hall.

Henry's new master was strict. Lo Bai Hu—mid-fifties but looked ten years younger, well built, thick black hair streaked with bands of gray—wouldn't allow any of his students to fight until he deemed them ready. Lo's English was excellent, having learned it as a child at a British missionary school. "Too soon, Henry," he explained early on. "Your fighting skills are very good, as I'd expect from one of Baak's advanced students." Baak was the given name of Eric Kwan. "Before I let you attempt *beimo*, I need to see how you do against my best students."

It did not go well at first. While Henry could hold his own or even beat most of the intermediate students, against Sifu Lo's best five students, he was humbled. They manhandled him. Two months passed before Henry was allowed to attend *beimo*—as a spectator. His task was to observe and study the lessons from these almost anything-goes contests. Some combatants were surprisingly unskilled, whereas others were scary good. Four weeks later, Sifu Lo gave his blessing for Henry to participate. He lost. Barely. In the aftermath, Henry nursed a sore chest and bicep, reviewed his mistakes, and took pointers from his kung fu elder brothers (*sihing*) and his sifu. There followed the countless hours he and roommate Archie spent practicing in their tiny flat. Archie was an accomplished Western-style boxer who was also a black belt in Taekwondo before eagerly giving them up to study Wing Chun with Lo Bai Hu. Archie shared his wealth of knowledge with Henry. The two trained together every chance they could spare. Such was their lives. Little else mattered.

They were young men with excessive energy and a fire burning hot inside them.

# CHAPTER 15

By the time Janet's white Mazda neared her objective, the sun had dipped below the tree line. She'd navigated through congested Highway 494 rush hour traffic in the south metro, exiting onto East Bush Lake Road. The business center was nestled in a crowded office park in Edina, a wealthy inner suburb of Minneapolis. She turned into the lot and found a parking space. Glanced at her dashboard clock. Made it with time to spare!

The CPA firm was on the second floor of the office tower, where Nikki, the office manager and receptionist, greeted her. "Alan's on the phone," she said. "He should be winding things up soon." One of Nikki's many talents was her innate ability to predict the length of client phone calls. More importantly, their termination. Janet could never figure out if that was a skill the office manager had developed or some innate psychic ability. Didn't matter. Eight out of ten times, the woman was on target.

Nikki Valencia was the one and only employee of AZ & Associates, CPAs. The AZ being Alan Zhu, and the associates his two junior partners. Age-wise, she looked about fifty and had a buoyant personality. Hers was the first voice potential clients heard on the phone; she had a knack for making people feel special, as if they had just made her day.

Two minutes later, as predicted, the door at the end of the short hallway opened. Out stepped Alan Zhu. Short, slender, energetic, and dapper in a stylish ragg wool sweater and dark chinos, his wide grin gave his office manager a run for her money. "Janet! Great to see you. C'mon in."

A quick hug. Her hands felt the firm back muscles through his sweater. Alan was the same height as her, five foot five. Janet had known this man forever. Alan and Henry had grown up together and were best friends. He was like a second uncle to her, and on rare occasions, she sought his counsel. He ushered her into his small office, where she made herself comfortable in a clothbound chair. On the wall behind his desk hung framed certificates and licenses. Mounted on the wall behind her was a poster-sized photograph of a verdant bamboo forest taken from within. Sunlight streaked through the thick canopy of giant green stalks. Beautifully mysterious and soothing. Janet imagined Alan looking up from a dreary financial statement to rest his eyes on this calming scene.

He settled in his chair, adjusting his black-framed glasses to focus receptive brown eyes on his guest. "So, what brings you here?"

"This won't take long," she prefaced, knowing his time was valuable. It was Tuesday, a Wing Chun night. Alan would be heading into South Minneapolis shortly to teach class, which he did two evenings a week and three Saturday mornings a month, leaving one Saturday devoted entirely to his family.

Take your time," he said.

Janet swallowed, moistening her lips. "Christmas is in like five weeks. I'm trying something different this year for holiday gifts. Mom and Dad's are done. So is yours. My problem is Henry. He's tough to shop for."

"Been there. He's not big on material things."

"Tell me about it! I've been dropping hints for weeks."

Alan frowned thoughtfully. "Do you need to put in so much effort?"

"Yeah, I do. He's had a rough year—badly hurt, the ICU stay and long recovery, learning to walk again. On top of that, he's been my partner and mentor. I really want this year's gift to be special." Quite a mouthful and blurted out in one go.

Alan gave a little laugh. "Are you including yourself as part of his rough year?"

"Uh, not what I meant. You get my point, though."

"Where do I come in?"

"You know Henry better than anyone. I need some unique gift ideas. Any suggestions?"

"No, sorry."

"None?"

He shook his head. "Wish I could help. The last time I gave Henry a gift was in junior high. It was a Star Wars T-shirt."

"Oh, is he into Star Wars?"

"Not so much. I think he wore the T-shirt once."

"Bummer. Does he have other interests? Like art, books, movies. Even power tools he's talked about. I'm desperate!"

Alan couldn't help her.

"Yeah," she admitted, "kind of what I was expecting." All the same, she'd harbored a wish Alan might pull a rabbit out of the hat for her. No luck. And so she had to work up the nerve to tell him about her backup plan.

Sensing her discomfort, Alan looked back, somewhat mystified. "Is this why you wanted to see me? I could've told you this over the phone. You didn't have to make a special trip."

*Just do it.*

The little voice egged her on. Janet reached across the desk to rest her hand on top of his. "There's more." She could feel her face flush as the words teetered precipitously on the tip of her tongue. "Tell me about Kay McAdams."

Alan stiffened. "Like what?"

"Does Henry talk about her?"

"Rarely."

She could feel his resistance. Took her hand off his. "Too sensitive a subject?"

"Not really. Years ago, it was. Kay hardly ever comes up in our conversations these days."

"Kay's not a taboo subject or anything?"

"No." Alan compressed his lips, waiting for her to get to the point.

"You're probably wondering why I brought this up?"

"Well, yeah."

She swallowed. Rushed to say, "That's why I wanted to see you in person. I need your opinion." In truth, she wanted to *see* his reaction as she felt herself about to walk out over a deep gorge on a thin tightrope. "Do you think a reminder of Kay would upset Henry?"

"What kind of reminder? A photo? A hair ribbon?"

"Any of those. Some physical memento."

Alan thought it over. "I don't know," he said in a faraway voice. After a bit, he came back. "Probably not. A lot of time has passed. You're probably safe."

"Good," she muttered, daring to feel upbeat. *Maybe her plan had a chance!*

Wary eyes leveled on her. "Janet, where are you going with this?"

Her stomach tensed. "Well, for Henry's special present, I was thinking of contacting Kay's parents to see if they'd be willing to send a personal trinket or photo of her as a keepsake."

There.

The words were out. Out and at large.

Alan's eyes went wide. "I don't know. That might not be a good idea, contacting the McAdamses. They might not want to talk about their murdered daughter."

"I know! This could turn into a bad dumpster fire."

"Uh, *yeah.* And you still want to do it? How about painting a nice watercolor for Henry?"

"Nah, I did that two years ago. I need something special."

"This idea. You're serious about it?"

"Contacting Kay's parents? You bet. Is it that bad an idea?"

Alan was skeptical. "It could backfire on you."

Hearing him say it only made that outcome seem more likely. Yet it still didn't deter her. "I know it's a touchy subject," she pressed on with heat, perhaps trying to convince herself, "but it has been over twenty years. I know Kay's parents'll never stop hurting from her loss. What I'm hoping is the pain's dulled by now. If I approach them respectfully, they might say yes."

"They might also tell you to stay the hell away from them."

"They might," she nodded. Which was her fear, ripping the scab off an old wound that should have been left alone and upsetting everyone. Merry Christmas, guys! What a difference a few hours made. In the fresh light of morning, the idea seemed inspired. Now, in the dark of evening, it seemed anything but that.

*Don't upset Kay's parents. Don't risk hurting Henry.*

Solid advice.

Advice she wasn't going to take. She looked again to Alan, who was slowly rocking back and forth in his chair, patiently listening. Then, with a half smile, he said, "You're going to do it, aren't you?"

Her eyebrows shrugged. "Yeah."

"I'm not surprised. Did you talk to your parents?"

"I did. Dad's on the fence. Mom agrees with you. Thinks it's a bad idea to contact the McAdamses. She's also apprehensive about Henry's reaction."

"That's what's really bothering you, isn't it?"

"If I piss off the McAdamses, I'll be sorry but won't ever have to deal with them again. I'll survive. But if Henry's upset at me, it could mess up our relationship."

"And you think this memento of Kay's will do—what?"

She took a full second before answering. "That it'll give him some peace of mind? Lighten his heart? Maybe bring back some good memories." Even Janet could hear the doubt in her voice, wondering if this was all simply wishful thinking on her part. More likely her "great" idea would blow up in her face.

"I see..." Alan rubbed the side of his jaw, contemplating what she'd said. "It might work," he opined, though with reservations.

Janet prepared herself for disappointment. "Be honest. D'you think Henry'll have a bad reaction?"

"I can't say."

"I'm concerned he'll get depressed. Or angry."

"You're probably safe there. As you said, a lot of time's gone by. It's not like the first year after Kay died." Alan shook his head at the memory. Then offered a philosophical half-smile. "You're young, Janet. You live long enough and deal with enough crap, it toughens you up. It has been over twenty years."

She nodded slowly, wondering, "What happened to him back then? I know a little. Maybe if I knew, I'd understand better."

"Henry never told you?"

"Not in any detail. He didn't volunteer much like the memory was too painful. Would you tell me, Alan?" Janet coaxed with bright puppy dog eyes.

His brow furrowed as he thought it over. Eventually, with noticeable reluctance, he gave a nod. "I'll tell you. You're family, so it should be okay." Alan settled in his chair and collected his thoughts.

A tingle ran up Janet's spine. A curtain into the past was about to be pulled aside to reveal the darkest moment of her Uncle Henry's life. She leaned forward with anticipation.

Alan spoke in a subdued, detached voice as one casting his mind back through time and space, resurrecting ghostly images long undisturbed. "It was our senior year at Stanford. Mid-October was a busy time for all of us. Henry and Kay had been dating seriously for months. Both had tough class schedules and couldn't see each other as much." Alan gazed blankly ahead as if it was all unfolding before him. "On that last day, they'd arranged a quick lunch at a popular burger joint near campus, a chance to spend a little time together. Kay was feeling overwhelmed by her classes, which was unlike her. She was an A student who worked a part-time job. The pressure was getting to her, and she needed some tender loving care. She needed Henry. Needed to be with him. But he had plans. It was a regular Wing Chun training night. Henry hated to miss training with Eric Kwan, the reason we moved to California for school."

Alan paused to make sure Janet was following. A second later, he continued. "Kay asked Henry to skip class that one time—for her. He said no. But said he'd work harder to find time for her, even offering to skip the Saturday morning class with Kwan so he and Kay could spend the day together." Alan frowned and shook his head. "Kay got upset. She'd never been mad at Henry before but was then, accusing him of not really caring for her if he wasn't willing to give up one measly kung fu class. She reminded him of times she'd adjusted her schedule for him. Then she walked out. He'd never seen her like that, so angry and hurt. Henry was stunned and just sat there. She left angry, but he didn't go after her. He's kicked himself for that ever since."

There came a silence.

It took Alan a few seconds to find his voice again, laboring to continue. "Later that evening, Henry called Kay's dorm room to apologize. He'd screwed up and knew it. Except it wasn't Kay who answered the phone; it was her roommate, Jo. And Jo was a basket case, a sobbing mess. The police had just left after informing Jo that her roommate was dead. Kay had gone out by herself earlier and had been attacked and killed by a mugger."

Janet let out a gasp.

She could hear the sadness in Alan's voice, practically feel it, realizing for the first time how much the tragedy had affected him personally. "What happened to Kay was terrible. Shocking. She was one of a kind. One of those rare people who made you feel blessed to be around her. Unforgettable—"

He stopped cold, averting his face, the memory of it too vivid. Only then did Janet understand his initial reluctance to tell the story. At first, she thought his pauses were an attempt to conjure up a half-forgotten time, but now she realized the memories were crystal clear. No, the hesitations had been Alan trying not to react to them. He'd been more than a spectator; he'd also known Kay's friendship and had felt the impact of her murder.

Janet felt lousy for asking him to dredge up the memories.

From behind his glasses, Alan's eyes filled with an emotion she couldn't quite decipher: sadness, pain, worry. "Henry was broken. It was a bad time. *Very bad.*"

Janet swallowed hard, inching forward. "You helped him through it." She was keen to give him much-deserved credit.

"Me…and others." Alan's voice was heavy.

"Yeah."

"I never want to see him go through that again."

She thought it best not to say anything and give Alan a moment to himself.

After a bit, he picked up the story again. "It took time, and it was rough, but Henry pulled himself together to get his degree. Although by then, he was a different person."

"Different, how?"

Alan grappled for the right words. "Hurting. Angry. A little reckless. Like he'd lost his reason for living."

"Is that why he went to Hong Kong?"

"Yes. To lose himself. To find himself. To redeem himself."

Having finished his foray down memory lane, Alan settled back to adjust his sweater sleeve, looking for Janet's reaction.

Truth was she didn't know what she was feeling. How strange to be told a terrible watershed moment in the life of a man she'd known since she'd first learned to walk. Janet was in kindergarten during this time, ancient history to one who was making orange and green Play-Doh animals, albeit all too recent to those who'd lived through the murder of Kay McAdams. By the time Alan had finished his story, Janet was on the verge of tears.

"Thank you," her voice trembled.

"Does that help with your decision?" Alan asked.

Her lips smushed together as she stroked an eyebrow. "It does. Makes me feel what I'm doing is more important than ever. So yeah, I'm going through with it." She made a fatalistic sound. "Which could be the dumbest thing I'll ever do! But I've got to do it. Does that make any sense?"

"It does if you think it's right."

"More than ever."

"Be careful," he cautioned with a benign half smile.

"I'm still in the research phase, trying to locate Kay's parents. So much time has passed; they might not be alive, or they've moved. Or when I call, I might chicken out at the last second."

"Which wouldn't be a bad thing."

Janet heaved a sigh that climbed up from her depths. "I really want this to be a positive thing for everyone, especially Henry." Her eyebrows arched. "Am I crazy for thinking this'll work?"

Alan assured, "No, you're not. You have a good heart. It's your secret weapon and the reason you could succeed."

Her eyes welled as that heart filled with gratitude.

\# \# \#

After dance rehearsals ended, Henry decided to gas up his car on the way home, stopping at a Fuel and Go across the street from a busy strip mall. He'd taken an alternate route to St. Louis Park from Minneapolis, one that skirted the bottom of Gillette, to stop at a popular gas station. Bright lights streamed down from the pump canopy, an island of dazzle against the black night sky. Henry grabbed the squeegee brush from the pump bucket and wiped each window. It had been a long day. Not a difficult one, mainly fruitless and mentally draining. More bad breaks and muddled results. Tomorrow will be no different, he thought. During the drive, he'd had some new ideas, though it was too late in the day to act coherently on them. He parked the thoughts for review in the morning—

And then it happened.

Henry was squeegeeing the rear passenger's window when—out of nowhere—he was shoved hard from behind and slammed into his car. A hand pushed forcefully on one shoulder while something hard—*a knife or gun?*—was thrust into his lower back.

"Don't move!" ordered a gruff voice, inches from his ear. Hot breath pulsed at the back of his neck.

His entire nervous system pegged to the red zone. Hearing. Sense of touch. Vision. Decades of training and experience kicked in. His body was off balance and reacted, feet adjusting under him. Knees bent. Done within two heartbeats. Brain neurons fired up like Fourth of July bottle rockets.

The fingers on his shoulder clenched.

The pressure triggered an explosive spin like a Tasmanian devil, sloughing off the attacker's hand. The object jammed against his back slipped away, then was knocked aside by his downward chopping arm (*gaun sau*). The same arm continued its arc, his hand still gripping the rubber squeegee brush, swinging upward. He slammed the aluminum shaft into his attacker's neck, hooked the squeegee blade behind, and yanked the startled face into the full kinetic fury of a *biu jee* overhead elbow that crashed into the other's collarbone. Not wasting a second, he launched forward with a powerful forearm strike to the chest, backed by the force of his entire body, that sent his attacker tumbling back five yards, dropping to the concrete like a pallet of bricks.

Henry—heart pounding like manic war drums—flicked his eyes every which way for the next threat.

There was none.

He swung back to the man on the ground. Only then noticing the police uniform, a Gillette PD uniform. The officer moaned, struggled painfully to a sitting position. "Shit, Lau, why'd you do that?" His hand went to his shoulder.

Officer Ken Ferguson. The jokester. Funny Man Ferguson. There'd been no weapon pressed against his back, Henry now realized. Most likely a finger. Still breathing rapidly, Henry speared him with a lethal look. "What the hell shit was that?"

"A joke, man. It was a joke."

"Are you fuckin' serious? You think that's funny? What kind of stupid, sick bastard are you?"

Ferguson sounded offended. "Geez, dial it down. You didn't have to go kung fu ape shit on me!"

Henry was having none of that. "Don't you dare blame me. This is all on you, Ferguson."

Rubbing his shoulder, the impetuous officer groaned, "I think you broke something."

*Hell, yeah! That'd been the point.*

Henry had targeted his attacker's clavicle, a thin yet vital structure that connects the shoulder to the chest. A mere five pounds of pressure is enough to snap it, rendering the arm virtually useless, as well as making any movement with that appendage agony. It was an autopilot response in a fight or flight moment for his life—or what Henry'd

153

perceived as life-threatening. He'd intended to incapacitate this attacker and deal with others. But Henry would never admit this; he didn't trust Ken Ferguson.

Henry's shoulders bunched at a sound.

Running feet.

He whirled round.

Another officer scrambled over from the far end of the parking lot where a Gillette police cruiser was parked. Felicia Chavez, recent transfer from Florida and the officer who'd been in charge of preserving the crime scene at the knife factory, rushed over and knelt by Ferguson. "Holy shit!" She tossed a worried, cautious glance toward Henry before attempting to help her comrade to his feet. He yelped in pain during the ungainly trip to become upright.

Eyes like razor wire glared at Chavez. "Were you part of this?"

She vigorously shook her head. "No way! I told Ferguson it was a dumb idea."

"Okay. Remember that when you're asked later." He tossed a chin jut toward the teetering Ferguson. "Take him to urgent care. Have him checked out."

"Will do, Detective."

Henry waited until Chavez had assisted Ferguson to the police cruiser, her charge grimacing the entire way down into the seat. The car drove away. It was then that Henry realized he was still holding the squeegee brush. He returned it to the mounted bucket, went to the Malibu and leaned his backside against the rear fender. Head bowed and eyes closed, he waited for his heartbeat to settle as his lungs continued to drag in short pulses of breath.

The body's reaction to danger can't be shut off like a light switch. A lot of people don't get that. He'd no idea the attack wasn't real. His mind and body had jacked into survival mode. As Wendy Chu remarked earlier in the evening, it was all real to him, with a life-and-death fear. It took a while for his internal alarm system to reset and for his mind and body to calm down. The older he got, the longer it seemed to take. And it didn't stop with that; there was wear and tear on the body and soul after these encounters.

There was always a toll to pay. A piece of him gone.

# CHAPTER 16

"You did *what*?" Chief Bowman eyeballed Henry early the following morning. His office. Door closed.

Henry had just finished relaying the details of the Fuel and Go incident from the night before.

"Jesus, Henry!"

The Samuel L. Jackson bobblehead behind Bowman shook its head as a dump truck wheeled by.

Henry had arrived at the station early, wanting to tell his side of the story before Ken Ferguson or anyone else could skew what happened. Having accomplished this, he now sat patiently for the chief's response. Bowman's rugged jaw tightened, drawing down the thick black mustache. Some heavy-duty reflection was going on as the chief contemplated the man sitting across from him. And then his eyes crinkled with amusement, and the silky voice erupted in a full-throated laugh.

*A good sign!*

"Chief?"

Bowman whacked the top of his desk. "God, I wish I'd been there to see it!" Then shook his head, scowling. "I don't get Ferguson. The man's a good cop. But why he continues to pull these lame-ass pranks and jokes, I don't know. What he did was inexcusable. Well, you may have cured him of that. I've broken my collarbone; for the next month, he'll really enjoy putting on his socks and underwear with one hand." Bowman chuckled.

Henry looked at him cautiously. "So, we're okay?"

"You bet your ass we are! There's no way Ferguson can justify his actions. It was irresponsible and dangerous. He should've known better than pulling a dumbass stunt like that with another cop, let alone you."

For the first time since he'd entered the chief's office, Henry felt the tension in his body dissolve. Bowman wasn't holding him responsible.

"Rest assured," Bowman cautioned, "I'll have plenty to say to Ferguson. It's high time he permanently stows his jokes and pranks in a trunk, locks it, and throws away the key."

"Appreciate it, Fred."

Bowman noticed Henry's guarded response. Cocked an eyebrow. "This really bothered you."

"You can't imagine. A stunt like that could go wrong in so many ways. And not just for Ferguson."

"You got that right." Glancing at the wall clock, Bowman said, "Roll call's in a few minutes. As an extra measure, I'll share Ferguson's ill-fated stunt and how it blew up on him. Be sure, I'll emphasize that kind of schoolyard antics will not be tolerated." Then the chief cracked a wry smile, clearly enjoying the moment. "I'll also strongly suggest to one and all that it's a very bad idea to sneak up behind Detective Henry Lau."

It got a chuckle from Henry.

He could afford to be lighthearted now with the situation behind him. He'd had his doubts about how the meeting would go. As a man who carried a badge and was a highly skilled martial artist, Henry had to walk a narrow path in public. Too much physical persuasion in the wrong situation and he could be accused of using excessive force. Another out-of-control cop. An unbearable charge for a man who'd devoted most of his life toward protecting the innocent. Which was why Henry had been furious at Ferguson for putting him at risk.

# # #

Roll call had finished. The station corridors were abuzz with uniformed and plain clothes men and women on their way to their daily assignments. Janet walked close to her uncle on the way back to their desks. "Well, you had an exciting night!" she said humorously, referencing Chief Bowman's recap of the Fuel and Go incident.

"Yeah," Henry grumbled.

She heard the disenchantment in his voice. Looked carefully at him. The youngish, usually agreeable face appeared uneasy under the black shag and its few threads of silver. The dark brown eyes seemed preoccupied, and there was a slackness in the smooth features that accentuated the idea that his mind was elsewhere. But there were too many people around. Janet waited until they'd reached the privacy of the Criminal Investigation Department before she pulled him aside.

"You seem distracted," she said. "What's going on? Tell me."

Her uncle was a private person who rarely spoke about his feelings, particularly the more disturbing ones. As he continued to waffle, Janet pressed as only she could. "You *are* going to tell me, aren't you?" Only the meanest troll could ignore that irresistible face, the same face of the adorable little girl who used to plead with her Uncle Henry to tell her a story, which he did because Henry Lau was no troll.

The pull of that face worked, as always. Henry sat on the edge of his desk and spoke barely above a murmur. "I'm tired of dealing with idiots and assholes. Seems there's a new crop of 'em every year. They never go away. People are less civil in public since the pandemic. More hate's out there." His gaze fell away.

The light went on for Janet.

Of course, this was still about Ken Ferguson. She remained silent, her face encouraging, letting Henry take the discussion where he wanted.

As if catching himself turning maudlin, his expression morphed back into a somewhat subdued version of his usually affable self. "But

I'm not special. Dealing with idiots and assholes is an occupational hazard in law enforcement."

He'd get no argument from her. Although, she felt there was more to it. Henry was more resilient than that. Dubious eyes inspected him. "This isn't just about Ferguson. What aren't you telling me?"

He spread his hands. "I'm not sure."

It was an answer Janet didn't like. "This talk about idiots and assholes. You're not thinking of quitting?" A note of dread in her voice.

Henry gave a dismissive gesture.

"I hope not," she came back, frowning. "You worked so hard. All those injuries. The months of healing and getting back in shape for work—"

"And to get back my life."

"That too. Did you get back your life?"

The answer didn't come right away, which bothered her.

He thought about it. "It has…mostly."

"What does that mean?"

"Some things I used to do take more effort."

"Your body's still healing," she stressed, troubled where the conversation was headed.

A mirthless laugh. "Yeah, everybody keeps telling me that. One after-effect I'm finding is I'm not as patient with some people as I used to be."

"Oh, I hope not."

Janet counted on his good nature and guiding hand. The job was stressful and could leave one emotionally shipwrecked. If Alan Zhu was a safe harbor, Uncle Henry was her home port. She'd hate to lose that. Yes, she could count on her parents' support and the support of friends, but it was this man who understood what it took to be a police detective and its daily hurdles. The others had no idea. Beyond this, there was the simple fact that she loved working with him.

Before Janet could comment further, a chorus of rowdy laughter grabbed their attention. She and Henry looked past the cubicles to the wide corridor beyond. Three patrol officers, in the middle of a lively discussion, were on their way to the garage. Passing them in the other direction was an athletic Nordic woman. Ragnhild Steinbakken, a Norwegian who spoke better English than a third of the station personnel, was one of the dispatchers. Tall and toned with striking features, her wheat-colored hair was done up in imposing shield maiden Viking braids. You didn't mess with Ragnhild, who'd once trained as an Olympic downhill skier for her home country. She waved a greeting to the detectives on her way to the dispatch room.

Henry waved back, smiling.

Clearing her throat, Janet tried to steer him back to their conversation before the interruption. "You were saying you were feeling less patient?"

"Oh, right." He shrugged. "It comes and goes. I don't know why." His demeanor became more cavalier when he saw her growing distress. "I'll be fine. I was having a *moment*. It's gone."

A moment triggered by Officer Ferguson, who should have known better. Annoyed, Janet could have done without the smartass officer and was relieved Bowman was dealing with him. She hoped there was no long-term emotional fallout for Henry. People—and she meant Ken Ferguson—needed to understand the consequences of their actions. In the next few minutes, she was pleased to see her uncle's good nature returning in little ways: the look in his eye, an easiness in his voice, a general lightness about him.

Then came doughnuts.

Janet was in the break room, enjoying a Boston cream doughnut, part of a box left by the police dispatch supervisor. Taking the last bite of a bear claw, a buxom Officer Anna Jankovic eyed the slender detective with annoyed admiration. "How can you eat those things and stay so skinny?"

Raising a single lean, well-defined eyebrow, Janet said the first thing that came to her. "Maybe 'cause I eat only one?" Which wasn't intended as a slam against the generously proportioned Jankovic, whose insatiable love of sweet, gooey confections was well-known at the station.

"Hmmm," the officer acknowledged, "my willpower does crumble whenever I get near these tasty fat applicators." She squinted at Janet's mouth. "You got some custard on your upper lip."

Janet's tongue emerged and deftly swiped her lip. "Better?"

"Much."

All the same, Janet decided a pitstop in front of the restroom mirror was advisable. Returning to her desk, she found Henry leaning back in his chair, staring at the ceiling tiles, lost in thought. Given their earlier conversation and his previous mood, she figured some levity might be in order. "Contemplating life, the universe? Or maybe what's for dinner?" She dropped in her chair and was delighted when he grinned back.

"None of the above," he said. "Blaine PD called with news."

She was all attention. "They found something, didn't they?"

"*They did.*" He sat up, pleased. "I was talking with Dan Hicks, who's going through stuff in Park's garage. In the recycling bin was a weekly newspaper. He'd found a half page from a yellow legal pad inside the fold. With words hand-lettered in a broad-tipped Sharpie."

"Oh?"

"Hicks emailed a photo. I was thinking about it when you walked in." Henry rotated the wide flatscreen. The display made Janet's blood run cold.

*I KNOW WHAT YOU DID! STEALING
IS A CRIME. YOUR SECRET WON'T
STAY SECRET FOR LONG. YOU'RE
GONNA PAY! I'LL MAKE SURE!*

Janet frowned. "What is that? A poison-pen letter? A blackmail note?"

"No payment demand."

"Good point. But—wow—this is an attention grabber!" Her face clouded as she attempted to suss it out. "What d'we make of this? Was Sam Park being threatened? Did he steal something? Is that the *secret*?"

"Who knows?"

"Not much to go on." Her nose wrinkled as she tried to puzzle out the message. "How old is this note? It was in the recycle bin. It could be months old, even older."

"Yep. Could be. The note was found in a two-week-old edition of the weekly newspaper."

"If the note's recent, why throw it out? Unless Park didn't think it was worth bothering about?"

Henry, who could never sit for too long without getting restless, got to his feet. "All we know for now is there's a threatening note. Is someone accusing Sam Park of stealing? Like what? Money? A pricey object? Taking credit he didn't deserve. Stealing someone's affections."

Janet's scalp tingled. "Oooh, the last one. Someone's affections. Is the note referring to Susan Zelinsky? We keep hearing about her and Park. What if somebody's jealous?"

"Like Joe Prescott?"

A vigorous nod. "The guy threatened people. Got fired for it. Is this another one of his threats?"

"Maybe, but I'm not sure. This poison-pen, blackmail note—whatever you call it—doesn't seem his style. Too well written. I've met the guy. Though I take your point," Henry added. "We can't ignore a possible Park and Zelinsky connection."

"How're we following up?"

"For the moment, we aren't. We have another suspect to question first."

"We do?"

"While you were on break, I got a call from Lori Deaver."

Janet couldn't place the name. "Who?"

"She works at Hancock Blades. Same department as Susan Zelinsky."

"Ah, the woman who ran out after you from the lobby. The CPA."

"Right."

"What'd she say?"

"Deaver's taking Zelinsky's murder hard. They were friends. She was looking through old text messages. One from two months ago caught her eye. Zelinsky mentions a new guy she was seeing, even made a joke about his name: John Adams."

"Like the second U.S. president. What about him?"

"Deaver remembers Zelinsky and Adams went out only four or five times before she ended it."

"Dumped him?" Janet was intrigued. "Another unhappy love interest?"

"We won't know until you ask him."

"*Me?*"

"If you'd be so kind. I tracked down Mr. Adams. He runs a plumbing supply company in Coon Rapids. I'm off to Blaine to see this note up close and personal. Also, to check out Park's house in case anything got overlooked."

"Good luck with that."

"Thanks. One other thing," Henry said. "You were at Zelinsky's home."

"Yeah, with Sergeant Hanson. Why?"

"Did you see an e-bike?"

"Uh, not that I recall. What's an e-bike have to do with anything?"

"It belongs to Lori Deaver. She loaned it to Zelinsky to try out for a few weeks. Zelinsky was going to return it on Monday—"

"But she never made it to work."

Henry nodded. "In the shock and excitement of the two deaths, Deaver forgot about the bike."

"I'll text Hanson. Maybe it was there and I didn't notice it." Janet's eyebrows turned down at a new idea. "If Zelinsky was returning the e-bike on Monday, maybe it's in her vehicle."

"Which is still missing."

Janet looked away, thinking with a sense of weariness how "missing" was the word for this investigation. Missing like Susan Zelinsky's car. Missing explanations for the poison-pen or pseudo-blackmail note found in Park's garage and the letter found at Zelinsky's. The missing meaning of the Post-it found on the floor in Park's office: "An Actionable Crime." And the missing identities of K.J. Hazzard, a name on that Post-it, and Ann or Nan Oreino, Evelyn Brown's mysterious Filippino woman. Lastly, the missing suspect responsible for two homicides.

Janet had no clue how all these threads were weaved together. Was worried she might never know, feeling she was too wooly-headed to sort them out or see the pattern they formed.

*Stupid concussion.*

# CHAPTER 17

Detective Hicks guided Henry through Samuel Park's home. There was always the chance some minor thing got overlooked during the initial sweep, which a second viewing might reveal. But no, Blaine PD had done an excellent job, although one thing near the top of Henry's to-do list was a closer inspection of Park's home office.

Pretty much any part of the house would be at home in an upscale furniture showroom display: good, simple taste, comfortably modest, stylish without being too showy. Standard upper middle-class fare. Nothing in the surroundings gave a clue as to the owner's unique taste.

That changed the moment Henry entered the home office. This was Sam Park's little oasis. The walls were painted in a soothing sage green. An L-shaped desk in the back dominated the room, decked out with the usual monitors, a laser printer, small cabinets, and ceiling track lighting. On the wall behind the desk hung a Korean tiger folk wall hanging. Henry vaguely remembered the tiger as an important symbol in Korean culture, supposedly driving away evil spirits. A large ceramic dinner plate with iron black and red painted fish was displayed on a shelf across the room. On a tiny credenza beneath it were three individually potted philodendrons in a tidy row. Several framed photographs rested here as well. One of Park's adult daughter. Several older ones with his wife, himself, and his daughter at least fifteen years earlier. The last photo of what Henry suspected was of a college-aged Sam Park with his parents. Samuel Park was a second-generation Korean American.

It was a room to reflect in, to get away from the outside world, a place to find harmony and focus. Henry appreciated the tranquil ambiance; he'd be at home in a place like this. Along the wall opposite the windows stood four tall wooden bookcases crammed with hardcovers, softcovers, glossy picture books, and heaps of old-fashioned pocket paperbacks. These piqued Henry's interest. He walked by every bookcase, scanning titles. Books on history, rows of mysteries, a few science and motivational subjects, including a short section on achieving business objectives.

Dan Hicks watched from nearby. A long, lean man with a Roman nose and an agreeable disposition, he stood with the patience of a shoe salesman waiting for a customer to decide between a pair of loafers. "Looking for anything in particular?"

"South America," came the reply.

"Say what?"

"Books on South America or countries there." At the end of his search, Henry turned to face Hicks and shrugged. "Nothing."

"You don't look disappointed."

"I'm not. Wasn't expecting to find anything."

"Then why look?"

"Just making sure."

"Why South America?"

"An angle I'm working on. Looks like a dead end." Or too obscure a reference, Henry thought. There was no hint of any interest or association with the southern continent in Park's home. Yet the open world atlas under Park's hand *had to mean something!* Was it, as Janet wondered, Park naming his killer? If not, what then?

Henry thanked Hicks and drove back to Gillette, first calling ahead to the knife factory to arrange an impromptu meeting. He found the CEO and CFO waiting for him in the same spacious conference room where he and Janet had first interviewed Aimee Hancock on Sunday. However, she was much more poised and put together today. Hancock sat with a pad of paper before her, writing a series of notes with a gel pen. Beneath snow-white bangs, restive eyes watched him distrustfully. Jim Karjala wore a tight expression and looked none too pleased to be there. From their stiff postures, Henry could tell both were braced for bad news, no doubt based on his previous death notification visit regarding Susan Zelinsky.

He sat across from them, unzipping his jacket, though not removing it. He didn't expect to be there long. He'd come with a plan and wanted to see how his suspicions played out in front of these two. "Thank you both for seeing me on such short notice."

Aimee Hancock gave a cursory nod. "Anything to help." Her eyes darted to the wall clock. "Will this take long? I have a sales and marketing meeting in twenty minutes."

Anything to help? Except for missing a meeting with staff, it seemed. Henry assured her, "We'll be finished before then."

The tight lines in her face eased. She set the pen aside, giving him her full attention.

Henry cleared his throat. "There's been a development, and I'd like your opinions."

Both executives looked back with interest, their curiosity whetted.

"We found this in Sam Park's home. It's some kind of threat." Henry displayed the photo of the poison-pen note from his smartphone.

Hancock and Karjala's eyes widened. They exchanged looks.

Setting aside his phone, Henry chose his following words with care. "This note refers to a theft. Mr. Park was your chief operations officer. Does it make sense for someone to accuse him of stealing from the company?"

"That's total bullshit," the CEO scoffed, her face incredulous. "Sam would never do that."

"Agreed!" Karjala threw in. "That makes no sense. The note must be bogus."

"You may be right," Henry acknowledged. "It's dangerous to read too much into it. It's why I'm here." He let them chew on that before continuing. He was about to tread on delicate ground and wanted more from them than knee-jerk answers. "You've both insisted Sam Park was an honest man. Is there any chance—no matter how remote—that he misappropriated money from the company?"

"*No way*," Karjala fired back. It seemed incomprehensible to him.

"Bear with me, please." Henry raised his palm. "Let's speak hypothetically. Say it's Employee X who's the operations director, not Park. Is there any way Employee X could siphon off payments meant for the company to himself?"

The chief financial officer bristled as if the mere suggestion of embezzlement was a personal affront. "Hypothetically, could that happen? Not without me knowing about it." Karjala tapped his finger on the table. "The director of operations oversees the day-to-day functions of the company. He works with department heads and supervisors. He has marginal contact with vendors or clients."

Henry continued. "Could Employee X call a vendor and request a change to an invoice payment?"

Karjala adjusted his glasses. Looked uncomfortable at the suggestion. "Well…yes. Technically, he could. But that'd be unusual. Whoever he spoke to would find that strange and would need an authorized person from our accounting department to confirm the change request." His eyes flared behind the lenses. "It's a safeguard. To prevent just anyone from contacting our vendors and customers. Only certain people are authorized to make those requests, which means Sam Park, or Employee X, couldn't do it without it coming back to my department." Karjala stabbed a finger toward Henry. "And if a request like that came in, I'd be told."

"What about mail? Could he intercept a check from a vendor and alter the payee to himself?"

Karjala snorted humorously. "He could. It would also be pretty dumb. Any check Sam or anyone altered to pay themselves causes an immediate problem. The check was payment for an invoice. If the payee were altered, we'd have an unpaid invoice. The account would be flagged for an outstanding invoice, and the vendor would be contacted. Then the vendor would tell us they made payment on such and such date, for such and such amount, on check number 1234, say. They could also show us a bank image of the check after it was deposited. The image would show the payee's name. We'd know immediately who the culprit was."

"I see. What if the payee was changed to Cash?"

"Even dumber! The bank would find that suspicious. We're not talking small checks here. We're a manufacturing plant. The amounts are in the thousands or tens of thousands of dollars. Sometimes more. For that amount, a bank would insist on asking who wanted that much cash. And even if Employee X got the cash, we'd have the same problem: a vendor with an unpaid invoice. That'd trigger an investigation on our side." Karjala's message was clear: the company had safeguards and methods in place to prevent this kind of theft. Having made his case, the CFO removed his eyewear, chewing on the bow with a confidence that suggested he knew he had his bases covered.

"Thank you," Henry said, beginning to understand. "So it would take someone either very clever or who has special knowledge to pull off a theft like this?"

"Yes," the other's eyes narrowed to make his next point. "Except, as I've told you, the numbers wouldn't add up. The accounting team would be all over it."

An impatient Aimee Hancock inhaled sharply. "Detective, why are you going on about this? Both Jim and I've told you Sam wasn't a thief. I'd stake my reputation on that." Irritation edged her voice. Henry noticed the way her eyes kept drifting to his cell phone.

"Is something bothering you, Ms. Hancock?"

She released a troubled breath. "That note you showed us, can I see it again?"

He slid over his phone. Deep blue eyes narrowed on the photo, studying the large black marker lettering. Her eyes flicked up again, and in them was certainty. "I wasn't sure earlier, but I'd swear I've seen this note before."

A startled Henry looked back. "You have? When?"

Hancock scoured her memory, squinting. "Two weeks ago. I'm positive that's Sam's handwriting."

"Wait. What?" Henry felt a rush of excitement.

"Sam's done whiteboard presentations with magic markers. Some of the letters—the S and G—look like how he writes them. The G has a tiny hook at the bar. Sam did that. And we have those yellow legal pads. I mean, I know every office has those, but Sam used them all the time." A realization reared up before her. "That's it! It was right before the senior staff meeting. Jim and I walked by Sam's door to get him. He was writing on a legal pad with a fat Sharpie pen. When he saw us, he tore the sheet off and put it upside down on his desk. Then, he stood up, grabbed the pad and a pen, and joined us. As the page flipped over, I got a glimpse of it. I remember the large black block letters. Remember, Jim?"

"Not really," Karjala admitted. "I wasn't paying attention."

"Sam was in a hurry. When he rounded his desk, he bumped his hip against it. You joked he should slow down."

"Okay, that part I do remember. Sam limped for an hour."

The meaning of this was not lost on Henry, who realized its significance. He leaned toward the factory owner. "Ms. Hancock, to make sure I heard you right, you're fairly certain the writing you saw in Mr. Park's office looked like this note. Could even *be* this note." He tapped the image on his phone.

The CEO nodded. There wasn't a shred of doubt in her face. "The more I look at it, the more I'm convinced this is Sam's handwriting. Oh!"—it suddenly occurred to her—"If Sam wrote that note, it wasn't him being accused of stealing. *He* was accusing *someone else.*"

There it was!

Aimee Hancock had just vocalized what had been lurking in Henry's thoughts for the past hour. She'd all but confirmed that Sam Park had authored the so-called poison-pen note.

Which begged the questions:

Why was the note found in his trash?

And more importantly, who was his intended recipient, and was this the reason Park was killed?

The Adams Commercial Plumbing Supply building looked oddly like a two-slot toaster lying on its side, an effect mainly driven by the long, narrow horizontal window treatment. Janet suspected a Sunbeam Wide Slot toaster had not been the architect's design inspiration. Nevertheless, the building reminded her of a giant version of the gadget on her kitchen counter.

Detective Janet Lau identified herself at the service desk and asked to see the owner, Mr. John Adams. She was shown to the back area by the office manager, a bouncy woman bursting with personality. Shaggy black hair, bright eyes, and a glowing, flawless oolong tea complexion completed the picture of a person who looked comfortable with herself and her situation in life.

"Please have a seat," the woman flashed a gleaming smile of perfect white teeth. "John's on the phone with a supplier. I'll let him know you're waiting. Can I get you something? Coffee? Water?"

"I'm good, thanks." Janet lowered herself onto a chair that had seen better days yet was still comfortable. Her gaze wandered over toward the office manager's desk. Tiny fingers adorned with glossy ruby nails danced across a keyboard as she focused on the computer screen. The desk plate in front of her said her name was Yolanda Aquino. Mounted on the file cabinet behind her by a magnet was a scenic postcard from Manila.

The capital of the Philippines.

Janet sat up. Now here was a coincidence! she thought. Evelyn Brown had mentioned a Filipino woman, Ann Oreino, for whom the two murder victims had said they needed to complete their mysterious project, a person whom Janet had been unable to locate. Janet glanced at the nameplate again. Yolanda Aquino. Not even close.

Strange coincidence, her running into a Filipina while in search of another.

Janet didn't like coincidences. They could get messy.

Before her thoughts got too tangled on the subject, the door across from her opened. Out stepped a man she assumed to be John Adams. Middle-aged, chubby, thinning hair and a recessed chin. A plaid flannel shirt strained to cover a well-stocked beer belly. A pair of stretch jeans did their best, given the limits of elasticized denim. His eyes brightened upon seeing her. "Detective Lau," he said in a melodic baritone voice, "sorry to keep you waiting." He gestured for her to enter his office, which was surprisingly sparse and practical. Nothing ostentatious. Everything in its place. No clutter but a space not particularly welcoming. The room had a sterile feel, a place where work was done without the need for homey adornments. The one touch of life was a glossy Schefflera soaking in the sun by the window that seemed to be staring enviously at the plants outside. "Please." He indicated a padded chair.

As Janet made herself comfortable, she was aware of his eyes looking her up and down. It bothered her.

"Lau," Adams said, firing up a memory. "That's a Cantonese name."

She shrugged.

He wasn't finished. "Did you know Lau was the surname of the Han dynasty emperor's family?"

She didn't know. Didn't care, either. Janet noticed Adams' smug expression, which told her all she needed to know. The man was a show-off, a know-it-all. She was unimpressed. Struggled to keep down her bile and maintain a neutral demeanor. "Mr. Adams, my family name has no bearing on why I'm here. Can we stay on topic?"

Apparently not. The man was on a roll and wouldn't be stopped. "You'll have to excuse me. I'm a history buff. Love weird factoids. Like the origins of words and family names. Yours, for instance. In high school, I had a classmate, Bobby Lau. No relation, I'm sure, but I learned his story." Adams wore a patronizing smirk that Janet desperately wanted to smack off his face. "I bet your family emigrated to America from the Guangdong Province."

"No, my grandparents came from Fujian Province." She enjoyed correcting this irritating blowhard way too much.

Adams looked back, confused. "They spoke Cantonese, didn't they?"

"No, Mandarin."

"That can't be," he insisted.

"*Guān nǐ pì shì*," she replied. In Mandarin. ("None of your fucking business.")

Adams went silent

She glowered at him. *This arrogant son of a bitch was mansplaining her own family to her!*

Janet was beginning to see why Susan Zelinsky became disenchanted with this dude. Butterflies generally fluttered in her belly at confrontations, except this jerk was pissing her off, and that always had a way of scattering the flutter bugs.

It didn't get better. Adams kept going. "You must be wrong," he was ill-advised to say. "Fujian Province is also Cantonese. It means that—"

"*Mister Adams*," she broke in sternly, "I know where my grandparents came from and what language they spoke. *Drop the geography lesson.* I'm here on police business."

An awkward pause followed. A chastened John Adams cleared his throat. "Yes. Of course. Go ahead. You're here about Susan."

"Susan Zelinsky."

"Right. I saw on the news that her body was found somewhere in Bloomington."

Janet could hear the pain in his voice, even a little confusion. The brash know-it-all from a minute ago was now a soft-spoken shadow of his former self. It was evident he had feelings for Susan.

"Just awful. Awful." Adams squeezed out a weak smile. "I'm not sure how helpful I'll be."

"We won't know until we try." Be nice, her mother used to say. Don't be rude. Then Abby Lau would tell her only daughter: *But don't let people walk all over you.*

The pull of Janet's soft caramel eyes seemed to settle Adams, who gave a go-ahead nod. She went on. "How did you meet Susan?"

"It was July at an Anoka County Libraries thing. They hosted a five-week creative writing class. Every Tuesday evening into August."

"Did you see her outside of class?"

He seemed surprised she knew that. "Um, a few times."

"Were you in a relationship with her?"

"No. It wasn't like that. A few weeks after our class ended, I sent her a message asking if she wanted to grab a coffee."

"Was that the extent of it?"

"Pretty much."

"What does that mean?"

"One time, we went out to dinner." He smiled at the memory.

Janet heard the fondness in his voice. "Did you want more than being Susan's friend?"

"Nothing happened," he replied, "if that's what you're asking."

Too defensive, she thought. Worth exploring. Janet played dumb. "What d'you mean by 'nothing happened'?" she asked with innocent eyes, playing off her youth.

Adams squirmed. Several seconds ticked by before he muttered, "Sex."

With disarming directness, Janet came back, "Did you want sex from Susan?"

A little too on the nose. Adams looked visibly uncomfortable, probably because a woman had asked the question. "Um…it was on my mind," he began. "But it wasn't high on the list—"

"*Pardon*?" she jumped in. "You have a list? What list?"

A startled Adams waved her off. "No, no. That came out wrong. It's not what I meant." A look that resembled panic registered on his face. "You gotta believe me, I'm no weirdo who preys on women. I…uh…I don't date much. I'm rusty. What I was trying to say was it was nice spending time with someone who liked what I liked. We were hanging out together, that's all. There was never any talk about sex," he was at pains to point out. A fleshy hand came up to wipe sweat from his forehead.

Janet let him squirm momentarily before continuing. "Susan ended things between you. Is that how you remember it?"

A reluctant nod. "Yeah, she was nice about it. Susan said she'd be busy working on something for the rest of the year and wouldn't have time for much else. I think that was an excuse to stop seeing me, but she was too nice to say so. I got too interested too fast. Scared her off."

And it still bothered him, Janet noticed. "How long ago was this?"

"October. Second week. Our first and last dinner."

"Was that the last time you had contact with her?"

"Yes."

"No emails, texts, or calls?"

The plumbing supplier frowned. "No, Susan'd said her piece. She was busy. I wasn't gonna force myself on her."

*Well, give him points for that.*

By the way John Adams kept his eyes on her, Janet could tell he was gauging her reaction to the narrative he'd given. Now, she started to wonder how truthful he'd been. When she took too much time to react to his statement, he grumbled, "You don't believe me. Look, I'm no stalker creep. Okay? After our dinner, I never saw or spoke with Susan again." He crossed his arms.

A thought came to her. "Is that why you took the class, to meet women?"

"Yeah," he admitted, a little embarrassed, "but I also like poetry and short stories."

Janet's lips quirked a hat tip to his honesty. She'd encountered guys like him in her first watercolor classes, men who seemed more interested in trolling for women than improving their painting skills.

Straightening up, Janet cleared her throat. "Just one more thing, Mr. Adams. Do you know if Susan was dating anyone?"

A headshake followed. "Never came up, and I never asked."

"Did anything make you think she was in a relationship with anyone?"

"No."

A long shot, but worth a try. Janet was fishing and hoped for a lucky strike. "What about people in general? Did Susan ever talk to you about friends, family, coworkers?"

"Sometimes."

"Anyone in particular recently?"

At ease now that she'd moved on from his personal life, Adams pressed his lips together, thinking. "There was one time she got amped up about a guy at work."

*Bingo!* "Go on," Janet said, the back of her neck tingling. "When was this?"

"Late September."

"This guy Susan was 'amped' about. Did she give you a name?" *Perhaps Samuel Park?*

"Uh, she might've. I'm not good with names…"

"Please try."

"Nope," he came back after an effort. "Sorry."

"Was the name Sam?"

"No."

"No?" She couldn't hide her disappointment.

Adams gave it another try, massaging his forehead. Seconds later, he sat up. "Got it. Tom."

"*Tom?* Tom Marsh?"

"Dunno the last name."

"Why was Susan amped?"

"Some info this Tom dude gave her. Can't say what, only that Suze got excited."

*Now that was interesting!*

Detective Janet Lau's imagination was on high alert. Tom Marsh. Shipping and receiving manager at Hancock Blades, the only other person who was in the knife factory when the body of Samuel Park was discovered. Marsh and Zelinsky? What was going on there? Janet had no idea but knew she'd spend the rest of the day trying to find out.

# CHAPTER 18

Instead of returning to the station after leaving the knife factory, Henry took a detour in the opposite direction. Windjammer Coffee was bustling when he got there. As he placed his order, he learned that his barista was taking nursing classes at a nearby college. Pleasantries exchanged, he moved to the Pick Up area at the far end of the counter.

Glenda wiped her hands against her green apron before personally handing Henry his paper cup. "One medium hot skim latte." She flashed a practiced yet sincere smile, this one particularly heartfelt. "Thanks again for helping out the other day." A sly reference to the obnoxious cigar-smoker. Glenda was being tactful, as there were other customers nearby.

"Did our friends come back?" Henry inquired.

"No," she mouthed, relieved and grateful in one.

"Good. I wanted to make sure."

"You're the best," her throaty voice almost sang.

He raised his coffee cup in salute. Glenda and her staff were hard-working people who didn't deserve to be harassed for doing their jobs.

Finding a quiet corner, he settled into an overstuffed armchair to enjoy the nineteenth-century sailing ship décor around him. He smiled at a placard on the wall with the coffee bar's slogan: *Sail into Great Flavor!* After a long sip, he rested an elbow against the armrest for a hard think. A change of scenery often helped jumpstart his brain. Uppermost in his mind was Aimee Hancock's validation that Sam Park had written the poison-pen letter.

Did this change Park's murder?

Not that he could tell right now, he thought. The note was found in Park's trash. Was it a change of mind? What if a previous threat had been sent, and the recipient discovered it came from Park? That'd be a motive for murder. For some, secrets must be kept at any cost.

*A secret worth killing for?*

*What was he missing?*

Henry sorted through everything he and Janet had discovered, believing the answer was mockingly inches out of reach. Park's poison-pen note mentioned *stealing* and a *secret*, and the Post-it note found in his office referred to *An Actionable Crime*. Whose crime? K.J. Hazzard's? The name on the Post-it. Or was Hazzard a source? An informant who had dirt on someone?

Relaxing in the chair in this little oasis, Henry had hoped for a glimmer of inspiration.

Turned out, inspiration had the day off.

While waiting for a brainstorm, he turned toward the enticing smell of warm cinnamon and sugar glaze. A woman in a striped cardigan sweater was nibbling on a heated cinnamon roll at a nearby table. He smiled. The pastry reminded him of a few hours earlier when Janet had returned from her doughnut break and was bubbling with questions about the new note found in Park's recycle bin. At one point, Janet paused, troubled that she was asking him too many questions. Never, he'd told her unequivocally, appreciating her passion to learn.

As a teenager, he'd been worse. With chagrin, he recalled bombarding his first Wing Chun teacher with endless questions during the beginning months of his training. Eventually, Sifu Chiang-Li had to pull him aside.

"You're young, Henry. Hungry to learn. Asking questions is good. Too many questions at one time is not good."

"Why, Sifu?"

"You won't remember the answers."

At the time, that nugget of wisdom was lost on Henry's sixteen-year-old brain. "I don't understand."

His sifu, whose cool-headedness, confidence, kindness, and impressive fighting skills Henry sought to emulate, had to be less obtuse. "It's like this: I teach you three new things today. Then, before you can master those three things, you ask for more."

"I learn quickly, Sifu."

Chiang-Li knew better and directed his eager student to follow him. They stopped by the school's entrance, where students left their belongings and street shoes. "Henry, take off your shoes."

He slipped off his kung fu shoes.

"Hand them to me."

He did as instructed.

Chiang-Li held up the footwear. "Each shoe is a lesson. There's more than you see on the surface. There's the bottom, the stitching, the laces, the cushion inside, the wear patterns. Hidden depths." He tossed a shoe to Henry, who caught it. Then he tossed the other. "You have two hands. You can look at each shoe and study its details and see the differences." Next, the wily master bent down to the floor and grabbed more shoes. One at a time, he tossed them at Henry. "Don't drop any!" Six shoes later, Henry struggled to hang on to them all. One slipped out of his grasp to bounce on the stained wood floor. He clutched the remaining shoes against his chest.

Chiang-Li laughed. "You have too many shoes. Can you tell me the details, the hidden depths, of any of them now?"

"No."

The message was clear. The brain can deal with only so much at one time. Overload it with too much information, and you don't have time to examine the subtleties.

"It's not about technique, Henry," his sifu stressed, as always. "Good kung fu is about understanding energy, sensitivity, timing, and distance. Techniques will fail, depending on your opponent. You have to be able to adapt. Search for the hidden truths. That comes from a real understanding of why we do what we do."

That lesson had opened Henry's mind to looking beyond the surface. A student could spend a lifetime peering into this deep well, absorbing new insights with each viewing. Over the years, one's knowledge expanded with discoveries that cannot be taught, only revealed. It's the difference between an amateur street musician and a Beethoven. Both musicians use the same Western diatonic scale, yet a Beethoven can add depth, layers, and nuances unimaginable to the amateur. The same notes but different results. This was the lesson Henry's first teacher had drummed into his beginning students.

Later, under Eric Kwan's tutelage, Henry's kung fu knowledge and skills deepened. It was the reason he'd moved to San Jose for college. After four years with Kwan, Henry Lau was a sharp blade of steel, albeit one in need of tempering to become battle-hardened. The forge hammers for which lay in Hong Kong.

Those first months in this new place made him feel like a fish out of water as he endured rough living conditions and the daily grind of living in a strange new world. Hard training. More *beimo* matches. Henry took his lumps, learned from his successes and failures, working diligently to improve. Most of the fighting contests took place on Kai Tung Street, across from Kan Jee's Noodle Shop, on the roof of a low-rise walk-up apartment above a hand-crafted mahjong tile store. Large, colorful advertising signboards hung on neighboring buildings, adding a tawdry circus feel to the gathering. With no protective gear, most *beimo* matches were over in less than forty seconds, few lasting longer than a minute or two. Real fights end quickly. It was during the seventh month of his stay when Henry went up against a cocky gang thug named Sammy Hong. Arrogant, strong, unnervingly fierce, his ugly face sporting a shaggy Kublai Khan mustache and wispy chin whiskers, Hong was a semiregular combatant because he almost always won. He mowed down his opponents like a charging musk ox. Henry had his ass handed to him in less than a minute, which impressed his fellow students for having lasted that long with Hong. Hollow comfort to sore ribs, a stiff neck, and a bruised ego.

Days later, in his post-fight analysis, Sifu Lo didn't mince his words. "I've been watching you. Your instincts are good but need fine-tuning. Where you get in trouble is against highly aggressive fighters. You don't attack soon enough. Or you back away too much. Your defense collapses against that much aggression." Lo Bai Hu's authoritative voice cut deep. Yet Henry knew Lo spoke the truth.

Not wanting to complain, Henry nonetheless needed to justify his actions. "It's not easy fighting back when you're getting hit hard."

Sifu Lo smiled patiently, his eyes staring into the back of his student's brain. "Then you have only three choices: you can run away, stop your opponent from hitting you, or hit him first so he can't hit you. Smother his attack with yours."

Easy to say, hard to do. Lo had been a respected fighter in his day and was a revered teacher with the experience to back up his words. Lo elaborated. "Raw aggression is the hardest thing to stop. A fighter with raw aggression doesn't need a lot of martial arts ability. They charge at you, expecting to get punched. They don't mind. They'll take your punch to swarm on you with their punches." Lo placed a gentle hand on Henry's shoulder. "Fighting someone with this much aggression is like trying to stop a runaway bus. Sammy Hong doesn't have high fighting skills. What he has are good skills and a surplus of aggression. It's his biggest weapon."

A crestfallen Henry asked, "How do I beat him?"

"Don't think about beating him. Work on your skills. Improve your defense. Learn to better read your opponent's movements. Attack hard and fast but at angles to neutralize his aggression. Remember to use soft power. Cultivate your *fajin*, Henry, your own explosive power." Lo thumped a hand on his student's chest. "Basic skills over and over, that's how you do it. Bruce Lee had a saying, 'I fear not the man who has practiced 10,000 kicks once, but I fear the man who has practiced one kick 10,000 times.'"

So much to master. Could he do it? There were times during that first year in Hong Kong when an overwhelmed Henry Lau wondered if he'd bitten off more than he could chew.

The first thing Janet did after leaving John Adams' was text Henry, hoping he was still at the knife factory. He wasn't. He was long gone, so she drove to Hancock Blades to talk to Tom Marsh. Unfortunately, Tammy the receptionist had disappointing news.

"Oh, sorry, Detective. Tom's out of the office for the rest of the week."

*That was unexpected. Now what?*

Tammy continued, "Is there someone else who can help you?"

"Um...I don't know..."

"Paul Winslow is Tom's backup. Would you like to talk to him?"

Might as well, she figured, having come all this way. What did she have to lose? "Thank you," Janet replied, somewhat disheartened. Perhaps there was a way to salvage this visit.

With an apologetic shrug, Tammy looked up after checking her phone console. "Paul's not answering the phone. He might've stepped away or is dealing with a shipper. I know he's there. If you can wait a minute, Linda's relieving me; I'll take you back myself."

In no time, Janet was escorted near a long row of conveyor rollers, an endless train of cardboard boxes riding across them. Workers were everywhere. By a tall storage rack, Janet saw a man maneuvering a pallet jack loaded with a stack of shrink-wrapped cartons. Tall and gangly, he sported a striking handlebar mustache that would have been the envy of any Victorian gentleman. He also had large hands, which he wiped against slate-colored coveralls. He joined his visitors. Introductions were made. Tammy left them alone. Janet swung toward the towering flagpole, tilting her neck back to meet his gaze.

Paul Winslow cranked a polite smile that jiggled the curled ends of his showy lip foliage. "I remember you, Detective. You were here the other day with your partner."

"Yes, talking to Tom. I'm sorry, did we meet then?"

"Nope. I was over by Dock 2 loading a truck. But I remembered seeing you," he added with a twinkle of interest as if the moment had been noteworthy.

She didn't know what to make of that. Should she be flattered? Creeped out? Janet decided to move on. "Tom's why I'm here, Mr. Winslow. I was told he's out, and you're covering for him?"

"Yep."

Her brow creased. "I'm a little confused. Two Hancock employees have been murdered. Isn't it an odd time for Tom to be away right now?"

"It's deer hunting season, Detective. Tom takes PTO around this time every year. He plans for this all year and works extra hours to make sure he's all caught up. The man works hard. He deserves time off."

"Do you know where he is?"

"Rochester. There through the weekend."

"He's back on Monday, though."

"Yep."

Monday was too far away; she wanted answers now. No harm in asking the shipping manager's right-hand man about Zelinsky's conversation with Marsh. Maybe she'd get lucky. Her neck was getting stiff from cranking it back to look up at him. *Man, this dude was tall.* She felt like a Chihuahua next to an Irish Wolfhound.

She asked, "Did you know Susan Zelinsky?"

"The lady in accounting who died? Didn't know her but knew who she was. I rarely get to that side of the building."

"Susan's the reason I'm here. She was in your area a few weeks ago talking with Tom. You didn't happen to see them?"

"You bet."

"You did?" Her scalp tingled. "I suppose you didn't catch anything they said. A phrase? A word?"

Winslow's stylish mustache twitched sideways. "It gets kinda noisy here at times. I wasn't close—"

Janet's shoulders sagged.

"But," Winslow said, "I walked by and caught one word."

"Which was…?"

"Guns."

"*Guns*? You sure? Maybe it only sounded like guns."

"Nope. I'm pretty sure. Like I said, Tom's a hunter. He knows firearms. Likes talking about them. There's a look he gets when he does. He had that look."

"Let me get this straight. You think Tom was talking to Susan about guns?"

"Yeah."

"Was he answering a question about guns? Or volunteering info?"

Winslow made a hapless gesture. "Can't say."

The tingle was back, crawling up her scalp. Janet stepped closer, even though it meant she had to tilt her head farther back to make eye contact with her high-rise companion. "I'm sorry, I have to make sure, Mr. Winslow," she stressed. "You're pretty sure the word Tom Marsh said to Susan was guns. G-U-N-S."

Winslow bobbed his head. "Uh-huh. The more I think about it, the more I'm certain. Now that we're talking, I remember something else.

A second or two later, Tom said the word Glock. That's a brand of gun made in Austria."

That she knew. Janet carried a Glock 22. Nevertheless, the mention of a popular service pistol cemented his story. She felt optimistic. Although a firearm wasn't used in either homicide, the mere thought that Zelinsky recently had been speaking to Marsh about guns demanded a follow-up. The only way to verify this was for Janet to talk to the man himself.

"Do you have Tom's cell number? I need to talk to him."

Winslow laughed. "Good luck with that! I'll give you his number. I doubt you'll reach him. Tom's likely in a deer stand. When he goes away like this, he's off the grid. Doesn't want to be disturbed by nobody. You can leave a message, though you probably won't get a call back for a few days."

Such was life. She'd take whatever she could get.

Winslow walked her back to the lobby, where she thanked him for his time. Signing out and returning her visitor badge, Janet rubbed the back of her neck.

"Detective Lau," greeted Aimee Hancock, emerging from the executive suite and looking sharp in a pressed white shirt, ochre pants, and black pumps. "I asked Tammy to buzz me when you came back," explaining her sudden appearance. Shock white peek-a-boo bangs parted enough to reveal inquisitive black eyebrows. "Do you have a minute?"

Janet said she did. The CEO guided her into the nearest conference room. Closed the door and flashed a vacant smile. "Your partner was here earlier about the poison-pen note found at Sam's. Are you here about the same thing?"

"No, something else."

"Tammy said you wanted to see Tom Marsh. May I ask what about?"

"Information. Ms. Zelinsky and Mr. Marsh had a conversation that could have a bearing on the murders. He's on PTO."

"Like clockwork. Every November, Tom's got to bag his deer. Was Paul able to help you?" Hancock asked with what seemed a little too much interest.

Janet was suspicious. Decided to be cagey in her reply. "Yes, he was, thanks." And left it there without going into details, smiling innocently. If the factory owner wanted the down low, she could ask Winslow herself.

"Ah, good. If there's anything I can do to help, please let me know."

Janet considered her.

*Well, she had just volunteered.*

An emboldened Janet seized the opportunity. "There is one thing. Larry Stenson and you. Is something going on between you we should know about?"

A frosty Hancock replied, "That doesn't concern you."

Janet wasn't going to fold that easily. "Stenson has been seen leaving his office every day at the same time for weeks. During one of those absences, the mayor is with you at La Pâtisserie in what looked like an intimate moment. Is that an everyday thing? You couldn't help noticing I was there."

"It was personal." The CEO's hackles were up. "Nothing to do with either death."

Janet could almost feel the heat from the woman, like standing in front of a blast furnace. Janet wasn't backing off. "Ms. Hancock, I'm a homicide investigator. Two of your employees have been murdered. *I* decide what's relevant, not you."

Aimee Hancock bridled. "We're done here." Without another word, she ripped open the door to the executive suite and beat an indignant retreat.

Okay then, Janet thought, that could've gone better.

# CHAPTER 19

At home that evening, Janet ate a light dinner of leftover chicken and rice hotdish. Leftovers for the third night in a row. After doing her brain exercises—which were getting pretty boring by now—she devised plans for the next day. Then she flopped onto her sofa and pressed her back deep into the soft cushion, her slender body rigged out in a roomy sweatshirt and black leggings, her feet bare. Janet never wore socks at home. Even during the Arctic cold of a Minnesota winter, at home her feet remained uncovered. Sure, January might blow a slight chill on her toes. She didn't mind; it was a fair tradeoff from the suffocating bondage that was hosiery.

Janet glanced at the analog wall clock with its black hands and red sweeping second hand, marking off each second like a white knuckle countdown. She steeled herself for the task ahead. Had been stalling all evening. In a minute, she'd call *the* number. She'd worked hard to get that phone number. Hoped it was still current. With her police resources and ingenuity, Janet had located the original police report of Kay McAdams' mugging and killing. She'd also found her obituary in a late October 1999 edition of the Sacramento Bee, her hometown newspaper. From this, Janet learned the names of Kay's parents and family. The obituary photo of Kay broke Janet's heart. So young, so beautiful, a face brimming with vitality, a life with such promise. A sobering thought gave Janet pause: when Kay died, she was five years younger than Janet's age now. Henry was also only twenty-two, far too young to deal with such a gut-wrenching tragedy.

Once again, the warning whispered like a voice in the wind: *Bad idea raking up something this sensitive. You'll upset Kay's parents. You'll upset Henry.* The pit of her stomach rumbled as if a tiny goblin was trampolining inside to get her to pay attention. Janet disregarded the warning. Was determined to make the call as apprehensive eyes flicked toward the fridge. Was she in need of a glass of liquid courage? No wine, she decided; she could do this without a crutch. Time to put on her big girl pants, as her mother used to say. Janet expelled a breath, lowering her head, a curtain of dark brown hair falling across her eyes. She tucked long strands behind her ears, sucked in a deep breath, then punched in the number on her cell.

And waited.

One ring…

Two…

Four rings later, Janet began to think she'd have to leave a message, which she was hoping to avoid. No telling where she'd be when—or even if—the return call came. Talking to a homicide suspect? That would be awkward.

Then, on the fifth ring—

A click. "Hello?" came the tentative voice of an older woman.

Janet's chest tightened. *Here goes!* "Hello, may I speak to Beth McAdams?"

"This is she."

*Omigod, it's her!* Janet pulled in a breath that went down to the bottom of her belly. "My name is Janet Lau. I'm calling from Minnesota. Are you the mother of Kay McAdams?"

There came an uneasy silence.

Janet wished she could see the woman's reaction.

Finally came the guarded reply. "What's this about?"

Afraid she was about to get hung up on, Janet blurted, "I don't mean any trouble, Mrs. McAdams. I'm sorry to bother you. My uncle is Henry Lau. He was a classmate of your daughter's at Stanford."

"Henry?" A change of tone and oddly surprised. "Yes, I remember. He was such a nice boy. Very polite. It's been so long…You say he's your uncle?"

"Yes, ma'am."

"How is he?"

Relief tamed the jumping goblin in Janet's belly. She'd been prepared for an angry Beth McAdams telling her to go away, but the woman sounded genuinely interested. Janet gave a quick recap of Henry's life, touching on the highlights, including his being a senior police detective for the city of Gillette. Janet ended with the pedestrian-car accident in April, his weeks in ICU, and subsequent recovery.

"How terrible!" breathed Beth McAdams. "They don't know who ran him down or why?"

"No. Looks like a random drunk driver."

"Good Lord! I can't imagine. All those broken bones and internal injuries. And he had to learn how to walk again?"

"It was a rough couple of months."

"But he's okay now?"

"Yes, ma'am. He's been back on duty for over seven weeks. Which is why I wanted to reach out to you." *Okay, so far so good. Kay's mother is still on the line. But now, the tricky part.* Janet steeled herself. "I know Henry loved Kay. He doesn't talk much about her; I think it hurts too much. He told me once—though not in so many words—that her death was a big reason he became a police detective. To help people." Janet swallowed, dearly hanging onto her composure. "Even though he looks well on the outside, inside he still hurts."

"We all do, dear," said the voice on the other end of the line.

"Of course. Sorry, I'm rambling. I didn't mean—"

"It's all right," assured Kay's mother.

"What I'm getting at is Henry's been a great teacher. Has been so patient with me. He's such a good guy and had such a bad thing happen to him earlier this year…I…I'd like to give him a little peace of mind if I can." Janet rushed out her idea for a unique, meaningful Christmas present. "Um, I was wondering, Mrs. McAdams, if it's not any trouble—" Janet's voice wavered.

"Are you all right?"

"I'm a little nervous."

"Of me? Oh, please don't be. You were saying?"

Janet gulped in a breath to steady her nerves. "If it's no bother, I was wondering if you might have a trinket of Kay's or something from her time at Stanford that you'd be willing to part with to give Henry. A memento. I don't think he has anything of hers. It would mean so much to him."

Or so she hoped.

An agonizing silence followed. Finally, Beth McAdams said, "I might have something…"

"Oh, you think so?"

"How strange you should call now after all this time. Last summer, my husband Alex and I went through some of Kay's old boxes. We kept everything. Inside one box were her college notebooks. One was her final notebook. Mixed in with her notes is a draft of a letter Kay was writing…to Henry."

*"What?"* Janet's heart thumped.

"The letter was from the day she—the day she was killed. It was written hours before. I can send you the notebook."

"Oh my god," Janet breathed. "Are you sure? Don't you want to keep it?"

A sigh of resignation followed. "We've had it for twenty years. Most of that time, it sat in a box in the garage. We hadn't looked at it in years. Until July. In a way, it's too painful a reminder, it being from her last day. Besides, we have other things that have more meaning to us: stuffed animals, clothing, photos and letters, and home videos." Mrs. McAdams made an ironic sound. "That's what I meant when I said it was strange that you're calling now. Alex and I had completely forgotten about the letter to Henry. When we saw it again, we wondered if we should try to find him, but we had no idea where he was. Out of the blue, months later, you call. It's like it was meant to be!" There was a smile in her voice.

Janet was floored. *Meant to be.* "Thank you! Oh, wait, is it a *nice* letter?" She remembered that Henry and Kay had argued. The last thing she wanted was to give her uncle a Dear John breakup letter from his dead girlfriend for Christmas!

Mercifully, Beth McAdams blunted her worries. "It's a nice letter. Hard to explain over the phone. After you read it, you can decide. If you don't want to give the notebook to Henry, return it to us."

"Oh, I can't tell you how much this means to me! Thank you. I was afraid my call would upset you."

"It's all good, dear. I'm getting too old to hang on to bad feelings." Her voice lightened. "And you seem like a lovely person, thinking of your uncle."

"I just hope he likes it."

"From what you've told me, he seems like a good man. The gift is coming from you; that's all that matters. Where should I mail the notebook?"

Janet gave her work address, thanked Kay's mother profusely, and ended the call. Jumping up, she danced a bare-footed victory on her living room carpet.

A week after getting mauled by Sammy Hong, Henry, still discouraged, sought further insight from Sifu Lo. He'd worked on his teacher's suggestions yet believed he was missing something, so approached his master again to ask specifically what he had done wrong.

In a rare humor, Lo had chuckled. "What you did wrong was fight Sammy Hong."

Henry wasn't amused. But he swallowed his pride. Deep learning comes from making yourself open to receiving knowledge.

Lo Bai Hu could see his frustration and took pity on him. "The point of *beimo* is to test your skills in real situations. You fought a powerful opponent. You tell me, Henry. What did you learn?"

"That I have a long way to go."

Lo nodded. "There's a saying in martial arts: *I can beat a thousand men, but a thousand men can beat me.* Do you know what that means?"

He did. Learned it long ago. "It means no one is unbeatable."

"Good. It's an important lesson. Knowing there are times you will lose should make you cautious. You need to know when it's wise not to fight. What it *doesn't* mean is you shouldn't be afraid to fight *if you have to*." Lo winked at Henry. "Remember, winning without fighting is the highest skill in all martial arts."

Henry appreciated the sentiment. It was deep. Only it didn't satisfy his present need, and his master sensed that.

"Someday," Lo said, "you'll understand what I just told you. You don't have enough experience with the world. I'll show you one thing."

Lo asked Henry to assume his ready stance. Then Lo dropped to a squat with impressive agility for a man of his fifty-five years. Sturdily built with broad shoulders and well-defined muscles, he moved with the fluidity of a man half his age. He pressed a finger on Henry's shoe behind the foot pad. "This is the *Yongquan* meridian point, also called 'the bubbling well.' It's a major pressure point in the body."

This Henry knew. Both his previous sifus had emphasized the same acupuncture point. Regardless, he listened carefully to what his master had to say. The first Wing Chun form centered around lining up the bubbling well with other body points, long practice of which cultivated sensitivity to energy pathways within the body.

"Footwork is the key to combat." Sifu Lo rose to his full height in one easy motion. "Your feet are your foundation. The bubbling well is your balance point. Watch your opponent's feet. Does he move off his *Yongquan*? If he does, he's vulnerable."

Smiling, Lo Bai Hu began peppering Henry with heavy punches, jabs, forearms, elbows, and kicks, all of which the latter neutralized, though with difficulty as the intensity progressed. Lo commented, "Don't tighten up. Stay relaxed. Use your body, not your strength. Pivot—but just enough to evade the attack. No more." Lo upped the ferocity of his attacks.

Henry struggled with them.

"Stay calm," Lo said. "No angry karate guy face." Suddenly, Lo's hands leaked between Henry's defense to pull down his arm, jerking his weight forward. Before Henry could recover, Lo stepped in with an explosive forearm to the chest that sent his student flying backward.

On his knees, a bent over Henry rubbed his chest. Sifu Lo, not even out of breath, smiled broadly. "Better! It took me longer to uproot you. Do you know why I was able to?"

"I couldn't redirect your attacks. They were too strong. I felt my weight move off the bubbling well."

"Yes! Very good. Your body absorbed the energy instead of redirecting it. I felt it in your arms and knew I could move in without any resistance from you. Remember these things," Lo emphasized as if imparting a great truth, then added: "All the techniques in the world are meaningless otherwise."

Henry was starting to understand. Began to see subtleties he previously hadn't. More importantly, in the months to come, his body started to assimilate them, which meant he could summon them without thinking.

Small victories.

# CHAPTER 20

The new morning brought good news. Shortly after breakfast, Janet received a text from Sergeant Cheri Hanson. Minutes after Janet arrived at the Gillette police station, Hanson pinged her again. She was in the lobby.

"We have a visitor," Janet announced, entering the detective's alcove.

Henry, dutifully updating reports, looked over. Steps behind her came a full-figured woman in an unzipped winter coat. Barley-colored hair dangled at her shoulders.

Janet said, "It's Sergeant Hanson from Bloomington PD."

Henry stood up to shake her hand. "Hey, Cheri. It's been a while."

"Too long," Hanson smiled.

Was that a touch of wistfulness? Janet thought she heard. She noticed Hanson had also dialed back the huskiness in her voice. It was softer. She also wore a hint of makeup. "The sergeant has news," Janet added, bothered by the nearby foot traffic. "Um, it's a little busy here. Maybe somewhere more private?"

They relocated to a small conference room near Evidence Storage. Hanson sat at the table, coat off, nursing a steaming coffee mug. "Susan Zelinsky's Subaru Forester was found late last night. It was abandoned at a Dealco Warehouse in Bloomington about a mile from where her body was found. The SUV was parked at the farthest end of the lot, just out of range of store cameras. I checked the video to see if the cameras had caught the vehicle driving through the lot. No go. Whoever left the car there knew what they were doing."

Henry and Janet shared a look. "Well, that's progress," he said. "What about inside the vehicle?"

"Like an e-bike?" Hanson suggested after a heavy slurp of Columbian Dark Roast. When it came to her morning cup of joe, Cheri Hanson was a high-octane gal who craved the bold and the bitter. "No. I checked. No e-bike in Zelinsky's garage either."

"Interesting," Henry replied.

Hanson continued. "Dirt and brown grass clippings were found in the SUV cargo bay. Perhaps an e-bike had been there. Our forensics techs are still processing the vehicle. One thing they found was this." She reached over to her coat, pulled out a plastic evidence bag, and set it on the table before them. Inside the bag was a standard-sized yellow Post-it note with writing.

Janet read the words aloud. "' How to prove malfeasance? Need hard proof!'" She looked at the others. "Serious stuff." She squinted at the bag's contents. "Looks like Zelinsky's handwriting. Her note. Her car. Makes sense."

"Only Zelinsky's latent prints are on it," Hanson informed, tapping the plastic bag. "Check this out. A pinhole. See it?" Her head swung toward Janet. "Remember the corkboard in Zelinsky's home office? It was bare. No notes or papers, only push pins. This baby looks like it came from her corkboard." Hanson next posed the question they were all wondering. "Did Zelinsky drop the Post-it in her car, or did the killer? Her killer dumped her body. They likely used her car and got rid of it afterward. They had Zelinsky's keys, using them to access her townhouse. Maybe the same person cleaned off her corkboard. If so, this little guy might've got lost in the process."

"Plausible," agreed Henry, nodding. After a beat, he turned to Janet. "Did you catch the significance of the message?"

*Uh, no. Crap, what'd she miss?* She inspected the yellow square, uncertain what he'd meant.

"Malfeasance," he clued her in. "Interesting choice of words, don't you think?"

"Hang on." Janet fished out her smartphone, looking up the word. "I've got an inkling…" Soft brown eyes widened. "Ah ha." She read the display: "' Malfeasance: wrongdoing, especially of a public official.'" Janet caught her partner's nod of approval. It took a second for her to get it. "*Oh yeah!* 'Public official,'" she quoted.

A perplexed Sergeant Hanson darted her eyes between them. "What am I missing?"

Henry addressed her with a note of caution. "What I'm about to tell you goes no further than this room."

Hanson nodded.

First, a caveat. "We have zero evidence of any wrongdoing—I repeat, zero. All this is speculation, but there's an unsubstantiated suspicion that a city of Gillette politician may be involved with one of the knife factory suspects."

The sergeant's lips pressed together. "And that means…?"

"We aren't sure ourselves, so I can't be more specific. It may be nothing. We're still working it out. But the mention of malfeasance is a little too close for comfort. I don't like it. Anytime politicians are connected with a homicide investigation, you walk on eggshells."

Janet was glad Henry hadn't referred to Larry Stenson by name. While she believed she could trust the Bloomington detective's discretion, Janet also knew Stenson's name might accidentally slip out in passing. An offhand chat with her boss or a colleague and, before you knew it, Stenson's name would travel along the metro police grapevine and reach the mayor. In all fairness to His Honor, it was best to keep his name out of the investigation until they had evidence of inappropriate behavior. As Henry had emphasized, there was no evidence of wrongdoing on his part, merely a suggestive moment between Stenson and his sister-in-law at a French bakery. Suggestive. That's all. Maybe nothing more. Yet the discovery of this Post-it written in Susan Zelinsky's hand shined a light on the scene at La Pâtisserie.

Malfeasance.

Wrongdoing.

*Especially of a public official.*

Janet's eyebrows jumped up. "Holy shit!" Her hand smacked the conference table. All eyes turned to her. In a breathless voice, she said, "What if we got it wrong?"

"How so?" Henry squinted back.

Janet spread out her hands as if saying get-ready-for-this. "Our two murder victims were spending an unusual amount of time together. Several people have said as much. Gossip is that Sam Park and Susan Zelinsky were working on a private project that nobody else knew about. They told nobody." Janet was chuffed, eyes shining. "What if this private project was an investigation? That Post-it asks: 'How to prove malfeasance?'" She raised her index finger to mark the point. Then, "Another Post-it we found in Park's office talks about 'An Actionable Crime.'" Up went another finger. "And we also have the so-called poison-pen letter written by Park, which accuses someone of stealing." A third finger stood proud as Janet caught her breath. Her next words resonated like a brass bell. *"What if they were investigating some local politician's criminal involvement with the knife factory?"*

Henry grinned. "I'm liking this idea. It explains a lot."

Cheri Hanson, for whom all this was new info, was burning with curiosity. "Sounds juicy! You think whoever Park and Zelinsky were investigating got wind of it and decided to stop them."

"Yeah." Janet nodded enthusiastically.

"And you guys still aren't clueing me in on who this local politician is?"

Janet wasn't comfortable with the idea and looked at Henry to make the call. His answer pleased her. In his most diplomatic manner, he replied, "Not yet, Sergeant." He sounded sincere and apologetic, even disappointed. "As I said, this is all based on a vague insinuation. It could be a false lead, and I don't want to prejudice your thoughts against this person. I hope you understand."

Not pleased but not upset, Hanson lifted her shoulders in resignation. "I get it. Early days. But if this turns out to be a real thing, I expect to be filled in."

Henry nodded. "Of course. I'll do it personally."

A delighted Hanson gave a thumbs-up.

Watching from the sidelines, Janet found this exchange entertaining. The Bloomington detective was smiling a lot more than the other day when Janet was with her. Gee, what could be the difference?

Henry leaned closer to the sergeant. "Cheri, it was thoughtful of you to hand-deliver the Post-it note. You could've emailed a photo."

Hanson's eyes landed on him softly. As did her voice. "My pleasure. It's been ages since I was in Gillette. I don't get up this way often enough."

Cheri, dial it down a notch, Janet mused. You're coming on a little strong.

The sergeant presented her business card and slid it toward him. "Janet has my number, and now you do too. Call me if you need something...or"—she added suggestively—"just to talk."

*Nope. Dial back wasn't gonna happen.*

Janet decided to sit back and enjoy the show.


Only after Hanson left and the detectives were back at their desks did they feel safe talking about the new discovery. Walls have ears, even in a police station. Janet's uneasiness about a slip of the tongue didn't apply only to Sergeant Hanson. She and Henry also had to be careful not to blurt out the mayor's name in their building. Particularly in their building.

Safely ensconced behind her desk, Janet said in a stage whisper, "Larry Freakin' Stenson needs to be looked at deeper."

A distracted nod from Henry, who leaned back in his ergonomic chair, his left hand squeezing a stress ball he kept in his desk drawer, the smooth features of his face lost in thought. "Do you find it strange how many of these little yellow notes keep showing up?"

"Now you mention it, a little."

"I don't know what to make of them."

"Me neither."

Henry made a face. "Maybe we need to take a step back. This new note Hanson showed us. We can't be certain Zelinsky wrote 'malfeasance' with the strict definition in mind. What we need is to find out what she and Park were working on."

Janet swiveled in her chair, a nervous habit to blow off energy. "I'll call IT for an update. Yesterday, they said they'd found 'stuff' on Park's laptop and were combing through it."

"Good. I'd bet money those computers hold the secret. *Damn.*" Henry smacked his forehead. "We forgot to ask Hanson about Zelinsky's PC."

Janet's arm reached for her cell phone. "I'll give her a quick call. See how close her forensic guys are—" She jerked upright. Set aside her phone and smiled mischievously at her partner. "What am I doing? Shouldn't you be the one calling Sergeant Hanson? She did give you her card. Didn't you say you'd call her *personally*?" Janet fluttered her eyelashes coquettishly.

Henry grumbled, "Please don't do that."

# CHAPTER 21

Henry was on the move. If he sat for too long, he got antsy. Too much restless energy. It'd been like that since he was a kid. He had to keep moving. A bit like how a great white shark can never stop swimming or it will suffocate, Henry had two basic modes: rest and kinetic energy. Nothing much in-between. His mind lost focus if he didn't move his legs every so often. Had to get his blood pumping. At the station, he frequently could be seen walking the halls. Occasionally, he'd go outside. He did his best thinking while walking. This time, he opted for a brisk walk outdoors sans jacket, hands stuffed in his trouser pockets for a Tour de Parking Lot.

It was a sunny thirty-three degrees. Brisk. Stimulating. With his loose-limbed stride, he glided across the asphalt to the adjoining sidewalk. By this time in November, most trees had already dropped their foliage, apart from a few red oaks, miserly to give up their colorful leaves. On the steps of a Tudor-style house across the street sat three jack-o'-lanterns, somewhat the worst for wear this long after Halloween. While two doors down, an inflatable Thanksgiving turkey balloon swayed on the front lawn in a light breeze. Much like Henry's thoughts, which were shifting all over the place. The new note from Hanson. The previous notes and messages. The relationship innuendo about Park and Zelinsky; their secret project. Disjointed parts of a much larger whole, as if someone had scattered pieces of a jigsaw puzzle on the floor, except half the pieces were missing, and he and Janet didn't have the cover picture to guide them on how the pieces fit together.

*Some key thing was missing.*
*Something that would make sense of it all.*

He turned a corner, returning to the station's front entrance. Honking from above caused him to lift his eyes. Four swans flew several hundred feet overhead. He smiled at their outstretched necks, and long white wings beating against the air. As a child and teenager, he'd seen few of these elegant creatures in the metro area; now they were everywhere, as were great blue herons and bald eagles. Seeing these graceful birds was a reminder of how Nature, if left alone, finds a way to repair itself and even thrive.

A valuable lesson that. It gave him comfort to think that things can always improve.

Inside the station lobby, Henry walked by the reception counter and opened the ballistic-resistant door to slip into the dispatch room for a brief word with Ragnhild Steinbakken. Exiting a minute later, he glimpsed a moving figure at the end of the corridor. Someone he thought he recognized. He tried to catch up. Past the Tactical Planning Room, he hung a left at Evidence Storage, then another left and paused at the Men's Locker Room doorway. A metallic door swung open. The only person in the room was a medium-height man in a zip-up hoodie with the hood down, wearing loose-fitting drawstring linen trousers. His right arm was in a sling.

Officer Ken Ferguson.

Henry wanted to see how Ferguson was doing. Thought it would be a show of goodwill to check on him. No hard feelings. However, before he could utter a word, Henry was distracted by the injured officer fumbling with his duty boot in front of his gear locker. His sling hand couldn't keep a grip on it. He grimaced, and the black boot tumbled out of his grasp, landing on the floor with a loud thud.

Henry stood motionless in the doorway. Surveyed Ferguson, the sling, the boot. The world stopped. Like he was peering through a haze of smoke. In an uncanny out-of-body sensation, he felt what he was witnessing was significant.

*Why?*

*And why did it make him think of Sam Park's office?*

Ferguson was bending down for his boot when he noticed Henry. Quickly straightening, he looked uneasily at the man who'd put him in the sling.

With a cordial smile, Henry asked, "How's it going, Ferguson? Feeling better?" It was an attempt to make peace.

The other edged back a step, his body tensing. "Good. I'm good." While his mouth said *good,* the rest of him was saying *keep away from me.*

Seeing how skittish he was, Henry remained in the doorway, pretending there was no tension between them. "Glad to hear it. How's the sling?"

"Still getting used to it. Broken collar bone."

In reply, a grim nod of acknowledgment. "Taking PTO?"

"For a few days. Back Monday to work a desk job until this heals." Ferguson hitched the sling shoulder.

"See you around, then."

The other came back with a curt nod. "Yeah."

Awkward, Henry thought as he walked back to the Criminal Investigation Division, but he'd made an effort. Had wanted to show Ferguson there was no remaining animosity on his part about the Fuel and Go incident. If Ferguson harbored any ill will, well, that was on him.

Janet smiled at the text from Sergeant Cheri Hanson and felt optimistic. Things were looking up. Just then, Henry strode into their alcove and noticed the look on her face.

"What's up? You look pleased as punch."

"Good news. Got a text from Hanson. Bloomington PD's made progress on Zelinsky's home computer. They should have files for us tomorrow. And five minutes ago, I got a call from our IT guys. They're promising me a report on Park's laptop before end of the day." She felt her cheeks flush with anticipation.

"Finally!" Henry's fingers closed into a fist.

He stopped and dug out his cell. Read a message. "That was Ragnhild. I asked her to watch the security cameras and text me when she saw the mayor's car return to the lot." An exaggerated clearing of throat followed. "He's back from his mysterious daily excursion that his sister-in-law was so closed-mouthed about. I say it's time we give His Honor a chance to explain. Care to join me? Or would you prefer I did this solo?"

"Let me do it." Janet jumped out of her chair and snatched her coat. "I'll talk to him. Alone, if that's okay."

"Fine with me. Go get 'em."

Janet rushed for the exit, throwing on her coat as her feet pounded against the floor. "Make a hole!" she yelled, and people jumped out of her way. She was chuffed, firing on all pistons. Wanted to seize the initiative and square off with the mayor alone without the protective crutch of her senior partner. She needed to do this for herself. Bolting out of the lobby, Janet raced across the parking lot toward City Hall. The mayor's car was in its reserved spot; he was still in the driver's seat. As he opened the door to step out, she put on the brakes, slowing to a less frenetic pace so she wouldn't be breathless. Being a man of some girth, it took extra seconds for the mayor to climb out of his vehicle. By the time he placed a foot on asphalt, Janet had closed the gap.

"Mr. Mayor," she called. An unforeseen benefit of her run was her heart was beating like a drum, too busy to be bothered about anything as trivial as a bout of nerves.

Stenson shut his door, turning at his name.

"Mr. Mayor, if I can have a minute of your time." There was an urgency in her voice.

His face was hopeful. "Do you have an update?" Then reconsidered. "Should you be talking to me? Chief Bowman made it clear he didn't want me speaking directly to you."

"This is different. I'm coming to you. Can we talk privately? I need only a minute."

"Of course." Stenson glanced round and considered the City Hall building scant yards away before gesturing behind him. "It's a bit nippy out here. Let's sit in my car."

Sitting in the mayor's car also meant he wouldn't be seen walking into City Hall with a Gillette police detective. How much did that matter? she wondered. Inside the cocoon of Stenson's Ford Expedition, the mayor of Gillette looked at her inquisitively. "What can I do for you, Detective?"

Janet drew in a preparatory breath. "Another Hancock Blades employee has been murdered."

The mayor's heavy jowls tightened, his face somber though not surprised. Hardly a news flash, it seemed, what with his family connections. He already knew about Zelinsky.

Janet held his gaze, her voice flat to pound home her next point. "We're now dealing with two homicides. Both victims were working together on a private project, a project—it's been suggested—concerning a politician, perhaps an investigation."

Larry Stenson had been listening politely until that moment. As soon as the words 'politician' and 'investigation' dropped, his entire demeanor changed. His body stiffened.

"Mr. Mayor," Janet forged on, "you're the only politician we know with a connection to the knife factory via your wife's sister, whom I saw you with the other day at La Pâtisserie in what looked like an intimate conversation. Aimee Hancock was touching your arm rather

206

tenderly. I'm sorry to ask you this, sir, but exactly what is your relationship with the CEO of Hancock Blades?"

That landed like a one-ton anvil. Stenson looked back gruffly, fleshy lips curling back. "It's personal. Has nothing to do with your investigation. And I don't particularly like my private life poked at, Detective."

Her voice turned blunt. "And I don't particularly like poking into private lives." *Screw being respectful. She was pissed at his evasion.* "Let me remind you that two people are dead, both employees at your sister-in-law's factory. Whether you like it or not, you have a connection to these murders. I'm not accusing you of anything." She paused to let him appreciate the point before continuing. "My job is to find the truth. When people hide things from me, it makes me wonder why and forces me to look deeper."

On the verge of boiling over, Larry Stenson huffed, "This is unacceptable."

No matter. Janet wasn't leaving until she got what she came for. "Please answer my question, Mr. Mayor. What is your relationship with Aimee Hancock?"

"Detective, I don't like what you're insinuating. I'm not having an affair with my sister-in-law. Not even close! It was a private, very personal moment between us. That's all you need to know."

"A personal moment in a public space between the mayor of Gillette and the owner of the crime scene. I don't enjoy intruding into your life, sir. If I'm going to eliminate you as a suspect, I need a truthful answer."

"*Suspect?*" Stenson came back, alarmed. "I'm a suspect?"

"I didn't say that. I said if I'm to eliminate you as a suspect, I need you to tell me the truth."

His face clouded as he weighed his options. Pudgy fingers curled into a fist and tapped the steering wheel.

Janet waited. Outwardly calm, inwardly a bundle of nerves. Career suicide in the making, cornering her boss' boss. Perhaps not the smartest thing to do. But if it did mean the end of her career, so be it. She had a job to do and wouldn't compromise her integrity.

"Fine," he spat, pointing a warning finger at her. "I'll tell you, but I expect you to treat this information as sensitive. I don't want it getting out. Got that?"

Stenson was a large man, and she felt small and boxed in.

The mayor of Gillette scowled at the dashboard before turning to Janet. The heavy lips pressed together. When he spoke again, his tone was disarmingly candid. "I've been diagnosed with cancer. Prostate cancer. Very early stage. My PSA number is in the bad zone, just slightly. For the past three weeks, I've been driving to Methodist Hospital in St. Louis Park for radiation therapy. I go five days a week. Most days, I'm in and out in thirty to forty minutes. I've got another two weeks to go." He looked her straight in the eye. What he said next came straight from the heart. "I've only told four people about my cancer. What you saw at La Pâtisserie wasn't a romantic fling; I was telling Aimee about my cancer and treatment. It was the first she'd heard of it." Stenson indicated the glove compartment. Asked Janet to open it. "See that orange paper? Pull it out."

In her hand was a radiation treatment parking permit for the cancer center at Methodist Hospital with an expiration date at the end of December. She returned it to the glove box. Snapped shut the door.

"Thank you, Mr. Mayor," she offered in a subdued voice. "That was very personal. I'm sorry I had to intrude. I understand now. My partner and I will be discreet."

Stenson was not mollified. Was still annoyed. "Now do you believe me? I can't believe I had to do this."

"And I apologized." She surrendered no ground. "You were inconvenienced, but I'll remind you that two people are dead.

Murdered. We don't yet know if the murderer is finished. Who might be next." She tossed the last in for good measure, hoping it might stuff a cork in him.

It worked.

The mayor blinked back. It hadn't occurred to him that he or other family members could be potential targets. The stiff creases in his jowls slackened, and a speck of apprehension appeared in his eyes.

Janet decided to toss out a nugget of wisdom from her Grandma Lau. "Unanswered questions are like holes in the ground. Something will fill them and not always what you want. You've answered my question, Mr. Mayor, and I believe you. I'll let you get on with your day."

That seemed to appease him. "You're right," he conceded. "You're just doing your job. I was out of line, Detective. My cancer is highly treatable. We caught it early. I'm trying to prevent my cancer from becoming general knowledge until after treatment is over and I have my follow-up labs. People hear a word like cancer and go off on wild tangents. They make up lies. I don't want to give my constituents concerns or my opponents ammunition to use against me—when there's nothing there. Lies can ruin lives, Detective."

"Which is why truth matters," she returned with a charm that could tame a wolverine.

With a half smile, a more agreeable Mayor Larry Stenson nodded. "If we're done here…"

"We are. Good luck with your treatments."

Walking back to the station, Janet reflected on what Stenson had said. *Lies can ruin lives.* Yes, they can. On the other hand, so can the truth. Some fear the truth.

And will do anything to stop it from coming out.

Anything.

# CHAPTER 22

Henry fought the urge to follow Janet as she rushed out to intercept Larry Stenson. For an instant, he'd considered watching from the lobby before deciding against it. He had faith she could handle herself, and the best way to show he believed that was to let her be. He was her partner and mentor, not her nursemaid. Janet had wanted to deal with Stenson on her own. Even if the incident turned sideways on her, it could still be beneficial. From his own misadventures, he knew unpleasant experiences are sometimes the best teaching moments.

Minutes earlier, he'd had a fresh reminder of that.

Seeing a banged-up Ken Ferguson had shaken the memory tree, dropping more echoes of Hong Kong to the ground. Ferguson's sling arm had shoved one potent memory back on center stage. For months after the bruising and humbling experience of being Sammy Hong's punching bag, Henry thought hard about everything he'd ever learned in martial arts, searching deeper into things he'd thought he already knew. It was then that Eric Kwan's words came back to him.

"A teacher can teach only so much," Kwan had said. "It's up to the student to embrace the knowledge and make it work. That means thousands of hours of practice and thought. Less is more, as the saying goes. Wing Chun doesn't have large, flowery movements. Simplicity. Efficiency. Be like water. Water is soft. Yet water can knock down an elephant and erode mountains."

Sifu Lo had encouraged Henry not to seek stronger, bigger movements but smaller, more precise actions and attack with relaxed aggression. More techniques weren't the solution; perfecting what he already knew and improving his responses was the answer.

Master the basics.

Use relaxed aggression.

Smother your opponent.

Know in an instant when to yield to an opponent's attack to dissolve it and when to shut it down.

Only a few truly master these concepts.

More challenge matches followed. More wins, fewer losses. With every match, Henry learned more about himself. And then, half a year after he'd first fought and lost to Sammy Hong, the two met again. It was a rose-colored twilight evening on a tenement rooftop on Kai Tung Street. The roof was dimly illuminated by the anemic glow of a string of bare incandescent bulbs strung between poles. Two dozen men of all stripes had gathered to test their skills. Their teachers and elders hung back to observe. Seeing Sammy Hong among the crowd made Henry's stomach churn. Somehow, he knew that when his turn came to enter the open space, the man to face him would be Hong.

Sure enough, it was Hong who stepped out to fight him, who seemed bigger and meaner-looking than Henry remembered, built like an ox with a face and disposition to match: heavy brow, broad nose, wispy mustache, chin whiskers, and cruel eyes fixed on his sacrificial lamb.

Henry's breath caught in his throat.

*Maybe you should run.*

*You can still run.*

No, he couldn't; he had to do this, come what may. Henry swallowed his fear and readied himself.

True to his nature, Hong wasted no time, thundering forward. Henry deftly avoided being mauled by sledgehammer fists, even getting in a few strikes of his own, which, to his dismay, seemed to bounce off the brute like insignificant drops of rain. Months of persistent training paid off as Henry broke free of grasping arms, dropping to the floor with a desperate sidekick to Hong's forward knee, scrambling to his feet just in time to avoid a headbutt to his chest, but not the hammer fist that followed. He sank to the floor in silent agony. His ribs on fire, he squinted through a haze of pain as Sammy Hong lurched in front of him with an indescribable look before turning to limp toward the sidelines.

Henry had lost.

Again.

However, this time Sammy Hong had not left the encounter unscathed.

In fact, he was very much scathed, suffering a broken kneecap and a contusion to a bicep that had turned a deep purple days later. Yet after Sifu Lo had shared the news with Henry, it did little to deaden his disappointment.

"I still lost," a dejected Henry came back, nursing sore muscles and a bruised rib from Hong's headbutt, his arm in a sling. "Why can't I get this right!"

Lo didn't go easy on him. "You tried too hard to win. There will always be someone better than you. You need to be a tactician. Fight your battles, not theirs. Control your emotions. You got angry."

The younger man was at a loss. "You say that, yet my anger helped me move quicker and attack harder."

Sifu Lo shook his head. "Emotion gives you an adrenaline rush. That's good to a point. But it's not sustainable. Emotion will tense the body and block your energy."

Henry wanted to say something but decided against it. He needed to listen to what his master was telling him.

Lo's voice softened while his gaze remained firm. "You must learn to keep your mind and body relaxed to win against the Sammy Hongs of the world. You might not have noticed. In the end, Hong looked at you with respect. I saw it in his eyes."

"Not that it did me a lot of good."

"You don't know that. It might be the reason he stopped and walked away."

This was too much for Henry, who wasn't in the mood for mysterious platitudes.

Perhaps sensing this, Lo added with a paternalistic gentleness, "Your heart still holds too much anger and grief. It's what holds you back. You must let go of them."

"How do I do that? It's been so long…"

"There I can't help you. You must figure that out for yourself. But know this, Henry, you will never lose your grief; it will always be a part of you. What you need to do is smother your grief with goodness."

Henry nodded, wanting that more than almost anything. The ache in his heart had been part of him for so long; he could no longer remember what it was like not to feel the crush of that weight.

Sifu Lo advised, "Making peace with the world is more important for you than kung fu. Do this and you can overcome great odds. Don't get me wrong. You fought well against Hong. You've learned to focus your *fajin* explosive strikes on a tough opponent. Now, you must learn something far more difficult: you must learn to harness your soft energy to defeat a difficult opponent without hurting him. You cannot do this until your heart has found tranquility."

As usual, Lo Bai Hu was right. Not everyone learned the subtleties and nuances of a fighting art; many stopped at impressive, easier-to-attain levels. These days, people are in a hurry. They don't have the patience to look beyond the superficial. Henry swallowed his pride, knowing he still had much to learn.

Seeing Ken Ferguson's arm in the sling had brought it all back and with all the old emotions.

Like a punch to the face.

# CHAPTER 23

"Cancer, huh?"

"Yeah," Janet confirmed as she concluded her update on Stenson.

Henry chewed on this. "Therapy visits do explain his daily disappearances…if not a few other things."

She made a noise of agreement, sitting up in her chair. Clasped between her hands was a steaming mug of Earl Gray tea. Too hot to drink, she nonetheless enjoyed the warmth seeping into her fingers and the rising steam with a hint of mint. After clashing with the mayor, she was still easing back into her comfort zone. Curious how that brief encounter with His Honor seemed to drain the life force out of her, making her feel like a deflated beach ball.

"By the way, good work, partner."

She shrugged thanks, the corner of her mouth tugging back.

They spent the next minutes discussing the mayor's health and how it affected the homicide investigations, if at all. Then, Henry excused himself. He had to get to Hennepin County Government Center to testify in court on another case. While he was away, Janet busied herself with phone calls, internet searches, and tackling her stack of paperwork, all the while expecting Bowman to summon her to his office. About Stenson. It'd be like the mayor to complain about her parking lot skirmish with him.

But it didn't happen.

A call came late in the afternoon, though not from her boss; it was IT informing her they'd collated Samuel Park's work laptop computer files. She was emailed a server hyperlink that she breathlessly dove into. She opened a slew of files and folders. None of particular interest, all work-related. Twenty minutes in, she noticed a shortcut on the desktop labeled "Project A."

She clicked the link—

And a shiver ran up her spine at the names of the files and subfolders.

One after the other, she clicked open files for a quick scan of the contents. Then she hit paydirt: a large Word doc named "Project A." She opened it and gasped at the contents. Janet looked over at Henry's vacant desk. He'd be out for the rest of the day.

*He'd flip out when he saw this stuff!*

Diving back into the Word doc, she skimmed through more pages, stopping after a while, having seen enough. Needed to read the entire document in detail. And for that, she wanted a printout. The document was over 140 pages. Too big for her to read comfortably on her computer. This was a hands-on-with-a-highlighter read! Janet sent the file and a few others to the big multifunction copier all the detectives and uniformed officers shared. Her cheeks flushed with anticipation. Couldn't wait to get home, where she could read it all without interruption in the comfort of her favorite chair.

Minutes after walking into her apartment, she changed into black yoga pants and a long-sleeved cotton T-shirt. She sank into her comfy lounge chair, propping her bare feet on the ottoman, the fat document in her lap, a yellow highlighter in hand, and a gel pen nearby. Beside her was a berry container of carrot sticks and cashews and raisins. Twenty-eight minutes into the document, Janet glanced at the kitchen wall clock, set down the pages, and reached for her cell to text two words to Henry:

*CALL ME!*

Eight minutes later, her phone rang.

"What's up?" Henry said. "You used all caps."

Barely able to contain her excitement, Janet told him she had Park's files from IT. "I've combed through a lot of them. Mostly nothing. But one file is called Project A, and it's the jackpot. Answers a *huge* question," she raced on, her voice speeding up. "Big surprise, too! Pulls the rug out of everything we know." She stopped to catch her breath. "It's—"

"*Wait.*" Henry cut her off. "Have you eaten yet?"

Janet eyed the little container of munchies without enthusiasm. "Erm, no…"

"Me neither. I've been in court all afternoon. Still downtown. Just got back to my car. Tired and hungry as hell. Let's eat somewhere. My treat. You can tell me everything over a decent meal."

Motivating Janet Lau to get dressed again to go out on a cold, dark night after a long day at work wasn't easy. An offering of food, especially at a nice restaurant, always worked. "Okay. Got someplace in mind?"

"No. I'm open to suggestions."

"I've got one, then. You want simple and fast or really good?"

A thoughtful pause. "Better than a burger joint. Nothing fancy."

"I have just the place. It's small, quiet, fabulous food."

"Sounds perfect. I can swing by and pick you up."

"Nah, I'm only a couple miles from it. I'll meet you there in thirty minutes. Sending you the address now."

The call ended. Janet eased out a breath. A little disappointed at not being able to drop the big news on him there and then, but recovered quickly, thinking it would be more enjoyable seeing his reaction when she did. She changed into more weather-appropriate clothing: a turtleneck waffle sweater and a flannel wrap skirt over her yoga pants. She slipped on ankle boots, snagged her hat, gloves, scarf, threw on her coat, and grabbed her keys from a cracked soup mug on an Arts and Crafts side table by the door. She froze in her tracks. Dug out her phone and strode over to the coffee table to take a photo of the cover sheet of the Project A printout. Now ready, she snatched her handbag and breezed out the door.

Janet was the first to arrive at Fantastico!, an intimate family restaurant in the Diamond Lake neighborhood of South Minneapolis that served rustic Italian cuisine. She asked for a secluded table and was seated in a corner beneath a large Picasso reprint set in an antique frame. Janet waited for her uncle as she nursed a glass of Pinot Grigio, looking through the big windows onto the dark canvas of Lyndale Avenue, dotted now by the red glow of brake lights from slow-moving rush hour traffic. No matter. They were outside, she inside, where it was warm and snug, and she could unwind after a lackluster day, apart from the info from IT. And she was itching to share that breakthrough with her senior partner.

She didn't have long to wait. Henry arrived minutes later, appearing at the far end of the long room that made up the bulk of the seating area. Per instructions, he'd parked in the rear lot and entered by the back door. Janet waved him over, smiling with approval. Her uncle looked pretty damn sharp, she thought, dressed in his charcoal gray power suit with a European cut. He'd changed into it to wear to court. He felt the suit gave him an extra edge in certain situations, and he wore it like battle armor when engaging with power brokers, the well-to-do, and others with pretensions of superiority. The suit gave Henry Lau the appearance of equal status. His sartorial finery, coupled with his natural poise and presence, lent his testimony in court an extra air of authority. By comparison, Janet felt slightly underdressed.

Only slightly.

Fantastico! wasn't a fancy, hoity-toity restaurant where the wait staff looked down at you if you used the wrong fork for your salad—God forbid! No, this was a cozy little neighborhood eatery that served high-quality meals with friendly service.

Henry joined her at the walnut table for two.

Seconds later, their server, Troy, returned to take Henry's drink order and tell him about the specials. The thin-hipped waiter's shoulder-length hair was fixed in a man bun.

After Troy departed, Janet glanced at Henry's thick black shag and made a disapproving face toward their server. "Don't ever do that with your hair."

Henry smiled. "Not to worry. It'll never happen."

Janet scrunched her nose and sat back. She was champing at the bit to get started but wanted to give him a minute to get settled before launching into her story. After Troy returned with Henry's beverage and got their dinner orders, Janet leaned toward him, clearing her throat. "Like I said over the phone, the big surprise comes in Park's Project A folder," she gushed like a schoolgirl sharing a juicy bit of gossip.

"Hold up." Henry raised his palm. "I want to hear all this, but can we wait until after we eat?" His eyes and voice softly entreated. "It's been ages since I've eaten at a nice place like this and not talked shop the whole time. Can we hold off and enjoy where we are?"

"Of course." Curbing her impatience, she smiled pleasantly. Did a mental reset. *Go with the flow. There's no rush.* He wanted to enjoy the pleasure of a fine dinner in good company without the specter of work—especially their brand of work as homicide investigators—intruding on it, at least for a few minutes. She appreciated that. It occurred to Janet that apart from her dinner earlier that week with Dani, it'd been way too long since she'd dined out with a friend. Months. She missed that. The demands of her new job often got in the way of her so-called social life.

The dinners came. While Henry enjoyed his grilled salmon with buttery whipped potatoes and grilled asparagus, Janet reveled in her squash and pumpkin ravioli with fresh handmade pasta, caramelized pears, and sage brown butter. Between bites, she asked her uncle about his court appearance. Yes, technically, court talk was still work-related; however, by mutual consent, it was distant enough from their active investigations to not count as verboten dinner chat. While Henry told a humorous story about the judge, Janet caught movement at the table seven feet away where an older couple had just been seated. The woman looked well into her sixties with hair dyed a shade of pumpkin orange that seemed oddly seasonally appropriate; though Janet earnestly believed it would take a woman a third her age to successfully pull off the look. Even from this distance, the color gave the impression the woman was wearing a pumpkin on her head. Probably not the look she was going for. The woman's male companion, of similar age, balding with a long nose, spoke softly, too softly for Janet to understand. However, the woman wasn't fully engaged in whatever he was saying. Every so often, she glanced toward Janet. Once, when she didn't realize Janet could see her, the woman was clearly checking her out.

Unable to stand it any longer, Janet leaned across the table, whispering to Henry, "Do I have food on my face or something?"

"No," he answered, puzzled.

"Do I look weird?"

"You look fine. Why d'you ask?"

"The woman at the next table keeps looking at me funny."

"Maybe it's me she's looking at."

"Now that you mention it, I think she does sometimes. Mainly me, though."

"Maybe she knows you."

Her forehead crinkled. "She doesn't look familiar. Oh, well. I'll ignore her as long as I'm not spilling something on myself."

Eventually, dinner plates were cleared, and two cappuccinos appeared. Janet used her tiny stir spoon to scoop up the foam. She loved slurping up the fresh foam before diving into the coffee.

Sitting back, his suit coat unbuttoned to reveal the full splendor of his satin blue necktie, Henry nodded with satisfaction. "That was tasty. Best meal I've had in a long time. Thanks for suggesting this place." He breathed out a contented sigh. "I'm good now. Ready whenever you are. What d'you find out?"

Janet scooched her chair closer and kept her voice low so as not to carry. "The Project A folder on Park's work laptop tells us what he and Zelinsky were up to." She held his gaze and didn't let go. "They weren't having an affair. They weren't investigating anyone or working on a secret report. Their project?" Her eyes opened wide. *"They were writing a book together, a mystery novel."* Even as the words came out, she was dumbstruck with amusement.

She waited for his reaction with bated breath.

He squinted back. "That's it? A novel?"

"Yep. Check out the title." Janet whipped out her smartphone and showed the photo she'd taken of the first page of the printed manuscript:

*An Actionable Crime*

*K.J. Hazzard*

Henry's eyes burned into the tiny screen. Then dawn broke on his face. "From the Post-it in Park's office."

Janet tapped the screen with her finger. "K.J. Hazzard. That's the author name they're using instead of their own. A made-up pen name."

Here, Troy discreetly appeared to leave the bill on the table and just as discreetly left, not wanting to disturb their conversation. Henry reached for his wallet and placed a VISA card on the guest check presenter.

"Thanks for dinner," Janet smiled.

"My pleasure. You earned it. Good work reading through that manuscript. Got any more goodies?"

"Oh, yeah. There's a to-do list. One item on it is *firearm research.*"

"That may explain why Zelinsky was talking to Marsh about guns. Book research."

"Something he can verify when he replies to my text."

"Good." Henry took a long sip from his cappuccino.

"There's more."

He laughed. "I bet there is."

A humorous glint flashed in Janet's eye. "Ann Oreino, the mysterious Filipino woman? She doesn't exist, either. We got her name from Evelyn Brown, who'd overheard part of a conversation. Halfway through reading the manuscript, it hit me. It's November! What Brown actually heard was Park and Zelinsky talking about NaNoWriMo."

"Sorry, what?"

"Yeah, never heard of it myself until a few days ago. NaNoWriMo is short for National Novel Writing Month. It's a thing done every November. Tons of wannabe writers do it." Janet summarized her dinner with Dani and how her friend Jay Kapur's science fiction novel came up. "Remember the exact words Brown used? She overheard Park and Zelinsky say they had to *'get something done by the end of the month for Ann Oreino.'* She didn't know what NaNoWriMo was, so her brain inserted a name instead."

"Makes sense. This novel, is it finished?"

Janet shook her head. "No. Around forty thousand words. It's a very rough draft. Choppy in parts. But I guess that's the whole point of this thing. Try to get fifty thousand words done by the end of the month, no matter how raw it looks. You go back later and start rewriting and polishing. The manuscript ends at chapter twenty. They had two weeks before the end of the month."

"Except they both died."

A thoughtful silence fell between them.

Janet settled back in her chair to finish her coffee. Then rested her hands in her lap, enjoying the warmth of the flannel skirt. Around her came the clatter of dishes, the sound of sizzling meat in the kitchen behind the long bar counter, the clunk of ice cubes swirling in drinks at nearby tables, and the sound of people in lively conversation. The restaurant was filling up with the after-work dinner crowd.

"You're right," Henry finally spoke with a new intensity. "This is the jackpot; it explains almost everything. If Bloomington PD finds the same document on Zelinsky's home PC, that'll be the clincher."

"Right. Oh, speaking of Susan Z., remember that Post-it found in her car, the one that asked how to prove malfeasance?"

Henry grunted. "Don't tell me. More research."

"Yessir! There's a character in the novel who's accused of some shady doings. Also, the so-called poison-pen note Blaine PD found in Park's recycle bin? A version of it shows up in chapter eighteen of the manuscript."

Henry clamped a hand to his forehead, eyes incredulous. "Huh! What looked like clues to our homicides weren't clues; they were scraps of novel research!"

"I know. Kind of disappointing."

"How so?"

"I thought we'd find our two murder victims were uncovering some major criminal enterprise or political corruption. But a novel? It's kind of anti-climactic." She heaved a sigh.

Henry chuckled. "You're a romantic."

"I suppose, but we still don't know why they were killed."

"Hang on…" Henry's brow darkened. He tapped his cappuccino cup, searching for a memory. "Park and Zelinsky kept the project secret. Look how long it took us to figure out what it was. This novel must be connected with their deaths. Could they have fictionalized something at their workplace or included something that might embarrass a coworker?"

"Not that I noticed in a quick read. The characters and location have nothing to do with a knife factory. Although the manuscript isn't finished."

"Maybe the truth isn't important," Henry wondered. "What matters is what people *thought* Park and Zelinsky were doing. Susan's work friend, Lori Deaver, said something I just remembered."

"What?"

"That people see what they want to see. People thought Park and Zelinsky were having an affair. They weren't. Was someone jealous enough to do something stupid?"

Janet nodded, seeing his point. It was all about perception and emotions.

Inspired, Henry continued. "Our victims both had important positions in the company. One was the chief operations officer, and the other was the senior cost accountant. What if an employee had something to hide and was worried they were about to be found out?"

"Oh." Janet's mouth formed a perfect O. She liked this idea; they were back to intrigue and dark doings.

"Think it over." Henry slid out of his chair. "While you do that, I'll visit the men's room."

Seconds later came the scritch of a chair leg scraping across the hard vinyl floor. The older couple at the nearby table were leaving. The pumpkin-haired woman waited as her dinner companion helped her on with a long wool coat as she cast an appraising eye toward Janet. Then, as if having made a decision, she stepped over.

"Marge, no," cautioned her distressed-looking date.

Marge had a message to deliver and would not be deterred. "You're young," she said pointedly to Janet. "Let me give you some advice, dear. Try to date someone closer to your age."

*Huh? What the—*

"Ewww," Janet glared back. "That man is my *uncle*." She stressed the last word, enjoying its effect on the meddlesome woman, who blinked awkwardly in stunned silence.

Marge backed away, her male companion placing a guiding hand on her back. He mouthed "sorry" to Janet before steering his pumpkin-haired date toward the exit.

With a giggle, Janet clapped her hands.

"What's so funny?" asked Henry, settling back into his chair.

Amused as all get out, Janet explained.

"Wait? What?" He stared at her. "That woman thought we were on a date?"

"Yeah."

Henry uttered a subterranean growl as he shook his head.

In a teasing mood, Janet said brightly, "Actually, as I think it over, this is the best date I've had in…oh, a year."

"This isn't a *date* date. We're having dinner together, discussing work."

"I know," she assured, still smiling. Of course he was right. Nothing creepy was going on here, despite what Marge of Orange thought. That said, for Janet, there was an added element to this moment. Being here, now, at this place, with this man who was her uncle and work partner, Janet felt comfortable and safe. No need to be smart or entertaining or clever or to hold back. She could be herself. And she wouldn't be judged for it. Her Uncle Henry listened to her, actually listened, not just waiting for her to finish so he could make his next point. He encouraged her to do things her way. He was not simply her beloved uncle but also a great friend. She felt a pang of sadness, knowing their work pairing would end in a few months. Chief Bowman had made that clear. If for that reason alone, she was determined to enjoy the time she and Henry had left working together.

Work…

Oh yeah. A pile of reading waited for her at home. It was going to be a late night. Yet with a belly full of a wonderful meal and the good company of her mentor, Janet Lau was in no hurry to leave.

# CHAPTER 24

A grumpy Evelyn Brown looked tiny behind the massive conference room table. The disheveled bundle of hair jammed behind the leopard claw clip suggested an abandoned bird's nest.

Janet took her time. Closed the door behind her slowly and took a chair opposite the executive assistant. It was late the next morning. Once again, Henry was testifying in court. She was on her own. Three updates had brought her here. The first from Cheri Hanson. "Our tech guys finished with Zelinsky's PC," Hanson related over the phone. "I'll forward their summary. They found the Project A file you asked about with the name K. J. Hazzard."

That earned a fist pump from Janet. *Further proof of Park and Zelinsky's collaboration!*

The other result came from a suggestion by Henry. He was a runner. So was Susan. Her body had been found outside in mid-November without a jacket, hat, or gloves, dressed in light-weight clothing and sneakers, wearing a single wireless earbud. Had Susan been out for a morning run when she was run over? It seemed likely, and if she were like him, she'd be out before sunrise when the streets were mainly empty. Henry had suggested rechecking her neighborhood. She probably had a regular route. Her attacker must have followed her. Hanson reported patrol officers had found the location where she was killed: a church parking lot next to an elementary school. A crushed earbud was found that matched the one on her body. There were also tire marks and a piece of a broken turn signal bezel. The weekend flurries had covered them but became visible after the thaw.

The third update was tucked inside the black faux leather portfolio she placed prominently on the table in front of her. It looked very official. Evelyn Brown's uneasy gaze lingered on the portfolio.

To enhance her aura of authority, Janet had plucked a feather from Henry's hat. He had his power suit; she'd changed into a tailored white shirt, a black blazer, and dark gray sculpted pants with black patent leather pumps: her investment banker VP outfit, as she liked to call it. Dressed to kill. Augmenting this, she'd also adopted a no-nonsense manner upon entering the lobby and maintained it. No cordial smile today.

She was all business.

Her hands rested on the portfolio as if protecting its contents.

Brown couldn't help but notice this. She shifted uncomfortably. "I don't know why it was necessary to shuffle me in here. I've got a lot of work to do."

Janet wasn't playing nice girl today. "Ms. Brown, I'll remind you that Ms. Hancock promised her staff would give me their full cooperation. I also figured it would be less disruptive if we talked here rather than at the police station."

A troubled Brown parted her lips to protest but closed them as Janet opened the portfolio and withdrew a document. "This came today, a police report from Indiana. You were convicted of a fifth-degree gross misdemeanor assault for slapping and kicking a woman. Served ninety days."

"That was forever ago! I was nineteen, crying out loud. What's that have to do with anything?"

"Tell me what happened."

"Why?" came the acerbic reply. "You've got the report in front of you."

"Just answer the question."

Brown's eyes stared at the table with such intensity they threatened to burn a hole in it. Drawing in a ragged breath, she said her piece. "I was in college. It was a bar fight. Some stupid sorority queen with a rich daddy was mouthing off to me, and I'd had enough of her. The drunk bitch got in my face, so I smacked her. She started crying and yelling and making threats. The bitch wouldn't leave me alone, so I slapped her again. When she tried to fight back, I kicked her."

Janet found it difficult to imagine this tiny woman coming out on top in a bar brawl, but she knew it was possible. Sometimes little dogs put up the scrappiest fight. She waited for more details, but Brown offered nothing further, so Janet swiped her finger under a section of the complaint. "You omitted the part where after you kicked her, your sorority friend fell back and broke her wrist in the fall."

Brown shrugged. "It was a college bar. The floor was slippery. The bitch was tanked."

"And you?"

"Yeah, I'd had some beers. So what? I was nineteen and had a temper. A fifth-degree charge is the lowest possible; I mean, you look at someone the wrong way and you can get charged with it. It's not like I beat her with a baseball bat. It was a couple slaps and a kick. I got nailed for it. I'm not sorry. The bitch deserved it. I did my time. I worked on anger management. This was over fifteen years ago! I've not had so much as a parking ticket since then." Brown glared back, exasperated at the injustice of the world. "Why does it matter now?"

"How's this? Two of your colleagues have been murdered. You have an assault conviction. From what I've seen and heard, you had feelings for Samuel Park." Janet locked eyes with Brown. "You also seem to have a low opinion of Susan Zelinsky. You pushed the idea she and Park were in a relationship."

The executive assistant sat with folded arms, rigid and silent. Janet could almost feel the resentment steaming off her.

"It bothered you that your boss and Susan might be in a love relationship. Did your jealousy make you kill Susan? Run her down to get rid of your competition? Using her key card, you came into the office to face down Sam Park. You poured out your feelings, and he rejected you. Enraged and hurt, you wanted to make him hurt too. Seeing the knife display, you grabbed the tiger claw blade and stabbed him."

"*No!*" A horrified Evelyn Brown shook her head. "That's not what happened." She pounded the table. "*I'd never hurt Sam*. I didn't kill anyone. I'm not that teenager anymore," her tear-streaked face insisted. "I didn't do this."

Janet had to admit that Brown was pretty convincing, though she knew from experience that some people were too good at lying to take them at face value. "I want to believe you, but you're not telling me everything. What are you holding back?"

"Nothing."

"Think again. When my partner and I spoke to you on Wednesday, you told us the way Mr. Park and Ms. Zelinsky were acting around each other, and it bothered you. But there was more. I sensed you were holding back about Sam Park. What was it?"

"I wasn't holding back."

"This isn't the time to play games. There *was* something, wasn't there?"

"It was nothing."

"Tell me."

Silence.

"Ms. Brown," Janet came down hard, "you're not helping yourself. *Tell me.*"

The woman's shoulders sagged under the weight of her emotions. "Like I said, it was nothing," she replied in an afflicted tone as if she were betraying the memory of her dead boss. "It happened last week.

Jim Karjala was in Sam's office. They were talking. Don't ask me about what; I didn't hear what they said. I only heard their voices, not the words. Well, Sam kind of snapped at Jim over something. Raised his voice. Sam never did that. It surprised me."

And that was it. A rare flash of temper. Janet didn't know what to make of it. She watched as the small woman looked back with pain-filled eyes. In a wounded voice barely above a whisper, she lamented, "I didn't kill anyone."

This time, Janet was inclined to believe her. She put the police report back in the portfolio and closed the cover. "Thank you, Ms. Brown. We're done here. You can go."

Only she didn't move. Remained seated, looking tiny and fragile.

"Are you okay?" Janet asked.

Brown said, "I've worked so hard to get past that old assault conviction, but it keeps haunting me. You wouldn't be talking to me now if it wasn't for that. One stupid act when I was a teenager, and I keep paying for it. It's not fair—" Her voice broke.

Janet felt sorry for her and wanted to say something but couldn't think of anything that didn't sound trite or patronizing, so she opened the conference room door for Brown, who shuffled out as if heading to a detention cell instead of her workstation.

*My job is so fun! (Not)*

Janet didn't like unnecessarily upsetting people. Growing up, she'd always been the "nice girl," the "smart girl," the one who got teased by high school mean girls for being "perfect." Well, she wasn't feeling perfect today. Detective Janet Lau had a job to do, which meant she occasionally had to get tough with people, which was not something that came easily to her. She had a strong dislike for pushy people, and the thought of being one, even momentarily, was upsetting. Seriously, she thought, it wasn't that bad, wasn't as if she'd browbeat Evelyn Brown. Yet getting tough with the executive assistant still bothered her. Janet sighed at the realization her classmates had been right: she *was* the nice girl.

At the reception desk, Janet asked to see Jim Karjala, wanting to get his side of Brown's story, only to learn the CFO was out of the office all day, attending a corporate financial tax seminar at the Minneapolis Convention Center.

She took the disappointment in stride, making a mental note to find out later what caused Sam Park to raise his voice at the company's main money man.

Returning to the station, her mood lightened when she saw what was stuffed in her In Box: a FedEx envelope. Her eyes dilated at the return address: Sacramento, California. *Oh yeah!* She'd forgotten about the package from Beth McAdams. For Henry. What had she sent? Janet was eager to see. Her fingers fumbled for the easy-open tear-off strip before stopping. *No, not now. Bad idea.* She clutched the envelope to her chest, glad her uncle was still in court and not there to see the package. He'd probably ask what it was. No, there was too much risk in opening it here; she'd wait until she got home, so hustled out to her car to lock the big envelope in her trunk where it'd be safe and secure and out of sight. She'd open it after dinner. It was Friday, and she had no plans for the evening.

# CHAPTER 25

For most of Henry's adult life, Saturday mornings were devoted to Wing Chun training. Regardless of other obligations and his exhaustive predawn daily workouts, Saturday mornings held a special place. He enjoyed the morning drive to the trendy Minneapolis Uptown neighborhood and Alan Zhu's sixth-floor Wing Chun studio. Henry had helped install the requisite wall of mirrors, the *mook yan jong* (wooden dummy) mounted against a side wall, and the three sandbags nearby. These were martial arts sandbags made of rugged canvas for the express purpose of repeatedly smashing one's fists into them. However, instead of actual sand, Alan filled his bags with popcorn kernels. Sand didn't like humidity and would absorb it and harden. Over time, punching a breathable sand-filled wall bag would feel like whacking concrete. On the other hand, popcorn kernels didn't absorb moisture and remained loose to absorb blows.

It was a few minutes into the third hour. Henry wore a forest green T-shirt, black baggy kung fu pants gathered at the ankle, socks, and traditional Chinese canvas rubber-soled shoes. He looked out a window, one of a row of eight double-hung sashes on the back wall. He gazed over the rooftops toward Hennepin Avenue with a peek of Lake Bde-Mka-Ska in the distance, the Dakota name for the largest lake in Minneapolis and one of its most popular. The soundtrack to his panoramic view was the muted thwap-thwap-thwap-thwap of knuckles pounding into the nearby wall bag. Henry was coaching a new student on the correct way to punch while across the room twenty-four other students were practicing two-person drills under the direction of Alan.

Henry turned. The sound and rhythm of the punching was off. The easy, steady, loose piston-like forward and back motion had turned into a knuckle-busting fusillade. "Stop," Henry said, stepping over.

The new student looked over. Mid-thirties, deep-set eyes, a fleshy nose above a Tom Selleck mustache.

In a nonjudgemental voice, Henry said, "That's not what I showed you. Soft and easy. You're trying to kill the bag."

The student, whose name was Chad, rose out of his stance. "I'm a regular at Iron Gloves Boxing Gym," he answered defensively. "I think I know how to punch."

*Fun. One of these guys. I'm good at this thing so I must know all about your completely different thing.*

"This is a Wing Chun class. That's not how we punch. If you want to learn this art, you need to set aside what you've already learned and open your mind."

Chad wasn't receptive to being corrected. Rather than persuading him with words, Henry went for the direct approach, placing his palms over his stomach. Smiling, he said, "Hit me with your hardest punch."

"Really?"

"Yes. Your best shot right here." Henry indicated the hands over his stomach, then adjusted his stance.

"You want me to hit you?"

"Yeah."

Chad fired off a hard right cross.

Contact was made. Henry barely moved. A slight wobble, if anything. "Nice," he said. "Your turn."

Chad covered his belly with his palms.

Henry stepped closer, his elbow by his waist and his fist about six inches from Chad's midsection. "Ready?"

A nod. He was braced for impact.

One second later, relaxed yet ready, Henry's fist exploded forward like the business end of a battering ram. No arm retraction. No windup. No yell. Just startling kinetic energy that made Chad shuffle back three steps and double over.

"Did you feel that?" Henry asked.

"Yeah," Chad wheezed, grimacing. He looked unwell.

"Did you see the difference between what you did and what I did?"

"Yes," a weak voice replied.

"Do you want to punch like that?"

"Yeah."

"Then practice what I showed you. There's a reason for it. At this stage, it's not about power. It's about body alignment and relaxation."

A chastened Chad returned to the wall bag and sent out a mechanical stream of loose piston-like punches that seemed to have little power to them, which, as Henry knew, was the point. The new student didn't know it but was training his muscle memory to maximize his power.

From across the room, Henry saw Alan grinning with approval. He was feeding a student punches, pulls, grabs, and strikes for his partner to counter.

Then everything changed.

The door swung open. Two men entered the *kwoon*.

One man was solid-looking with muscular shoulders, a long, rough face, and lank, pale blond hair. The gaudy jacket was unmistakable. It was Letterman Jacket Dude from the dance rehearsals, aka Jake Bosko. With him was an equally unsavory-looking man with a square jaw, a slash of a mouth, and hooded eyes. The two waltzed in, clearly scoping out the place. Bosko snorted with satisfaction when he spotted Henry, elbowing his companion.

Henry had a bad feeling about these guys.

As head of the school, it was Alan's responsibility to greet the visitors. He broke away from his training partner. With luck, Henry hoped, maybe Alan could deal with them on his own. But he had a sneaking suspicion the visitors hadn't come for a friendly visit, so he went over to help Alan.

Just in case.

"There's the man," Bosko scoffed. "I heard you hung out here. You're a hard guy to hunt down."

Hunt down.

Henry didn't like the sound of that. Ignoring the comment, he looked to Alan. While Henry was the more accomplished fighter, he always deferred to his best friend at his school as a show of respect.

Alan glanced between Henry and Jacket Dude. "You two know each other?"

"We've met," Henry confirmed but in an underwhelmed tone that caught his friend's attention.

An uneasy though polite Alan looked at his visitors. "What brings you by?"

Bosko jammed a finger toward Henry and proclaimed, "I'm here to challenge Lau to a fight. You were right. The dance studio was the wrong place and time. But we're in a dojo. You can't brush me off this time."

"A fight?" Alan repeated, concerned. "I can't sanction that."

"What's with you guys?" Bosko tossed up his hands in disbelief. "Too scared to get it on with a real fighter?" He made some obligatory shoulder feints.

Alan Zhu shook his head. "Not that. Insurance. I'm not risking liability on you. If you get hurt, how do I know you won't try to sue me or the building owners?"

The way Alan had said, "if you get hurt," came across more like "*when* you get hurt," which did not sit well with Bosko. "Fuck this. You aren't getting rid of me that easily. Not this time."

A tense silence followed.

With a tight expression, Alan motioned to the bellicose challenger. "Hang on." Then, he guided Henry away to the windows where they could speak privately. "What's going on?"

Henry summarized his encounter with Jacket Dude at the dance rehearsal.

Alan groaned. "One of *those* guys." Troublemakers. Every trade, profession, sport, or activity had its troublemaker, but those in martial arts seemed a special breed of obnoxious.

Henry asked, "What do you want to do?"

Alan frowned, removed his glasses, rubbed the corner of his eye. His irritation was plain as he replaced his eyewear. "Some bozo walks in and demands a fight. No, I don't think so. It's disrespectful and dangerous. There could be hell to pay from the insurance company or the landlord if that guy gets hurt and sues." He huffed out a breath. "I can tell them to leave, and if they don't, call the police."

It was private property; the visitors were threatening trouble. If Alan, the owner, asked them to leave and they didn't, it would justify his summoning Minneapolis PD. It also got Henry off the hook. He was a detective for the city of Gillette. This wasn't his jurisdiction. Plus, he doubted playing his I'm-a-cop card would go over well with this punk. Henry agreed with Alan's plan. "Try it. Say no. Ask them to leave. If they say no, insist they do. If for no other reason than to have done it."

A *pro forma* precaution, otherwise known as *cover your ass.*

"You think that guy's gonna leave if I tell him to?"

"Honestly? No. He tracked me down for a reason. He wants a fight."

"That's what worries me."

"You feel like taking him on?"

"Me?" Alan laughed.

"Relax. Just askin'." Henry wasn't being facetious. This was Alan's place; as owner and sole proprietor, defending its integrity and the safety of its students fell upon his shoulders. By rights, if this were an old-style traditional kung fu establishment, it should be head man Alan Zhu who fought off all troublemakers and put them in their place. But these were modern times, and they lived in a litigious society where lawsuits dropped like confetti. And there was one other thing. Almost everyone in the room understood that as knowledgeable and as accomplished as Sifu Alan was, it was Henry Lau who was the most skilled and battle-tested fighter. However, Henry respected his old friend far too much to make assumptions. As a gesture of respect, he'd asked Alan if he wanted to take on the troublemaker.

Alan came back with a wry grunt. "Maybe a few years ago. Too risky now at my age with a wife and two kids. Fighting that guy isn't important enough. Besides"—Alan cleared his throat impishly—"he called *you* out. He has no interest in me."

"We could stand our ground. Tell him to go away. He causes trouble; we call the lawyers."

"Ugh. Attorney fees. Court. Sounds messy."

Henry felt for Alan. All he was trying to do was run a friendly martial arts club where people got along. The last thing he needed was for some high testosterone bonehead drooling to prove himself to invade his space and harass his students or himself. Alan had always been there for Henry; he didn't need this crap in his life. Alan did have a family to think about, and, yes, it was Henry who Jacket Dude had in his sights. This wasn't Alan's problem; he knew deep down it was his.

And it was up to him to fix it.

"I have an idea…" Henry said.

A minute later, the pair crossed the worn oak floorboards to join their visitors. With an uncompromising face and a stern voice, Alan informed them that he didn't want trouble. He said there'd be no fight and wanted them to leave and never return. If they didn't, he'd call the police.

The *pro forma* statement had been made in front of witnesses.

At this point, if not before, Alan's students realized something unusual was happening. There was no way in a room smaller than a basketball half-court that they could not have heard their sifu's rebuke. The nearly two dozen students stopped what they were doing to gather in loose clusters behind their leader.

As expected, Jacket Dude and his friend remained defiant. Jake Bosko puffed out his chest. "I don't think so. The only way you're getting rid of us is if Lau fights me. Here and now."

All eyes fixed on Henry. Tension clung to the air as they waited for his response.

Four seconds ticked by on the wall clock.

"Okay," Henry agreed.

Bosko was taken aback. "You will?"

"Yes, and since you challenged me, I get to make the rules."

"Rules! What the f—"

"*Shut up.*" Henry cut him off with a look that could melt lead. He'd dangled the bait, and the lank-haired punk had swallowed it whole. Now it was his turn to make demands. "The rules are simple. We fight. The first one to get knocked down two times or tap out loses. If there's no clear winner after ten minutes, we stop and call it a draw. Clear enough?"

"Sure. I'm down with that."

"Good," Alan said, stepping up, part two of their coordinated plan. "You also have to sign a waiver."

"Waiver? The hell I will. I'm not signing anything."

Alan pressed. "All it says is you're responsible for your own safety and the safety of others and that you won't hold me, other students, the school, or the building owners responsible for any injuries."

"No way I'm signing that," Bosko snorted in a voice dripping with scorn.

"Everyone who works out in this space must sign it. No exceptions. You don't sign, you leave."

The other stewed indecisively for a count of three before he caved. "Okay," he grumbled, "I'll sign the stupid waiver."

Alan went to the storage closet and returned with a paper and pen.

Casting dubious eyes on the document, Jacket Dude muttered something unintelligible, put the paper against a nearby wall, and scratched his name, signature, and date. Then shoved both items into Alan's hands. "*Now,* can we do this?"

The other gave a nod.

"Good." Jake Bosko peeled off his jacket, handing it to his wingman. "I need to warm up. Lau's had all morning."

Alan, whose patience for this pushy clown was fading fast, told him, "You have two minutes."

"More'n enough time," Bosko scoffed, beginning his stretches that, suspiciously enough, showed off his muscular frame. Intimidation poses? His bulky frame was covered in a light knit pullover, baggy workout pants, cotton socks, and Air Jordan sneakers.

Meanwhile, Alan rounded up his students to explain what was about to happen. He added in a conspiratorial tone that he didn't trust the strangers. "If they try anything, be ready. Otherwise, do nothing." Then he instructed them to form a protective line in front of the wall of mirrors to protect the fighters from broken glass and the mirrors from the fighters.

While this was going on, Henry had returned to the line of windows to look out into the morning sky, his back toward Bosko. He wasn't taking this fight lightly, this or any fight. They were all serious, all potential life and death struggles—to him at least. What was about to happen wasn't a friendly bout but a challenge. He'd have preferred to tell Jacket Dude to go away and bother someone else, but he didn't want to leave Alan paying the price. Bosko wouldn't be satisfied until he got what he wanted, which was proving he was as good as, if not better than, Henry Lau.

Behind Henry's back, Bosko was now loosening up with snap punches, blocks, steps, and backspin kicks. Every so often, the lank-haired blond glanced over, only to see the rear of his opponent's shaggy head and the back of his forest green T-shirt.

Appearances aside, Henry wasn't ignoring him. Rather the opposite. He was playing a mind game on the younger man. While it appeared that he was indifferently gazing out across the rooftops of Uptown, in reality, he was studying his opponent's reflection in the window glass. Watching how he moved.

The restless silence was punctuated by Alan's voice. "Gentlemen, to your places."

Henry turned, hands behind his back.

It was time.

# CHAPTER 26

A hush of anticipation permeated the room. As the two combatants moved to the center space, curious murmurs passed among Alan's students.

Jake Bosko prowled over like a lumbering panda, ungainly and full of menace. He'd walked the same way the first time Henry had seen him at the dance studio when the young tough had tried egging him into a fight. But Bosko slunk away after Henry'd stared him down, slunk away with the same heavy-footed, shoulder-swaying gait. Which was good; he was consistent.

Bosko walked from his shoulders.

That pleased Henry.

Men walked in three ways: many top-heavy men, whose primary weapon is their ample upper body strength, often swayed their shoulders back and forth when they strode, almost like counterweights. They lead with their shoulders, using them to intimidate. For good reason. You didn't want these guys to get their paws on you. Yet a drawback to this upper body bulk was it shifted their center of gravity above their hips. It made them tippy—under certain situations. However, to exploit this potential weakness, you had to put yourself in danger of being mauled.

The second way men walk is from their hips, which describes the majority of the male gender. Although specific individuals elevate this means of locomotion to a refined level. Dancers, many athletes, and professional fighters move with an uncanny fluidity and a surprising kinetic burst; their legs and hips their greatest asset. These men are gazelles, quick and nimble.

The third way men moved—and by Henry's measure, the most dangerous—was from their knees.

Like him.

Like Eric Kwan and Lo Bai Hu.

The Leung Sheung branch of Wing Chun emphasizes developing the muscles that support the knee, hence the grueling first form stance. Strong knees are the lynchpin to movement. The knees support and control the rest of an upright body. Weak knees unbalance you. You can have the upper body strength of a Hercules, but if your knees buckle under stress, you'll collapse. The knee joint is also a vital energy pathway to the ground. The fighter who walks from his knees knows how to redirect incoming energy through his body into the ground, just as he knows how to draw energy up from the ground through his body into his fists. A fighter who walks from his knees can be difficult to deal with. Many students—whether Wing Chun or other fighting systems—never fully develop this ability, and it's nearly impossible to tell when someone has it by watching them.

While any accomplished fighter was a serious threat, those of the last group were the guys that concerned Henry the most.

But not the surly punk in front of him.

Jake Bosko walked from his shoulders. That gave Henry something to exploit, as did one other thing. As he watched his challenger do his warmups, Henry noticed he tended to lean toward his toes, which lifted his heel a fraction off the floor, which meant, for that instant, his balance, his root, was undermined. His weight shifted off his bubbling well, if Bosko even knew what that was.

Henry could use that.

Exploit those observations but with care. He had too much knowledge to *expect* to win this contest and enough experience not to be afraid of losing. This wasn't a life-or-death street battle. Even so, he never sloughed off a threat. *You underestimate your opponent's ability at your peril.*

Henry's best asset was his almost supernatural reaction time. However, like everyone, he had his deficiencies. Some fighters were bigger and stronger, some more aggressive, some faster, some more skillful. To compensate, he had studied strategy and tactics—and the way people moved. That and thousands of hours of Wing Chun sticky hand practice gave him the ability to tell from an opponent's body posture or from a touch what they were about to do. Often before they knew.

But there were no guarantees. Every contest had to be treated like a deadly threat.

Alan walked over to join them.

The time had come.

A middle-aged Henry Lau stood ready, hands at his side as he waited to take on the brash fighter who had so much to prove to himself and others. Relaxed yet focused, Henry drew in slow, measured breaths. He'd rely on his years of training and experience to get him through this. How strange, he thought, that he was neither excited nor anxious. Truth be told, he was more annoyed than anything at having to do this. It'd been years since anyone had challenged him. He'd hoped he'd reached a point in life when those days were behind him. Once again, he was reminded of the gunfighters of the old West. Here he was on his own dusty street, facing an eager young gun with an itchy trigger finger.

For Henry Lau, it was High Noon.

The two men stood ten feet apart, Bosko looking like a mad bull ready to charge. So much like Sammy Hong, Henry mused as he maintained a serene, indifferent exterior. Inside, every nerve in his body was alert.

And ready.

Alan pointed to the wall clock. "When I say 'Go,' you'll have ten minutes. No rounds. No stops. If time runs out, we're done. As you agreed: the first man to get knocked down two times or tap out loses. If there's no winner after ten minutes, we call the fight a draw. Agreed?"

A nod from both combatants.

"Okay. Get ready…GO."

Nothing much happened in the first seconds. Each man sized up the other as they circled, tested probes and feints. Most of the feints came from Bosko who loved a left jab. Henry barely reacted to them apart from a body shift this way or slight arm adjustment that way, or no reaction. He was like a cobra, always turning to face his attacker and poised to strike, waiting for the right moment. Bosko wasn't aware that with every step or shift he made, Henry watched his foot placement. Often solid, there was an occasional heel lift.

A few more indecisive ins and outs followed, then, screeching a fierce war cry, Bosko bunched his shoulders and thundered toward Henry like a bulldozer. A fake kick to the stomach led to a hop-step roundhouse that Henry intercepted with *kwan sau* (scissor arms), clamped the leg and jerked it sideways. A falling Bosko lurched forward, miraculously regaining his balance after Henry released his leg to counterstrike. The lank-haired dude deflected the incoming front kick, jumping in with a ferocious punch that Henry swatted away with *pak da*: the hand from one arm slapping the attack aside as the pile driver fist of the other arm rammed into Bosko's chest.

The blond-haired fighter's torso jerked violently backward as though yanked by a rope, his rump landing on the floorboards with a loud thump.

There came a startled silence; it had happened so quickly.

"That's one count against the challenger," Alan announced, suppressing his amusement. Encouraging murmurs sprang from a few students behind him before he motioned for silence.

Henry stood expressionless as if nothing had happened. He wasn't even breathing hard. But if you paid close attention, you would've seen an intense glint behind his watchful eyes.

His opponent was anything but sanguine. A snarling Bosko hauled himself back to his feet. Calloused fingers swept limp blond locks from eyes that glared daggers at the man who'd knocked him down. The need to mete out punishment blazed hot in them. With a clenched jaw, he shook out his joints and shuffled his weight from foot to foot to foot.

*No dancing!*

The ghost of Sifu Lo's voice boomed in Henry's mind. Jacket Dude was psyching himself up, getting his blood pumping. Helpful to a point. Yet if the threat of having your face pounded to mush wasn't enough to get your heart pumping, what good would a little dance do? Lo wasn't a fan of fancy foot movement. Did it make you quicker off the mark? Debatable. In his view, all the shuffling did was compromise your balance and waste energy. And Wing Chun was a close-range fighting system; its practitioners trained to close-in on their opponent and attack.

While Bosko psyched himself up, Henry slid the soles of his shoes across the floor in position and waited, the muscles in his legs coiled springs.

And then—

With explosive rage, Bosko charged at Henry, who warded off the barrage of punches and double kicks with surgical-like pivots and shifts, though not easily. He had to work for it. A surprisingly athletic twist of Bosko's knee slipped by Henry's forearm, clipping his thigh. He winced. Then a blistering spinning wheel kick followed toward Henry's face that his *biu jee* elbow barely swung up in time to intercept. He paused for a split second.

Except it wasn't just a pause.

It was a lure.

And Bosko seized it. Thinking Henry had left his lower abdomen unprotected, Bosko swiveled with a feint and swung a punch in a tight circular arc toward an unprotected kidney. Henry dropped his elbow, deflecting the strike. Bosko's clenched fingers opened and grabbed the elbow, trying to shove the bony joint into Henry's own ribs. But decades of sensitivity training kicked in. The instant he sensed a change of pressure, Henry's wrist rotated and pressed his palm down. Bosko's vice grip drew in and down, and Henry felt the other's weight shift beyond his toes.

The anger vanished from Bosko's face, replaced by alarm at the realization he was falling. Instinct to catch himself caused his fingers to loosen from Henry's elbow. In the hazy, otherworldly suspension of time between action and reaction, Henry fired off a rapid volley of four chain punches into Bosko's center mass. He staggered back. Wasting no time, Henry jumped toward him, slamming his entire body behind an explosive forearm strike to the chest that shocked Bosko backward. Like a bag of bricks, he crashed to the floor twenty-five feet away.

"That's two!" announced Alan. "The fight is over. Winner, Henry Lau."

The air burst with the sounds of cheers and applause from Alan's students.

Henry was not celebrating.

His expression remained neutral. Kept eyes on the brawny punk who'd righted himself into a sitting position, painfully rubbing his chest. Henry could've used a less severe strike, though he doubted if Jake Bosko would have taken the message seriously if he had. A more lenient ending would send the wrong message to him; he might've entertained the spurious thought that that was the best Henry could do. The thinking being that if he'd lasted a little longer, Bosko could have beaten him. No, this belligerent shithead needed his ass handed to him.

Broken bones or severe injuries would be overkill. What Henry wanted was for Jacket Dude to have grave doubts about trying a stunt like this again. For that to happen, Bosko needed to leave with a very sore souvenir of their encounter, sore enough to last a few days. Learning to temper his attacks to fit the situation had been difficult to master. Sifu Lo would approve.

Henry remained where he was. Did not move. If this had been a friendly demonstration between martial artists, he would've gone over and offered a helping hand to his opponent. But there'd been nothing friendly or sporting in this challenge. Henry wasn't letting his guard down for a second. "We're done here," he said sternly. "And I don't want to see any posts about this on social media. Don't want you distorting what happened. You lost. And I have a room full of witnesses who can back that up."

Having said his piece, Henry turned and walked back toward the row of windows.

That should have ended it.

Only it didn't.

Jake Bosko's friend came over to help him to his feet. He sloughed off the hand. The whole time the ill-mannered karateka struggled up, his gaze never left the man who'd bested him. A volcanic rage contorted his face as Bosko flung himself at Henry.

But Alan Zhu got in his way, shoving Bosko aside.

Bosko stumbled, regained his footing, and looked at Alan with murder in his eyes. Alan, shorter, lighter, and nearly two decades older, stood his ground, ready to take him on. With a growl of contempt, Bosko lumbered toward Alan like a wounded wildebeest, whipping out two front snap kicks followed by a spinning back kick. They all whizzed inches away from Alan as he stepped out of the way. He immediately came back with a fake counterpunch to Bosko's head, then shifted sideways to fire off a sidekick that took out the blond bruiser's leg.

Bosko face-planted on the floor.

There came a burst of cheers and applause from Alan's students. Henry grinned for his friend.

Slightly out of breath, Alan hovered over the fallen tough. "Don't do anything stupid when you get up. Just go. If you don't, we'll toss you out. And don't ever come back here again or make threats!" Alan was pissed.

This time when his buddy came over to help him up, Jake Bosko didn't refuse. He grudgingly snatched his flashy letterman jacket but didn't put it on. The pair went to the exit, Bosko limping heavily. The door closed with a heavy thud behind them.

Alan spent a celebratory minute with his students before breaking from them to join Henry at the windows, wiping his glasses on his T-shirt before putting them back on.

"Nice work!" Henry clamped a hand on his shoulder. "See, you could've taken him."

Alan was too much of a realist to believe that brand of baloney. His eyebrows inched up skeptically. "You softened him up for me. A lot."

Henry returned an enigmatic smile.

Seeing Alan rush in to stop the immature hothead from blindsiding him had been the only enjoyable thing about this unpleasant business. It touched Henry deeply that his friend, without hesitation, had put himself in danger to stop the attack. What Alan didn't know was Henry had kept an eye on Bosko's reflection in the window as he walked away. He was never in danger of being blindsided but didn't have the heart to tell his best friend that, not wanting to rob Alan of his selfless and gutsy deed.

Done in a room full of his students.

A moment that would be celebrated among them and remembered for a long time.

# CHAPTER 27

Monday morning ushered in a Canadian cold front, atypical that early in the season. Freezing windchills and a short burst of fresh heavy snow flirted with rush hour traffic. A rough way to start the new week, but Midwesterners know how to cope.

By 10:15, the Malibu was parked outside Hancock Blades. Henry and Janet were inside Jim Karjala's office. He wasn't a happy camper. "What's so important you had to meet in person?" the CFO complained. "A phone call wouldn't do?"

No, it wouldn't. We can't see your reaction over the phone, Janet did not say out loud but thought it. Here was a situation where she was glad her partner was there to take the lead.

Henry ignored the question and got straight to the point. "It's come to our attention that you had a heated discussion recently with Samuel Park. What was it about?"

Karjala's face was blank. "When was this? I don't remember."

"Last week in his office."

"Last week? Um, we did talk, but I wouldn't characterize it as heated."

"Mr. Park raised his voice at you."

"He might have. If he did, it was a blip. Obviously, I didn't pay attention to it."

"Why did he raise his voice?"

"If it's what I'm thinking, we were talking finances. Long-term strategies. The company's profitable, but profits have been shrinking over the past five quarters. Sam wanted to bring in auditors to find areas where we could make improvements."

"And you didn't want that?"

Karjala swung up his injured hand in a dismissive gesture. "I didn't think it was necessary. But I wasn't against it. If Sam really wanted to bring in auditors, I suggested we wait until early next year. We have enough to do at year end without dancing around a bunch of outsiders. Year end's already a headache."

"Mr. Park didn't want to wait?"

"No. Look, Sam understood cost and management but not accounting. Our software's outdated. Ask anyone in the accounting department. It's a mess. I've been hounding management for years to update our systems and software. But that'd cost a boatload of money, and the Hancock family doesn't want to pony up the funds." Jim Karjala shifted gears. "Auditors aren't going to know our systems; they'd need our people to hand-hold them through everything. That'd distract my team from their work. I *know* our financials like the back of my hand, Detectives. We're already cutting costs to the bone."

Informative as this was, Janet thought the CFO was straying from the question. Apparently, so did Henry, who said, "I take it Sam Park felt differently about bringing in auditors."

"Right. Pressure from Aimee to make the company more profitable. He was under some stress. That's why he might've raised his voice, a heat of the moment thing."

"Under stress?"

"Yeah."

"From what? You've seen signs of this?"

Karjala made a vague gesture. "Nothing concrete. More of a general impression. Sam was less chatty. Worked longer hours. That kind of thing."

Or, Janet wondered, were these longer hours devoted to his novel writing? It'd be easy to misinterpret Park's change in behavior. Did that contribute to the stress Karjala had noticed, trying to balance work and his private life? She also wasn't satisfied with his answer. "Mr.

Karjala," she interjected, "you weren't keen on Mr. Park bringing in auditors. Is it fair to say you didn't like him stepping on your toes?"

The money man grunted. "Does anyone like someone stepping on their toes, Detective? Did it bother me a little? Yeah."

His answer left Janet wanting, although she didn't know what else to ask. Neither did Henry, it seemed. The CFO had answered their question. Moments later, the detectives concluded their interview, bidding the finance man good day.

Signing out in the lobby a minute later, Janet noticed a ceramic bowl on the counter that hadn't been there earlier.

"Help yourself," Tammy said. "Those are from Lalani. She bakes during the holidays. They're macadamia nut shortbread cookies. I guess they're a favorite on the islands."

Henry reached inside the bowl. "Don't mind if I do. Janet?"

Well, if he was taking a dip, so would she. "Yes, please."

On the way back to the car, Janet's phone pinged. She looked at the message. "Guess what? I just got a reply from Tom Marsh about the text I sent last week."

"I take it he's back from his long weekend."

"Yup. He confirmed Susan Zelinsky was researching a book. Asked him about guns."

"More confirmation about the novel."

"Only we still don't have a motive for the killings," she reminded him.

"True. We're close, though; I can feel it—"

Henry's phone rang. He retrieved it from his bomber jacket.

Janet could faintly hear a woman's voice.

"Okay, sure, that'll work," he said, ending the call.

"Something good?" Janet wondered.

"That was Lori Deaver. She's taking a half day off and wants to meet at Southdale Mall around 11:45."

"Any idea why?"

"She has something to tell us. Whatever it is, she sounded anxious."

"Anxious?"

"Yeah. Almost afraid."

"What's she got to be afraid of?"

Henry shrugged. "We'll find out."

"How about you find out? You can drop me off at the station and go. A mountain of financial statements is waiting for me to comb through." It'd been only a few days since they'd gotten bank statements of their persons of interest, including a slew of financials from Hancock Blades. Janet had already started the tedium of pouring through them.

"You okay doing that? Want help?"

Oh, she desperately did but wanted a first crack at them herself. "Nah, I need the experience. Help may be coming. My friend Eva Vasquez from Minneapolis PD. I told you about her, didn't I?"

"Did you?"

"She works in Special Crimes Investigations as a financial analyst. Numbers are her thing. She's got some free time and is willing to give me some pointers."

The Southdale Mall in Edina has the distinction of being the world's first fully enclosed shopping mall, opening its doors in 1956. It had always made perfect sense to Henry that a climate-controlled shopping mall should first be built in cold Minnesota, where winter pitched its tent for at least four months of the year. Sometimes longer. The mall was fully decked out for the holidays: hanging stars, red and green ribbons, large green wreaths, decorated Christmas trees, and several wire-framed reindeer sparkling with tiny white lights.

Henry rode the escalator down to the spacious center court as jolly holiday music played from overhead speakers, his gaze searching through the meandering shoppers for Juiceopolis, which he spied near a sports memorabilia kiosk. Weaving between three gray-haired mall walkers, Henry angled toward a loose cluster of padded chairs where he recognized a pudgy brunette in teal-colored eyeglasses. Lori Deaver was slurping on what appeared to be some kind of strawberry smoothy. As he got nearer, he noticed an ACE bandage wrapped around her ankle.

"Ms. Deaver."

The chubby face flashed a smile of recognition. Perhaps relief, too? he thought. Henry lowered himself in the chair next to hers, mindful of his thigh, which was a little stiff after taking a knee from Jacket Dude on Saturday. It'd been no walk in the park dealing with Bosko. The guy had impressive fighting skills but no smarts. Maybe he'd learn a little humility after having his ass handed to him.

Shoppers ambled by, too busy with their lives and purchases to pay attention to anything else. Deaver looked uncomfortable, moistening her lips several times before launching into her story.

"Thanks for coming. I was here for an eye exam for new glasses," she said, a little breathless. "Um, I wanted to tell you something that happened at work on Friday. I was having lunch with Tammy, our receptionist. She's taking evening accounting classes and hopes to move into our department next year. She'd be great. She already knows so much about the company! Anyway, Tammy was showing off her new watch, a fitness tracker; it does all this cool stuff like monitoring her heart rate and steps." Deaver paused to take a quick sip on her straw. "I kinda froze at the word tracker. Then it hit me. Earlier this year, I bought a GPS tracker for my e-bike—"

Henry straightened, eyes narrowing on her. "Wait. Your e-bike has a GPS tracker?"

"Yeah, I thought it might come in handy. I never really used it, though. I always knew where the bike was, so I forgot about it until Tammy's comment. I fished out my phone and found the app, but it didn't work. It'd been too long. It got corrupted, I guess. I needed to reinstall the app. The problem was I needed the tracker ID number, which meant I had to wait till I got home, *except*"—Deaver inhaled dramatically—"when I got home, I slipped on ice in the driveway and fell. Twisted my ankle. It didn't feel broken—believe me, Detective, I know what a broken ankle feels like, so I packed my foot in ice and kept it elevated for half an hour. I wrapped it in this bandage and kept my foot propped up for the rest of the night. I didn't go out on Saturday; I was babying my ankle." Lori Deaver paused, looking slightly embarrassed. "Sorry, I'm wandering. Um, what I mean is I put off working on the tracker app till Sunday."

"Did it work?"

"It did! I've got a Bando 2000. The app found it in nothing flat. But I wasn't up to driving anywhere. I checked later that night, and the bike was in the same place." She gulped in a preparatory breath. "Since I had a half day off today, I figured I'd swing by the location this morning. I live in Gillette. The GPS tracker said the bike was in Gillette, so going there first wasn't a bother."

She hesitated as if finding the nerve to continue.

Henry recalled the anxiety in her voice when she'd called.

Deaver took two slurps of the strawberry slushie. With a nervous glance round, she leaned in conspiratorially. "I went to the coordinates and found the house. The GPS is accurate within twenty feet. I didn't see my e-bike, but it had to be on the property. I wasn't gonna trespass and search. I can't walk fast with this ankle, let alone run, thinking: 'What if the guy who's got my bike also killed Susan and Sam?'" She gave an involuntary shudder.

"What did you do?"

"Stayed in my car and searched the address on my cell. I came up with a name, a name I recognized. It made me real uncomfortable. That's when I knew I'd better book it. I kinda stalled all morning before figuring I should call you."

"Why? Whose house was it?"

"Lawrence Stenson...the Mayor of Gillette."

"Larry Stenson! Are you fucking kidding me?" Something like nausea appeared on Chief Bowman's face. He was pacing, glancing toward the door for the third time to ensure it was closed and that this conversation was not in danger of leaking outside. Henry and Janet stood quietly nearby. Bowman groaned as he rubbed the back of his neck, shooting a questioning glance at his detectives.

Janet had figured he'd not take the news well. She and Henry waited for his instructions.

The chief stroked the edge of his mustache thoughtfully before extending his hand. "Lemme see that printout." It was a street map of a Gillette neighborhood, a red dot centered near a street with GPS coordinates listed at the top and a street address displayed at the bottom. "Looks legit," Bowman's deep voice mumbled. "How did this woman know it's Stenson's house?"

Henry said, "She used a phone app to look up the address from the GPS coordinates. A property owner website search came back with Stenson's name."

"Sounds straightforward. Did you find the e-bike?"

"We haven't gone there yet. It's why we're here."

"Okay, get a warrant, go there with uniforms to search the property. Text me if you find anything. I don't have to tell you to be discreet."

"Whatever you say, Chief, though with a police black and white and us in the mayor's driveway, I'm not sure how discreet we can be."

Bowman made a throwaway gesture. "Do what you can."

# CHAPTER 28

The Mayor of Gillette looked a sickly green.

Janet Lau, occasional watercolorist with an extensive color palette, decided he was tilting toward a sap green, cadmium yellow combo.

It was three hours later. A tense quartet had gathered behind the closed door of Larry Stenson's office. Janet, Henry, the mayor, and Chief Bowman sat in leather bucket chairs around a small table. The mayor's official desk stood at the other end of the room. Around them, fine cherry wood paneling heightened the sense of bureaucratic officialdom. Janet could feel the edginess in the room, a funereal pall having descended on them. Stenson looked guilty as hell. Confused. A little scared. His paunchy belly pressed against the table edge. "So this bike thing was found behind my garage?"

"It was," Henry confirmed.

"Then someone dumped it there! I haven't looked back there in months. Probably neighborhood kids. Who knows how long that thing's been there?"

"Actually, Mister Mayor," Henry said, "the e-bike's been there since last Friday. It has a GPS tracker. Before that, it was with the murder victim in Bloomington."

"Whoa! Hold on." Stenson looked alarmed. "Murder victim? That's got nothing to do with me. Jesus! Just a whiff of this going public would ruin me. Hey, guys, I'm not involved with any of this." A pudgy hand came up to wipe a bead of sweat from his brow.

Chief Bowman raised his hand in assurance. "No one is accusing you of anything, Mayor. But the fact remains that an e-bike last known to be in possession by one of our homicide victims was found on your property, a homicide victim who worked for your sister-in-law's company. It's too much of a connection to ignore." The chief cleared his throat and made a quiet appeal. "Look, Larry, we're trying to help you. That's why we're meeting in private as a courtesy. If someone's setting you up, we need to find out who."

Stenson's thickset frame relaxed. "Uh. Thanks."

From where Janet sat, the mayor seemed to fidget too much for an innocent man. Maybe he was the nervous type, worried about his image. Or did he have something to hide?

"Wait,"—Stenson sat up—"Friday, you said? That's when the bike was dumped at my house? When Friday?"

"Early afternoon," Henry supplied.

Stenson grinned. "Ha! Couldn't've been me. Fran and I drove up to Duluth Friday morning. Went up right after breakfast. Spent the whole weekend there."

"Easily verifiable," Bowman remarked.

"You bet your ass it is! I'll give you names." A more confident Stenson glanced between the three of them. "What happens now?"

Chief Bowman made a conciliatory gesture. "We keep this meeting under wraps. The e-bike may be a distraction. Until we know otherwise, that's how we'll treat it."

Until we know otherwise.

A conditional phrase. One that didn't leave Stenson totally off the hook. Plain as day to Janet, although not to the mayor, who heard Bowman's words as an absolution of guilt.

"Good! Good!" He hoisted himself out of his chair, heavy-footing it over on tree trunk legs to shake Bowman's hand. "I want to thank all of you for your sensitivity in handling this." The mayor, in his Mayorness, made sure to pump the hands of both detectives as well.

Too confident, Janet thought. Politely dismissive now that he thought he'd been cleared of any wrongdoing.

A minute later, Bowman and his team walked across the parking lot. A breath of cold wind from behind blew them on. With no outside jacket, Bowman gave a little shudder. "What do you make of what just happened?" he asked over his shoulder.

Henry, who seemed impervious to the chill, casually remarked, "Went better than expected. I was waiting for Stenson to throw a hissy fit."

"Came close," Bowman snorted. "But, yeah, I think we avoided a disaster. You don't agree, Janet?" He saw her frown.

It wasn't a frown of disagreement; she was thinking. Turning toward him, her dark brown hair fluttered in the breeze. "That's not it," she said, "I'm working out something. Let's say Stenson is right; someone dumped the e-bike at his house. How would they know that would work? It's a bike. It was dumped behind his garage in a place you can't see from the house or the street. Who'd ever notice it?"

"Good point," Bowman nodded.

Encouraged by this, she continued. "And there was no anonymous phone tip to search the mayor's home. If you were trying to frame someone, wouldn't you want to make sure the police got the message and then found the thing you planted? It doesn't make sense!"

For the next three seconds, the only sounds that followed were the chuff of shoes against asphalt and the rumble of a car engine starting across the parking lot.

"Wait!" Janet suddenly said in a rush of clarity. "What if this mysterious person *knew* there was a GPS tracker on the e-bike and that it would be found?" Her slender eyebrows rose inquisitively. "Does that make sense?"

Both men wheeled their heads toward her with the same startled expression.

From the looks on their faces, neither had thought of that.

The first thing Henry did after he got back to his desk was to call Lori Deaver. "Got a minute?"

She said she did.

"I'm putting you on speaker," he informed.

The detectives huddled closer to his phone. Seconds later, they heard Deaver's voice. "What can I do for you, Detective?"

"I'm trying to clear up something. You said it was last Friday when you remembered having a GPS tracker installed on your e-bike. Correct?"

"Uh-huh."

"Where did this happen again?"

"At work, in the lunchroom. Tammy was showing me her new fitness tracker."

"Ah, that's right. Besides Tammy, who else was there?"

A long silence followed as she tried to remember. "It was the lunchroom. People were coming and going. But I remember Aimee Hancock waiting her turn at the coffee maker behind us. She was waiting for Jim's latte to finish."

"Jim Karjala?"

"Yeah, Aimee and Jim were talking about meeting with the sales department after getting their coffees."

Feeling he was on the verge of something important, Henry asked his next question with care. "Your GPS app, does it only show the current location of the e-bike? Or does it also keep a history? Like where it's been in the last week?"

"Oh, I don't know. I've never played with the features. Lemme see…" Thirty seconds passed as they heard Deaver's mutter to herself. And then, "Ha! Got it. Yeah, there's a log in the cloud. I found the right button. Oh, cool, this screen shows me where the bike's been in the past month with green connecting lines and other shit—er, stuff."

Inspired, Henry looked at Janet as he spoke into the phone, "Lori, can you send me an electronic file of the log history?"

"No problem, Detective. Give me time to figure out how."

"Thanks. You're a peach. Um, one other thing."

"Sure."

"Can you check with Tammy on something?"

A shiver ran up Janet's spine. The GPS tracker kept a log of where it had been! This could be the break they'd been hoping for.

# CHAPTER 29

Days later, the Chevy Malibu and a Gillette Police squad car appeared at the front entrance of the knife factory, parked at the front entrance to make a bold statement. Discretion was irrelevant. Henry, Janet, and a uniformed officer climbed the wide concrete steps to the tall glass doors. The detectives had barely arrived at the reception desk when the executive suite security door swung open. An agitated Aimee Hancock emerged, her eyes darting between the visitors. The uniformed officer was a new development and not a welcome one.

An all-business Henry greeted her. "Ms. Hancock, just the person I wanted to see."

The CEO's eyes remained on the uniformed officer. "What's going on?"

"Your office," Henry said in a peremptory manner.

Her face darkened under the platinum fringe bangs. "This looks serious."

"It is," was all he said, extending a hand toward the executive offices, the implication being that they needed to talk in private.

Distress reared up in the factory owner's face. She was about to speak when Henry's raised hand cut her off. He turned toward Janet. "You know what to do?"

She gave a quick nod.

Then back to Hancock. "Office," he said, this time more forcibly.

Moments later in her office, Aimee Hancock was too worked up to sit. She stood, a tightly coiled spring, eyeing the imperturbable man who stood a few yards away.

Henry surveyed the room, which had a distinctly feminine aesthetic: a slender desk with curved lines, pastel wall colors, a tropical painting with pink flamingoes, a shelf with several potted English ivies and spider plants. A cheerful room, one intended for relaxation and to stimulate creativity.

The antithesis of the reason for his visit.

Henry could see her uneasiness and the attempt to mask it by half-turning from him. He had an unpleasant task to perform and decided to just get on with it. "We're here to make an arrest."

The CEO snapped toward him. "Arrest?"

"Yes."

"Who?"

"Jim Karjala."

Her jaw dropped in disbelief. "*Jim?*"

"I know this comes as a shock. As we speak, my colleagues are taking Mr. Karjala into custody."

It took a few seconds for her to comprehend the full meaning of this. A hand flew to her mouth. "Wait, Jim killed Sam *and* Susan?"

"Yes."

"*Why?*"

"Karjala had a dirty secret. He believed Park and Zelinsky knew what it was and were going to reveal it, which would've upended his life and sent him to jail."

"Secret? What secret?"

"He was embezzling money from you."

Aimee Hancock looked ill. "He was?" After the initial shock faded, the businesswoman in her took over. "Uh, how much?"

"Somewhere in the neighborhood of $400,000."

She inhaled sharply. "Jim," she groaned. Betrayal rang in that one word of a sacred trust broken.

"We're still sorting through the financials with help from a specialist. Based on Karjala's bank records, it started eight years ago, around the time of his divorce."

"It was a bitter breakup. Jim went through a rough patch."

"Looks like online gambling got him through that rough patch. His credit card statements show regular payments to different wagering sites. Small payments at first. Larger and more frequently over time. He got addicted and dug himself into a huge hole. Owed lots. Emptied his savings and investments. This is when we think he started siphoning money from the company to cover his gambling debts."

With a dumbfounded groan, Hancock looked away. This was her third piece of terrible news in less than two weeks: the first being the deaths of two key employees and now the arrest of and theft by a trusted member of her team.

Henry continued. "Karjala was in a unique situation. As chief financial officer, he had total access to your company's accounting systems and databases. Complicated and somewhat archaic systems, I'm told."

"Jim's the only person who knows how all the pieces work together."

"And that's how he got away with it. He doctored the software carefully and only every so often, enough to make payments on his debt but not often enough or in large enough amounts to raise red flags. Hancock Blades remained highly profitable, which he hoped would keep you from asking too many questions."

"It obviously worked. I had no idea."

"The thefts stopped after four years. Karjala was attending Gamblers Anonymous and working on his addiction. But the fact remains he stole money from Hancock Blades. As CFO, his career would be over if his crime came out. And there was the threat of jail." Henry's voice darkened. "The threat of his crime being discovered hung over him. So when he believed your operations director and his best accountant had teamed up to secretly expose his embezzlement, he freaked out and went too far."

"Hold on. You're saying Sam and Susan *weren't* digging into our finances? Weren't they working together on some special project?"

"They were, but it had nothing to do with Karjala or Hancock Blades. Karjala got it wrong."

Her eyebrows inched upward. "What were they doing?"

For the first time in the meeting, Henry offered a qualified smile. "Actually, it was quite innocent..."

The City of Gillette Police Department had three interview rooms. Jim Karjala was in Interview Room One. Small, windowless, and soundproofed, it was large enough to accommodate a table and three chairs.

Janet closed the door and took the far-end chair, pad and pen, and her trusty black portfolio at the ready. Henry sat opposite their suspect, five feet away. Almost close enough to touch but just out of reach. This was her uncle's show. She was eager to watch him in action. Perhaps learn a thing or two.

Karjala was as rigid in his chair as the chair itself, bolted to the epoxy-coated concrete floor as a precaution against unruly suspects using the chair as a weapon. The CFO's back almost touched the white concrete block wall. Henry's position was a psychological tactic so Karjala would feel cornered. Even so, Henry remained respectful. Janet knew his preference was to get their man to volunteer information. There'd be no good cop / bad cop theatrics. Henry disliked bullies of any stripe, which applied doubly to law enforcement. His and Janet's game plan was simply to present their case, knowing their evidence was strong.

Slowly beginning to stir, Karjala shifted in his chair and removed his glasses to pinch the bridge of his nose. To Janet, his manner seemed contrived; he'd been caught unprepared for this situation and was hiding his true feelings behind a mask of indifference. But she could see the stress was getting to him. The gray temples seemed a shade grayer, and a worry crease had cut into his forehead.

Henry began with quiet authority. "Mr. Karjala, you're here to make a formal statement. We believe you killed Samuel Park and Susan Zelinsky. Can you tell us what happened?" A chance to unburden himself, that's the way Henry made it sound.

The other was not obliging. "You got the wrong guy, Detective."

Denial was always the first response. Janet had expected this. Thus began the back-and-forth contest between police and suspect, like a tennis match. Karjala had returned Henry's serve by declaring his innocence; now it was her partner's turn to volley.

But with force and topspin.

"Sorry, that won't wash. You're not fooling anyone. The proof's overwhelming. It's you, all right."

"Bullshit. What possible motive would I have for killing either of them?"

It was a high backcourt lob to make Henry scramble.

Except he was already in place. "Motive? To cover up the fact you've been embezzling money from Hancock Blades."

A wicked smash to the chest!

Karjala faltered at the kill shot. The crease in his brow deepened.

Henry didn't give him time to rebound, staying on the offensive. "You killed Park and Zelinsky because you were afraid they were days away from revealing your embezzlement."

Her uncle turned to her.

She was up.

It took Janet no time to get up to speed. She'd been ready for this all morning. "Your bank and credit card statements told us a lot," she said. "Pretty messy, but we finally noticed a few irregularities over the years. We know about the gambling debts and the unusual deposits." Janet flipped open the portfolio, removed a printout, and slid it across the table toward the CFO. "Confusing and hard to spot, but it's all there. Numbers don't lie, Mr. Karjala. For six years, your bank account wildly fluctuated."

"I got divorced," he replied. "My ex took a lot of assets."

Janet shook her head, bottom lip protruding. "Bad answer," she replied as if scolding a misbehaving child. "How does that explain *more* money coming into your personal bank account—lots more money—years after your breakup?"

Karjala shifted uncomfortably. Had no comeback.

Cutting him no slack, Janet went for the jugular. "Your divorce can't explain the weird money withdrawals and payments done at Hancock Blades during the same time period, a company *where you are the chief financial officer.* The dates of the debits from Hancock and the deposits into your account are within days of each other. Not just sometimes. *Every time!*" She flashed a satisfied smile at him. "It was tedious work pouring through the Hancock financials. Thankfully, I had help from a forensic accountant who's brilliant at finding discrepancies. She's the one who figured out you've been cooking the books." Janet slid over another report with orange highlighted sections. "Only you could figure out a way to steal money from the company and bury it under a pile of accounting hocus pocus."

Janet leaned in for emphasis. "Your one problem was Susan Zelinsky. Or so you thought. She was great at her job, a tenacious digger. You knew how good she was. At some point in the last few weeks, it alarmed you that she was on the verge of figuring out what you'd done. Her working closely with Sam Park must've given you a heart attack."

There.

She'd gotten in a few hits of her own, and it felt good. Karjala had been too smug. Too detached. Not anymore. He was starting to fidget, fingers opening and closing.

She glanced at Henry, whose lips pulled back with approval. Before the meeting, he'd complimented her on how doggedly she'd worked on the financials for Karjala and Hancock Blades, something he confessed he wouldn't have the patience for. That praise and his approval made her feel on top of the world.

The prisoner examined the printouts in front of him. After a while, he looked up with chilling indifference. "Numbers aren't proof of murder."

Janet sat up. *Whoa! Did he just admit to embezzlement?*

Perhaps not in so many words, she thought, but he didn't deny it.

Henry took up the challenge, locking eyes with the prisoner. "No, not proof of murder but a damn good motive." A count of two beats passed between them in silence as they stared at each other. Then Henry continued. "Like others at Hancock, you'd noticed how Park and Zelinsky were meeting regularly. You knew they were working on some private project. A secret project. Park's office is next to yours. Maybe you overheard things, things like *criminal activity, accountability, malfeasance, theft.* Words and phrases that alarmed you. Maybe you heard them talk about finishing their project by the end of the month. A looming deadline. You realized you had to act. Fast."

Henry edged closer. "You knew Susan was a morning runner. Early Saturday, before sunrise, you parked outside her home and waited. When she came out for her run, you followed her from a safe distance until she cut across a parking lot. That was your moment. It was dark. No one was around. She was listening to her iPad and didn't hear you come up from behind until it was too late. You ran her down, Jim. Afterward, you put her body in your car and drove back to her townhouse to search it, looking for the evidence she and Sam Park had on you. Evidence you didn't find. You decided not to leave Susan's body there, knowing her home would be the first place the police would look when she didn't show up for work. You transferred her body to her car and drove a mile away to dump her remains in an abandoned auto repair shop lot on Old Shakopee Road, hoping it'd be days or weeks before she was found. More time for you to figure out what to do."

The prisoner listened to the accusation stone-faced. Didn't offer a scintilla of denial or moral outrage, which Janet found noteworthy.

"After disposing of Susan's body," Henry went on, "you drove a few miles and left her car at the warehouse store parking lot. One piece of luck was finding an e-bike in the back of her SUV. After abandoning the car, you rode the e-bike back to your vehicle."

In reply came a snort of contempt.

Finally, a reaction! thought Janet. But nothing more. The man was too guarded. Was too good at keeping his emotions under wraps.

Henry cleared his throat. "You weren't finished, though. You had all Saturday to fret over what you'd done. Not having found the evidence you were looking for, on Sunday morning, you went to the office to—what?—search her desk. Probably Park's as well. You used Zelinsky's key card to enter the building to hide the fact it was you. What messed you up was Sam Park. He arrived after you. What happened? Did he find you searching his office?"

"No comment," Karjala said as if he were above it all.

Janet couldn't stand his cockiness and wanted to take him down a few pegs. She exhaled, reminding herself to be patient. Her turn was coming again.

Henry said, "There was a confrontation. It turned bad. You were in it up to your neck and couldn't back down. In a rage or desperation, you grabbed the tiger claw knife from the display and went after Park. Stabbed to silence him."

Here, Henry stopped.

An unsettling hush descended upon the small room like the stillness after a hailstorm.

The financial executive mocked: "Interesting story, Detective, except I didn't hear a shred of evidence that I killed anyone. It's all conjecture."

Henry smiled back. "We're not done yet."

# CHAPTER 30

It took most of Janet's self-control not to feel too pleased when the cocky smile died from the prisoner's face.

Henry didn't go easy on him. "You made a lot of mistakes. The biggest one was taking the e-bike. You should've left it at Susan's townhouse, but, no, you took it with you! That was a very dumb thing to do, Jim."

No more *Mister* Karjala, Janet noted.

Her turn again. She was going to enjoy this. From the portfolio, she removed more printouts: colorful maps with lines and dots. "We have these," she said.

"What are those?"

"Tracking maps. What you didn't know—at first—was the e-bike has a GPS tracker on it and that it keeps a log of *where it's been.*" Janet could swear Karjala flinched at those last words. "I'll keep this simple. In front of you are maps of the Twin Cities metro area and surrounding suburbs. The green dots are where the e-bike remained in place for up to ten minutes. Red dots are where it was stationary for sixty minutes or longer. The green lines show where the e-bike traveled. There are dates and GPS coordinates for each location. The e-bike was at Susan Zelinsky's townhouse on Saturday, the day she was killed. The green line shows it moving along Old Shakopee Road, where you dumped her body, then went to the DealCo Warehouse lot, where you abandoned her car. The green line returns to the townhouse and then travels to Eden Prairie *to your house.* You'd stashed the bike in your car to take home."

Henry shook his head. "Dumb, Jim, very dumb."

Ignoring him, Karjala leaned forward to study the printouts.

Janet continued. "The bike's a Bando 2000. The same make and model e-bike Lori Deaver loaned to Susan. It was at your house for several days. Then, all of a sudden, it shows up Friday afternoon at Mayor Stenson's property in Gillette." Janet feigned amazement as if wondering how such a thing was possible. "The bike didn't move on its own. You took it there."

"Interesting timing on that," Henry jumped in. "The bike shows up at Stenson's home on Friday at 1:35 p.m., less than fifty minutes after Lori Deaver mentioned in the Hancock lunchroom that her bike had a GPS tracker installed. You were in the lunchroom then. You overheard her." Henry gave a guttural laugh. "You must've crapped your pants when you heard that! But then relief the next minute after Deaver said she couldn't get the app working and would have to reinstall it at home later. That gave you a narrow time window to ditch the thing. You had to act immediately. You left work, drove home, and moved the e-bike off your property. But instead of dumping the bike in an open field or on a busy sidewalk, you stashed it behind Mayor Stenson's garage. Trying to throw up a smoke screen, were you? Use his relationship with his sister-in-law to confuse us?"

"Bullshit," Karjala growled, tossing up his hands. "I was in my office all afternoon."

"That's a lie. I asked Lori to check with Tammy if anyone had left the office after lunch. Tammy said you stepped out at 12:50 and returned around 1:48. Plenty of time to relocate the bike. I know; I drove the route myself. Are you paying attention, Jim?"

Oh he was, he really was! Janet enjoyed watching Karjala squirm and waited for Henry to drop the hammer on him.

"You should know," he said, "while we were taking you into custody, a separate team was searching your home. They found your other car. You drive a BMW to work, but we'd noticed from a DMV search that you also own a 2010 Titan Gray Metallic SAAB Sports

Sedan. It was in your garage and had recent front-end damage. And on the undercarriage is what looks like human hair and skin. The vehicle's been impounded. If the DNA matches Susan's, I don't know how you're going to explain how it got there."

Karjala inhaled a labored breath. "I want a lawyer."

"Sure, that's your right." Half-turning away, Henry looked back casually at the other as if sharing a confidence. "By the way, you should know you were wrong about Park and Zelinsky. They knew nothing about your embezzlement. No one did."

The CFO's eyebrows turned down.

Henry delivered the final blow. "Jim, your coworkers were writing a mystery novel together. A piece of fiction. It had nothing, absolutely *nothing*, to do with you. You killed them for no reason."

*You killed them for no reason.*

A harsh reality that.

Janet saw something indescribable cloud Karjala's face. Bitter realization? Chagrin? She couldn't tell. Trying to read this man was like looking for images on a blank canvas.

As he stewed in the private hell of his inner emotions, the finance man absently rubbed his bandaged finger.

That prompted Henry to ask, "How's the hand?"

Looking over, Karjala said, "Uh, fine. Why?"

"Dislocated fingers take months to heal. I bet your grip strength is nowhere near 100 percent."

"What of it?"

"Just wondering."

"We're through here. I want my lawyer."

Without further ado, the prisoner was taken back to a holding cell.

Afterward, Janet asked Henry, "What was that about Karjala's hand?"

Henry offered a puckish smile and told her to wait until they got to the privacy of the Criminal Investigation Department. He grabbed his stainless-steel water bottle and took a long chug before setting it down. "Dry mouth," he said. "Always gets me this time of year."

In the comfort of her chair and near the good vibes of her little bamboo plant, Janet repeated her question.

"Right. The dislocated finger. It played a key role in the case."

"It did?"

"The knife wasn't the only murder weapon in Sam Park's death. There was another."

"There was? This is the first I've heard of it."

"Actually, it isn't. You're the one who first brought it up."

"I did?"

He was on his feet, away from his desk. Henry's rangy body moved with athletic ease as he used his hands to illustrate his point. "Let's review. Jim Karjala stabbed Park with the karambit knife, wipes the hilt and drops it, then high tails it out of the building."

"Right."

A vigorous head shake. "Except that's not what happened."

Janet skewered him with a look. "It wasn't?"

"No, Karjala thought Park was dead. He wasn't. As you suggested, there was a little life left in him. As Karjala was heading toward the door, he heard something or saw movement. Sam Park was crawling across the carpet. We saw the marks. Karjala freaked. Park might have enough life left in him to call 911 and say who stabbed him. Karjala desperately scanned the office for something to finish the job. Maybe he thought about using the knife again, but then he saw the bookstand just beyond Park. Karjala grabbed the atlas, a heavy book, and cracked it hard over Park's head, who dropped to the carpet to die of his wounds."

"Ah, yes," Janet remembered. "The ME's report mentioned a contusion on the top of Park's head. So you're saying the world atlas was the second murder weapon."

"In a manner of speaking, yes."

"Okay, what about forensics? Wouldn't Karjala's DNA or fingerprints be on the atlas?"

"His and many others, including the cleaning people. That's the problem. Too much to make sense of."

"The open page to South America? How does that figure in?"

Henry picked up a manilla folder from his desk. Held it in both hands. "This is the world atlas, a large, heavy, hard-backed picture book. Karjala's about to crack it over Sam Park's head. The problem is Karjala doesn't have two strong hands. He has one. The other has a healing dislocated finger, still sore. I saw him struggle to open a ream of paper. It slipped from his grasp. The same thing happened with the atlas. The impact of bashing the atlas against Park's head wrenched the book from his hands. It fell to the floor, dropping by Park's head as he went down, opening to a random page. As luck would have it, Park's hand flopped onto the open page."

"Wow," Janet mouthed, nodding. Simple and plausible. It explained what happened. Also, hugely disappointing. "So there never was a dying clue…"

"No."

Well, that's a bummer, Janet thought; she'd loved the idea of deciphering a bizarre clue that would solve the murder. It had been exciting! A challenge for her analytical skills on an intriguing puzzle. Like a treasure hunt. Though, in hindsight, it was probably a little immature of her to have felt that way. The important thing, the only thing that mattered, was the murders had been solved, and the perpetrator was in custody. A new thought brought a crafty smile to her face. "You know, in a manner of speaking, the atlas *was* a dying message, just not one left by Sam Park."

"A bit of a stretch, but sure, why not?"

"Which means I was right about there being a dying message," Janet said with a note of pride.

"Fair enough,' he laughed.

"So what put you onto the real meaning of the atlas?"

"A couple of things. First was seeing Karjala fumbling with that ream of paper because of his poor grip. Next was seeing Ken Ferguson, with his arm in a sling, drop his boot in the locker room. Those images stuck in my head."

"Apparently!"

"But one thing kept nagging me from day one from the crime scene."

He'd hooked her now. What had she missed?

"Which was?" she had to ask.

Henry's hand swept out. "We know Park's injuries were fatal, with him having only seconds left to live. The marks on the carpet tell us he crawled across the floor, but it wasn't to get to the atlas. Maybe he was trying to get up or go to the phone. Crawling to the atlas would take too long. Paper, Post-it notes, and pens were on the floor near him. I kept wondering that if Sam Park had really wanted to leave us a dying message, why didn't he just grab a pen and paper to write it down?"

Janet rolled her eyes. "Oh!"

*Of course! Pens and paper were all around him. She should've thought of that.*

But as she thought about it further, she realized she shouldn't be so hard on herself. *Your head's still wonky from the concussion. You still aren't at the top of your game.*

*Yeah, go with that.*

# CHAPTER 31

Jim Karjala was charged and processed for the murders of Sam Park and Susan Zelinsky and was awaiting trial. The prosecutor thought she had a solid case against him. The evidence was strong. If things worked out, there'd be justice for the two murder victims. Which pleased Janet. Gave her a sense of accomplishment. That she could be an agent of justice was a big reason she'd wanted to work in homicide. Yet even agents of justice need a break now and again, and she was glad violent crime in Gillette was on holiday. Christmas was less than a week away. Too soon for her. Though she was glad for a break to catch up on paperwork, review inactive cases, and work on those still open. The extra downtime did wonders for her post-concussion recovery. For eight days in a row, there'd been no fuzzy brain episodes or sudden headaches! Could she be nearing the end of this stomach-hurling, dizzying rollercoaster ride?

In celebration of this came a night out in style. On a chilly Saturday, Janet, her parents, and her uncle Henry—all dressed to the nines—dined at a top-rated restaurant before heading to the vast Minneapolis campus of the University of Minnesota. They were ensconced on the main floor of Northrop Auditorium, an old-style classical structure with a magnificent proscenium arch stage, ornate columns, and plush stage curtains, waiting for the show to start.

Abby Lau, seated next to Henry, glanced around her. "These are *great* seats! We're so close to the stage."

Henry made a little flourish with his hand. "Complementary seats."

Sitting beside her mother, Janet bent forward to interject, "Payment for being a *dance* consultant." She scrunched her nose.

With a muted chuckle, Abby affectionately patted her daughter's arm. "Go easy on your uncle, honey. It was sweet of him to invite us." Abby's reddish-brown hair swung to the side as she surveyed the cavernous space quickly filling up around her. "It's been ages since we were here. Hasn't it, Doug?"

Her husband turned to look past Janet at her. "Twenty-three years," he said without hesitation or enthusiasm. "Some avant-garde ballet recital done to the songs of Jethro Tull."

A blank look from Janet.

Doug explained. "Way before your time. They're a British progressive folk rock band from the 1970s and the '80s, mainly. Their best years. The dance was a one-of-a-kind performance," he said like a man with a less than enthusiastic recollection of the event.

Abby's nose twitched. "Doug's taste in music is stuck in '90s soft rock. I *love* Tull. When she was a teenager, Mom got to meet Ian Anderson in Blackpool. Got his autograph. Way before selfies."

"Anderson's the frontman and singer," Janet's father explained, "and the songwriter and flute player."

"*The* rock and roll flute player," Abby amended. "Anyway, the ballet to *Aqualung* and *Cross-Eyed Mary* was hilarious! And the whole *Songs from the Wood* sequence left me breathless."

Her husband closed his mouth and refrained from further comment, smiling thinly. A promising diplomat was lost to the United States Foreign Service when the young Douglas Lau chose to pursue a career in accounting.

Janet stifled a laugh. For a precious instant, she'd gotten a glimpse of the Baby-Tee- stone-washed-denim-combat-boot-wearing college-aged Abby Lau. She'd known her mother had been a brainy top student, had fought for social causes, and was wise and loving in a way that she could only hope to emulate, yet seeing this fleeting throwback to the young adult Abby Campbell was a moment she'd long cherish.

After a quick introduction from the master of ceremonies, the lights went down, the audience hushed, and the music came up. For the next seventy-five minutes, performers in colorful costumes livened the stage: Greek folk dancers, a Norwegian Halling troupe, a Native American ensemble, followed by a Sub-Saharan African company. Each performed with their own lighting, stage props, and folk instruments to enthusiastic applause. And then the penultimate act came out: the Dorothy Travers Dance Company.

Unlike the previous acts that had begun with full-stage lighting, the China segment started in total darkness. Then, at the rise of sonorous and haunting Chinese strings, a percussive bamboo flute, and the beat of drums, a few key spots came up to illuminate the flat cutout building shapes. The effect sent a shiver up Janet's spine. Made her feel like she was entering a mysterious land in a distant time. Sustaining the somber mood, every dancer who appeared was dressed in simple yet stylish black satin traditional clothing with white collars and cuffs. Each short section progressed the story of a Wing Chun fighter encountering different Chinese kung fu masters in beautiful and exciting faux battles. Janet was entranced. Felt her heartbeat quicken as the story progressed.

Then came the final segment.

The dancers, all female, wore fitted black satin *hanfu* dresses over black leggings. They walked the Bagua circle around their master, hands and arms in their fighting-ready position, twisting and circling. Janet was swept along with the beauty and deadliness of their movements, occasionally looking at Henry, whose attention was trained on the lead dancer. The Bagua master's quick, athletic kicks and rapid hand changes were perfectly mimicked by her ten disciples, whose stoic faces reflected their absolute focus on their motions.

From the shadows entered the Wing Chun master to challenge the fighters. The music swelled as they clashed. One by one, he dispatched them swiftly until it was only the Bagua master and her challenger remaining. Janet leaned forward. Eyes wide. The two figures whirled around each other in a spirited, flirtatious fighting dance of attacks and countermoves. In the end, the Wing Chun fighter barely emerged victorious with a wicked fingertip strike to the throat—except, at the last second, out of respect, he checked it scant inches from its target. In appreciation, the Bagua master capitulated with a tilt of her head and a kung fu salute: an open palm covering a closed fist. This led to the closing scene in which the Wing Chun fighter was invited to join the other masters at a seat in the temple.

The lights came up. The audience erupted with applause, hoots, cheers, and whistles. Janet jumped to her feet, clapping giddily.

*Now this was a show!*

The final dance troupe closed the celebration: Mexican *chinelos* dancers in elaborate, bright costumes playing exuberant music that filled the auditorium with plenty of seasonal good cheer. The audience got to their feet to clap and dance along.

Afterward, the tide of humanity made for the exits, and Doug Lau enthused, "That was great! What a fun show. Thanks, Henry."

Abby and Janet chimed in their appreciation as well.

By this time in December, most of the state was covered in a blanket of snow. Sparkling crystals reflected streetlamps and headlights. Colorful strings of holiday lights hung from windows and buildings, giving joy and color to cold and dreary winter nights. Henry's older brother Doug chauffeured them to the western suburbs in his roomy Range Rover. Henry was the first to be dropped off at his St. Louis Park home. Goodbyes and hugs were given.

He was steps away from his back door when he turned at the sound of his name.

"Uncle Henry, wait!" Janet shuffled over, breathless. A wrapped box was in her outstretched hand. "It's your Christmas present. I know Christmas isn't 'til next week, but I want you to have it now."

There was a slight urgency in her voice as well as a hint of misgivings.

He accepted the colorful box, smiling broadly. "Janet, you didn't have to."

"*Yes, I did*," she insisted, lifting her chin to look at him, feeling like her awkward twelve-year-old self again. "Don't wait for Christmas. Open it tomorrow morning and message me what you think— *pleeeeze*." Big caramel eyes implored.

A bit puzzled, he nonetheless agreed. "What's inside this thing?"

"Something special."

"It can't wait?"

"No."

"Okay."

"You'll do it then? Open it tomorrow morning?"

"Sure."

"You promise?"

"I promise," he laughed.

"And you'll message me? Please, please."

"Okay."

"Good." Janet drew close to kiss his cheek. "I really hope you like the present," she whispered in his ear before dashing off to the waiting car, a lump in her throat.


The new morning came with the promise of good tidings. Fair weather and a mainly clean slate. After his usual predawn workout, Henry ate a light breakfast and gathered his thoughts for the day ahead. There was a new shelf he'd wanted to install in the basement laundry area, plus he'd been meaning to change a garage floodlight bulb. No point putting it off any longer. Later, he'd be off to Red Wing for lunch with an old school friend he hadn't seen in a decade. But before anything else, he remembered his promise the previous evening.

His eyes fell on the narrow box on his kitchen counter. The metallic red and green paper glistened under the morning sun that streamed through the kitchen sink window. Henry retrieved the present and went to his living room, where he dropped into a well-padded high-backed chair. He lightly shook the box. Nothing rattled.

For a second he held the box between his hands, recalling the odd tone in Janet's voice. So tentative. Why? he wondered.

He ripped the wrapping paper along a straight line, pulled it off, and let it fall to the floor. Opening the narrow cardboard box, he slid out a large, padded envelope and a Christmas card. The empty box fell by the wayside. The card's front depicted three dogs in Santa hats romping in the snow. Inside were these words:

*Uncle Henry, this year was a tough one for you. Your recovery's been amazing! Then, just when you get back on duty, you get stuck with me as your partner. LOL.*

*THANK YOU so much for your support these last months and for putting up with me. I couldn't have asked for a better mentor and work partner!! For all these things, I wanted to get you a REALLY special present this year.*

*Luv, Janet*

By now, his curiosity had crescendoed. Impatient fingers tore open the large cardboard envelope. He was perplexed by the contents: a plain blue college ruled 10.5 inch by 8-inch spiral-bound notebook. Inside the envelope, he found a handwritten note. His gaze went immediately to the name at the bottom.

Beth McAdams.

McAdams?

It took him a full second to make the connection. *Kay's mother?* He felt a weight press against his chest. It'd been ages since he'd last spoken with Kay's mom. The weight grew heavier as his eyes focused on the note.

> *Henry, it's been so long! I hope this finds you well. Your lovely niece updated me on your life. You've gone through so much! She asked me for a gift with special meaning. Be sure to look at the marked page. Happiness to you.*
>
> *Beth McAdams*

Setting aside the note, he peeled back the front cover of the spiral-bound notebook. He inhaled sharply when he saw the name inside: *Kay McAdams. Psychological Anthropology.* The page was full of notes in blue ballpoint pen done in Kay's distinctive cursive handwriting.

*Her class notes!*

His heart jumped. He flipped page after page. This was the handwriting he'd known so well. Henry gently pressed his fingertips on the page. Kay had held this notebook. Had written every word. The ink looked as fresh as the day her fingers had put pen to paper. As if she'd walked away minutes ago. Henry could feel her presence, and his heart filled. He quirked a wry smile at a doodle in the margin: a happy daisy. On another page was another doodle: a little cat face with prominent whiskers. Not just her detailed notes were here, but tiny bits of her personality.

And then he remembered Beth's note.

He saw the marker.

A red stick-on index tab stood proud on one page near the back. Henry flipped over to it.

More writing. Though not class notes.

In Kay's flowing hand was a draft of a letter. Several words had been crossed out and replaced. His throat went dry when he saw who the letter was addressed to and the date.

It was addressed to him.

The date was October 15, 1999.

The day Kay died.

The last day they'd seen each other.

The lunch at Rusty Bob's, while pleasant at first, went sour. He wasn't clear how the disagreement between them had started but figured it was his fault. Of the mistakes Henry Lau had made in his life, none cut as deep as the one he'd made that day. He'd said the wrong thing and hurt Kay. Frustrated and angry, for the first time ever, she walked out on him.

Hours later, she was killed by a hopped-up mugger.

He realized Kay must have written this letter shortly after leaving Rusty Bob's. When she was still angry.

*This can't be good.*

He swallowed hard. *Did he want to read this?* Stupid question. Of course he would. There was no way he couldn't read her last thoughts to him. He'd take his lumps, however bad. Owed her that much.

A cold tendril of dread squeezed his heart as he began to read the letter, a letter Kay never made it back home to send.

*Dear Henry,*

*We did not part well today. I'm sorry for that. These last few months with you have been wonderful. Lately, both our schedules have gotten crazy. We haven't been together much. I miss you. I really needed to be with you this evening. But you had plans and didn't want to change them. I got mad and left, thinking you were being selfish or that you didn't really care enough about me. Later, I realized it might've been unfair of me to demand that you drop your plans suddenly just because I wanted you to.*

*Maybe I was being selfish too. Sigh. You said you'd work harder to find time for us. I got mad because it didn't happen immediately. We could have talked about it better and worked it out.*

*School this quarter's got me frazzled, and I took it out on you. You offered to spend the day together this Saturday and drive to Mendocino. Please, can we do that? My feelings for you haven't changed. Can we get together this weekend to talk more and be good to each other?*

*Love Always,*
*Kay*

Henry was stunned. Even after his thoughtless answer to her at lunch, Kay still had the grace to see his point of view. He was wrong then. He *had* been selfish. And stupid. Yet in this unsent letter, Kay revealed the true beauty of her nature by sharing responsibility with him, a gesture he wasn't sure he deserved. And she even offered a tender olive branch.

*My feelings for you haven't changed.*

Words that meant everything to him.

He held the notebook closer and read the letter four more times, the last two through watery eyes. After he finished, Henry lowered his head and cast his mind back to a time in his youth when all dreams seemed possible.

*Well, this sucks!*

It was just past 10:30 Sunday morning, and Henry had not messaged her yet. Janet realized she should've asked him to open the present *first thing* in the morning, not at some unspecified time. She blew out a labored breath, reminding herself to be more patient, another of her self-improvement projects.

The rapid gurgle of boiling water caught her ear. The heavy click of her electric kettle's off switch followed. Sliding over her Snoopy mug, she drowned her English breakfast tea bag before adding a splash of milk. Then went to the window seat to stare out into the day, comfy in a sweatshirt, lounge pants, and bare feet.

Relaxation, however, was an aspirational concept, thanks to the unruly python squirming in her belly. Her nerves were on edge.

*Well, this just sucks! Suckity suck sucks!*

*What was she thinking, giving Kay's notebook to Henry? Why hadn't she listened to everyone?*

The morning was ticking by, and Henry hadn't texted. He must be super pissed off at her.

She tossed back her head and uttered a little moan.

Then came a loud ping from the coffee table.

Janet jumped and snatched up her phone.

A text!

From Henry.

Janet gulped down a breath. A trembling finger swiped the screen. Her heart caught in her throat as she read the message:

> *Best gift ever! UR the best!*
> *THANKYOU!!!*

She leaped up, throwing a mighty fist in the air. *He wasn't angry! She hadn't fucked up! Oh, yeah! Your instincts were spot on!* She flung herself onto the sofa, arms overhead, flutter-kicking bare feet in triumph. Maybe, just maybe, her gift might ease the burden her uncle had carried for so many years. If that happened, this would be one of the best things she'd ever done.

And the thought of that brought a smile that went all the way to her eyes.

Thank you for reading *Tiger Claw!* If you enjoyed it, please consider posting a short review on Amazon. A few words are always helpful to an author. You might also enjoy the first Henry Lau / Janet Lau mystery:

# The Lost Dragon Murder
### --Winner of the Best Independent Book Award
### --Finalist for the Midwest Book Award
### --Finalist for the Silver Falchion Award

*The murder of an art expert and the disappearance of a priceless artifact propels Detective Henry Lau into the nebulous world of ancient antiquities. Complicating matters is a parade of dodgy suspects who wouldn't know a truthful statement if it bit them on the leg.*

"…A perfect story to curl up with on a winter's night."
--*Ellen Hart, Mystery Writers of America Grandmaster*

BookLocker. ISBN: 978-1-64719-892-3